THE OTHER SIDE
OF FOREVER

By the Author

Uncomplicate It

The Other Side of Forever

THE OTHER SIDE OF FOREVER

by
Kel McCord

2025

THE OTHER SIDE OF FOREVER
© 2025 BY KEL MCCORD. ALL RIGHTS RESERVED.

ISBN 13: 978-1-63679-812-7

THIS TRADE PAPERBACK ORIGINAL IS PUBLISHED BY
BOLD STROKES BOOKS, INC.
P.O. BOX 249
VALLEY FALLS, NY 12185

FIRST EDITION: NOVEMBER 2025

CREDITS
EDITOR: CINDY CRESAP
PRODUCTION DESIGN: STACIA SEAMAN
COVER DESIGN BY TAMMY SEIDICK

Acknowledgments

I started writing because I needed something to do on Wednesday nights. My wife's work schedule had her out of the house until almost 9 p.m. every Wednesday, and I needed something to do other than sit around and feel lonely. Yes, I could have joined a bowling league or found another option, but my best friend encouraged me to put my anxious energy to good use and write the kind of stories I wanted to read. As the world around us continues to evolve and we don't know up from down some days, the one thing I've told myself is that we need more stories with happy endings—even if that means we have to write them ourselves. What started as a way to pass the time has turned into something so much more, and I hope that my stories can help others to escape, even if it's just for a few hours.

I want to thank my wife, who is the greatest supporter I could ever ask for. This hobby has essentially become a second full-time job, and she shows love and support in more ways than I could ever imagine.

The team at Bold Strokes Books is phenomenal. They continue to help teach and guide me through this process and I am ever thankful.

Again, I want to thank you, the reader. Without you, none of this is possible, and it means the world to me to get to share my stories.

To my Wife—

I don't want to get to forever unless you're in it.

CHAPTER ONE

Kenzie McCall loved Valentine's Day. It wasn't so much that she loved heart-shaped candy and Cupid decorations, or that she liked exchanging overpriced chocolate with her partner. In fact, this year, Kenzie found herself very much single. But being single on Valentine's Day wasn't bringing her down. What Kenzie loved most were love songs. Since she was a songwriter, Valentine's Day for Kenzie was practically Christmas. Singing love songs while happy couples doted on one another was what she thrived on. Yes, thousands of fans screaming her name would be much more thrilling, but for now, Kenzie would take any audience she could get.

She played with the ends of her hair when her phone buzzed on the bathroom counter. *Shit.* It was Jenni. "Hello?"

"Where are you?" Jenni sounded frantic.

"I'm almost there. I'm only three blocks away."

Kenzie gave herself a final once-over in the mirror on the back of her bathroom door. Playing guitar with her hair down was impractical, but she was playing for tips tonight. Somehow the end of the month came faster every month, and while songwriting was her passion, the paycheck was sporadic. Her favorite pair of dark skinny jeans, a white camisole, and a flowing red sweater completed her look. Just festive enough but not too revealing to get any husbands in trouble for tipping extra—or wives. She looked at her top for the third time, making sure she couldn't see her bra through the sheer shirt. She felt good. She looked good. Her hair, while annoying that it was down, was having a good day, and for whatever reason, so were her breasts.

"Dammit, Kenz. You live three blocks away. You haven't even left yet?"

Kenzie knew that tone. "I'm sorry, Jenni. I was on a roll tonight and totally lost track of time. I promise I can walk fast." Kenzie was never on time. Everyone who knew her knew that fact. She would argue that it wasn't her fault. She often got caught up in the moment and lost track of time between the constant guitar, piano, or whatever instrument she played that day. When the melody hit and the lyrics flowed, she was in her own world. Meteors could strike and Kenzie might not notice if the chord progression was just right.

"I'm leaving now. I'll be there in ten." Kenzie threw her saddlebag over one shoulder and picked up her guitar case in her free hand.

Jenni let out a sigh. "Find me the second you get here. I need to show you how the new setup works."

"I'll see you soon, Jenni."

Kenzie thanked her lucky stars the rain held off, as drizzle in the Pacific Northwest was all too common in February. She wore tall brown boots because they would look great onstage, not because they were functional. Fortunately, the walk was only a few blocks.

Pressed, the coffee and wine bar, opened just three years ago in the Portland suburb. Business continued to thrive even though Pressed didn't have a large kitchen, and Jenni made it clear she had no intentions of becoming a chef, but on special occasions, Jenni would cater dinners. Valentine's Day quickly became her most popular night of the year, with tickets selling out all three years of the event.

The fun and festive decorations looked like Cupid threw up all over the place between the pink and red hearts and angel cutouts. At one point, Pressed was some kind of industrial building. Jenni refinished the old hardwood floors and kept the exposed air ducts to the vaulted ceilings. Industrial chic, as she called it. Kenzie never quite understood what it meant, but Pressed had always been popular, so she assumed that Jenni knew what she was doing.

"There you are."

Kenzie snapped her head around to see a stressed Jenni. Her

short black hair was gelled straight up this evening, almost making spikes.

"You look great." The tight black shirt and red leather pants hugged Jenni's small frame. She could have sworn the ends of Jenni's mouth turned up, but it faded quickly.

"Flattery will get you nowhere." Jenni spoke fast.

"It used to get me a lot of places." Kenzie nudged her shoulder into Jenni's hoping to relieve some of this tension.

"Well, it will get you nowhere tonight." Jenni's mood remained unchanged.

Kenzie and Jenni had tried to date. They tried for months but could never make it work. Yes, there was physical attraction. And yes, they had sexual chemistry, but outside of the bedroom, there wasn't much there. Kenzie was so close to catching her big break with Global Studios that she couldn't focus on anything or anyone else. Pressed consumed every ounce of Jenni's attention, so why Jenni was upset when their relationship wasn't more serious was beyond Kenzie. Neither of them were at a place in their lives for a serious relationship. When Jenni said that things weren't working, Kenzie didn't argue or fight to stay. Life was too short to be in a partnership like that. So she let Jenni go, at least in the romantic sense.

Kenzie couldn't take her eyes off Jenni. Damn, she looked good. If she thought she could sleep with her no strings attached, she would. But her thirty-two years of life taught her that one, you could rarely sleep with a woman with no strings attached, and two, that was especially true on Valentine's Day.

"Stop eyeing me and let me show you the new setup."

"What? I wasn't eyeing you." She totally was but didn't think she was that obvious.

"Whatever. Did you bring your tablet?"

Kenzie set her guitar on the carpeted stage and retrieved the tablet.

"Gimme." Jenni motioned for it.

Normally, Kenzie would have played around a little longer. Make Jenni work for it. Make her flirt for it, but tonight was not a night to mess with her, and she turned it over.

"Here." Jenni set the tablet on the music stand in front of them.

"It's a new program. It links to the chord sheets you already use, but I can send you songs and have them jump to the front of your queue."

"This is the new technology I needed to rush here for? It seems pretty straightforward. Also, why do you need to send me songs? I'll be taking requests."

Jenni looked up to the ceiling. "So I can read the room." She said it as if it was the most obvious answer on the planet. "If I'm back at the bar and hear a couple mentioning a song, or you go off on some tangent that isn't working, I can send you a song and bring things back to center."

"When have I ever gone off on a tangent that wasn't working?" Kenzie took pride in her ability to know the audience and play appropriate songs.

"Remember the afternoon you tried to play nothing but nineties hip-hop?"

"Okay." Kenzie raised her palms. "That worked, and people were into it."

"That's not what the online reviews said later."

"What? One angry guy online and now I need you censoring me?"

"Let's take a deep breath here." She waved her arms for Kenzie to breathe in and out and Kenzie reluctantly agreed. She changed her tone and spoke softer. "Kenz, I love your playing. You know that. This is just a new thing I want to try, so try it for me? Please?"

Kenzie never could say no to those big brown eyes. "Okay, but I reserve the right to veto power."

"No." Jenni shook her head and looked around the room, still frantic. "Just play the songs you're asked, okay?"

"Fine."

"The first seating starts in ten minutes."

"I'm ready."

Jenni took the small step down and headed toward the bar area at the back of the room. A long counter filled one end with a monstrosity of an espresso machine behind it. Big chalkboards with handwritten drink names hung on the exposed brick walls. To the left of that was another long counter with wine glasses hanging upside down from a rack. The large built-in wine rack would have been impressive if Kenzie liked wine. It had never been her drink of choice, but she obliged when Jenni insisted she try something new.

Kenzie moved her guitar to the small wooden divider directly behind the stool. She pulled out her pride and joy—a jumbo Epiphone six-string that she'd had since college. She owned multiple guitars, but this was the best one for this room. The oversized body lent itself to heavier bass tones that filled the open space and held a larger sound to mimic a full band. Jenni grew tired of writing her name out on a chalkboard and opted to make her a "McKenzie McCall" sign. The cursive lettering was cutesier than Kenzie might have picked out herself, but she appreciated the trouble Jenni went to.

She set the sign up against the microphone stand. Tonight, it was her job to set the mood. She was just supposed to be background music—someday she'd get to be the center of attention, but not tonight. This made-up holiday was the perfect opportunity for her to see what songs were still popular, as well as sneak in a few of her own originals. She grabbed a pick from the holder on top of her guitar and strummed an E chord. Was there anything better than a perfectly tuned guitar? If there was, she couldn't think of it.

Kenzie moved through her standard repertoire. A little Elvis, some Paul McCartney, Etta James. She paused after finishing her version of "At Last."

"Alright, lovebirds," she said, using her best late night radio host voice. "Just a reminder that I am taking requests tonight. If you have something you want your special someone to hear, come on up and let me know." Kenzie startled as her tablet blinked. Jenni sent a song to the top of her queue. She shook her head, annoyed that Jenni thought she was going down a tangent already. She clicked on the song and made eye contact with Jenni, who poured wine behind the bar. "Seriously?" she mouthed. Jenni just nodded.

Kenzie started with her best rendition of the Eric Clapton song. She hadn't heard it in forever and tried to hear the guitar riff in her mind to find the notes of the verse. She played the intro four times until she could remember the song and she started in.

Then, at the start of the second verse, the room stopped. A table front and center had just turned over and a new couple entered. A tall woman with long brown hair wearing the perfect little black dress approached the newly open table. Kenzie realized that now she would at least have someone nice to look at for the next hour or so. Her olive skin looked smooth to the touch. The woman must have been cold after leaving her coat at the door, but it was worth it for how good she looked in that dress. The capped sleeves revealed toned arms and the V-neck dipped just low enough to reveal a tasteful amount of cleavage.

Another person appeared behind the little black dress woman and pulled her chair out for her. Of course she was going to have a date. It was Valentine's Day. That was the whole point. The date had short brown hair cut close around the ears and wore a black suit with a white shirt but open collar. As the date turned around to pull out the other chair, the obvious hips and breasts could only be those of a woman. *And she plays for my team.*

Little black dress woman adjusted herself in the chair. She looked uncomfortable. Then as Kenzie got to the end of the verse, the woman looked up. They locked eyes and held each other's gaze until the woman's date interrupted her and she quickly looked away.

Kenzie continued with her set list with minimal interruptions from Jenni. She was able to sneak in a few of the new singles she was working on. It was hard to gauge the reaction from the busy room, but no one talked over her, so that was a good sign.

She strummed the last chord of the song, and little black dress woman's date approached her. Kenzie held off on starting the next song in case she was coming for a request. The woman pulled her wallet out of her back pocket and grabbed a few ones. She dropped them in the tip jar next to the "McKenzie McCall" sign.

"Are you still taking requests?"

"Of course. What would you like?"

The woman leaned in and whispered something in Kenzie's ear.

Kenzie wrinkled her forehead. "Seriously?"

"It's our song." The date looked offended. "Can you play it or not?"

Kenzie shook her head. "I can play it. Coming right up." Kenzie scrolled on her tablet until she found the chords she needed. She made eye contact with little black dress woman as she said, "This one is a special request." She started the intro. It wasn't that Kenzie didn't like Jewel. She was a talented songwriter and she had admired her work for years. It was just that this particular song was overplayed, and like Kenzie experienced many a time, not one of the songwriter's best. However, it was catchy and people liked it, so it lived on. Kenzie reminded herself that tonight wasn't about her. It wasn't about playing songs she liked or entertaining herself. It was about creating a mood for the patrons, and if she was being honest with herself, doing something to help Jenni.

Kenzie got to the chorus. She didn't belt it out by any means, but picked up her volume and put her own passion into it. She imagined singing to her own lover on this day. What would it be like to tell someone you were meant to be together forever? Little black dress woman pushed herself back from her chair quickly. Not in a way that signaled she just needed to use the restroom, but in an aggressive "I need to get out of here" kind of way. She threw her napkin on the table and stormed off. Her heels echoed on the floor even over Kenzie's playing. She didn't stop at the coat check but pushed the glass doors open with both hands, and just like that, she was gone.

Cʜᴀᴘᴛᴇʀ Tᴡᴏ

Rachel Park hated Valentine's Day. She hated pink. She hated red hearts. She hated the baby Cupid decorations and the idea that some all-knowing baby held responsibility for the love choices of full-grown adults. More than all of that, she hated those little heart candies with the stupid sayings. Not only did they taste like chalk, but now they tried to seem relevant, saying stupid things like "Text Me" or whatever.

Rachel stalled in the bathroom, psyching herself up for the date night ahead. Her hair fell down in loose curls, and she wore her favorite little black dress. It didn't scream Valentine's Day, but Rachel had never been the type to wear pink and she wasn't about to start now.

She didn't know what to do about Laurel. She couldn't explain it, but it wasn't working. Laurel was nice enough and had been great to Rachel for their nearly nine months together, but something was missing. There was no spark. She didn't know if she had ever felt a spark. Yes, at the beginning they had passion, but once the newness wore off, there wasn't anything left.

Laurel had planned this dinner for months. Ever since the tickets had gone on sale, it was all she could talk about. This dinner had been planned almost as long as they had been together. For Rachel to leave her now seemed just cruel. And that's if she even wanted to leave her. This dinner, their "special Valentine's dinner," as she kept calling it, was all she had talked about all week. Plus, things weren't all bad with Laurel.

More than anything, Rachel wanted to be a mother. She

yearned for it in a way that surprised even herself. At thirty-one, her biological clock ticked stronger each month. Laurel wanted kids just as much as Rachel did. On paper everything seemed perfect. They both had good careers and financially were ready for a family, but something just wasn't right. Which was ridiculous. Fairy tales weren't real and happily ever afters didn't exist. If Rachel was with someone who was perfectly fine and had the same goals as her, why did staying seem so hard?

"Ready, babe?" Laurel called from the living room.

"Be right out." She gave herself a final once-over, especially pleased with how her hair cooperated this evening.

Laurel helped her into her long black jacket. "Right on time. Like always."

Goose bumps formed on Rachel's arms as she handed her jacket to the coat check at the front of the restaurant. Pressed was only a few blocks from her office. She'd passed by it many times but had never stopped in. Even though red and pink hearts littered the space, she loved it. She could tell that on a normal day, the vaulted ceilings and industrial decor would be a cool place to hang out.

Laurel pulled the chair out for her. It annoyed Rachel no end. The implication that she couldn't pull out her own chair insulted her. She let out a sharp breath, trying to rid her mind of those thoughts. It was a nice thing to do. Her girlfriend was just trying to be nice. She shifted on the wooden chair, trying to get comfortable. Her ears perked up. How long had it been since she'd heard this song?

Her father loved Eric Clapton. He kept a record player in his study and spent countless evenings teaching Rachel why records sounded superior to digital recordings. Hearing this song from a woman's voice sounded different, but she liked it. And what a voice the woman had. The "McKenzie McCall" sign propped against the microphone stand partially blocked the long legs of the performer.

Well, McKenzie, I'm sure you have a day job, but your voice is great. She tried not to get distracted by the good looks of McKenzie McCall either. She looked nothing like Laurel. She looked nothing like the few girls Rachel had dated, and yet Rachel found herself drawn to her. She could get lost in those blue eyes, and my God, she wanted to run her fingers through that long, blond hair. Laurel's voice snapped her from her wandering thoughts.

"You like this place, babe?"

Rachel refocused on her. "Yes," she replied. "It's great." She looked around, taking in the space some more. "I pass by here all the time, but have never actually stopped in."

"I come by for coffee about once a week. It looks way different tonight with all the tables and decorations."

Their food arrived, and the flavors in the simple chicken with vegetables were much more than Rachel expected. When Laurel had shared they were going to a coffee shop for Valentine's Day, Rachel didn't know what to think. The whole night sounded awful to her, but Laurel acted so excited that she'd sucked it up and played along.

"I found the cutest house online today." Laurel patted her thigh.

"Shoot. No phones at dinner."

"I think we could break the rule if you wanted."

"No. No. I want us to keep working on being present."

Being present at meals was a recent development. Not that Rachel didn't want to give Laurel her full attention, but when her job was to be available all hours of the day, it was hard to detach.

"It's in this new development. Super kid friendly. There's a playground in the middle and a community pool."

"Oh?"

"I was thinking we could go take a look this weekend."

"Are you planning to buy a house?"

"For us."

Looking at houses was a big step. Where was this coming from? "Don't you think it might be a little soon for that? We don't even live together."

"Yet. We are going to move in together eventually, aren't we?"

Shit.

"Families live in houses and you are absolutely going to love this one. Just humor me and look at it. Okay?"

Where was the harm in looking at a house? Open houses could be fun. "You're right. Even if we aren't moving in together right now, it could be fun to see what we might want in the future."

"Exactly. You. Me. A few kids running around. Maybe a dog."

It was the picture Rachel dreamed of, but something didn't sit right. She couldn't explain it. When she tried to picture the future with Laurel standing next to her, she didn't feel any sense of excitement.

"I'll be right back." Laurel pushed her chair back from the table.

Rachel resisted the urge to check her phone. It was a work night, and she was on a huge case. Normally, she wouldn't go out the night before she had to be at court in the morning, but Valentine's Day became the exception. She thought of all the unread emails waiting for her. Surely one quick glance couldn't hurt. *No. I need to be a good girlfriend tonight. Whatever is on my phone can wait.* She grabbed her clutch purse, unable to keep herself from her phone. Just as she unzipped it, Laurel returned. Rachel put her clutch back down. "I'm sorry."

"I thought we agreed no more phones at meals."

"We did." Now Rachel truly felt like a jerk. They had both agreed to try and have less screen time while together since they both had jobs that ate up most of their waking hours. It was sweet the way Laurel cared about their relationship and wanted to work on it. But it was hard to work on a relationship and three major cases at the same time. She wished Laurel would give her just a little more breathing room when work was so busy, but clearly that was not possible on Valentine's Day.

"I requested a song for us," Laurel said.

"Oh?" Rachel tried to sound playful. It was a sweet thing to do. Laurel was being sweet. She needed to focus on that.

"It's our song." Laurel held a cheesy grin that Rachel couldn't help but smile at.

"I love our song." McKenzie McCall looked right at her as she said, "This one is a special request." Rachel's heartbeat ticked up. She furrowed her brow as the song started. This wasn't Bruno Mars. Or if it was, it was the weirdest rendition ever. What was this song? It kept going, and it hit her. Jewel. Seriously? This is what Laurel thought their song was?

Rachel shook her head and tried to mask her annoyance. It was a cute idea. She needed to focus on that. Laurel looked down at her lap. Her face contorted into a weird expression. Nervous maybe?

"Babe, I—" Laurel cleared her throat. "I—" She tried to start and then stopped again. "I have loved you since the moment I laid eyes on you. Not only do I want to look at houses with you, I want to build a future with you. You are it for me and I know that deep down, I was meant for you and you were meant for me." Laurel slid a small black box across the table to Rachel.

"What's this?" Rachel hesitated. She feared she knew exactly what the box contained and hoped to God she was wrong.

Laurel looked up, small tears forming in the corner of her eyes. "Open it."

Rachel took the box. She opened the hinged lid to reveal a gold engagement ring with a pear-shaped diamond. The ring's band surrounded a pink candy heart that read "Marry Me."

"Oh my God!" She pushed the box away. Her heart pounded in her chest. Her mind spun with thoughts, unable to land on a coherent one. She couldn't speak. Her heartbeat rang in her ears. It became the only sound in the room. Not knowing what else to do, she threw her napkin on the table and stormed out.

CHAPTER THREE

"Sorry I had to meet so late." Rachel met Ashley sitting at a small table in the middle of Pressed. Rachel's sister insisted on taking her for a drink Friday night. They hadn't had sister time in ages, and Ashley wanted to hear the whole story of the proposal. It seemed weird going back to the place Laurel had proposed, but it was close to Rachel's firm and a bar would be too loud to talk. Plus, there was a wine Rachel had eyed on Valentine's Day and wanted to try.

Ashley pulled her into a hug. "It's no problem at all. I know my baby sister is some kind of big-shot lawyer these days."

The red and pink hearts had long disappeared, and Rachel liked the vibe much better tonight. Rachel and Ashley looked so much alike multiple people mistook them for twins. Ashley shared the same brown hair, but hers stopped just above her shoulder. Having two children filled her face and hips out rounder than her younger days, but their resemblance remained unmistakable.

"I don't know about big shot, but certainly busy."

"I'll say. I'm surprised you could even pencil me in."

"I knew better than to fight my big sister."

"I always knew you were smart."

A waitress with a black pixie cut arrived, delivered two glasses of red wine, and quickly disappeared.

"I took the liberty of ordering," Ashley said. "You're going to love this."

Rachel swirled the glass in her hand and inhaled. Leather, coffee, and a hit of currant. "Is this what I think it is?"

Ashley nodded. "It is."

Wine tasting was something they did together. They loved learning all they could about the process and sampling all the various blends Oregon wine country offered. Rachel took a small sip and swirled the Pinot Noir over her tongue. Her eyes rolled back into her head as she swallowed. Heaven in a glass.

"Right?" Ashley said after her own sip.

"This is even better than I remember." Rachel took another sip, and the wine warmed her throat. "There is nothing better than a glass of wine after a day of kicking ass in court."

"Is there anything else we might be celebrating tonight?" Ashley looked to Rachel's left hand.

"There is nothing in my personal life to celebrate."

"So, you said no?"

"I said not yet."

"Start over. I need to hear the whole story."

"Laurel apologized for proposing in such a public place. She said she knew it was unfair, but she just got caught up in the moment. She thought it would be romantic."

"So, you said?"

"I told her to ask me again later."

"Ask again later? What's the holdup?"

"If we're going to spend forever together, then what's the rush?" Rachel shrugged. She still struggled to find the words to describe the conflict in her mind.

"When Patrick proposed to me, I couldn't wait to marry him. I don't even think we waited five months from proposal until wedding day." Ashley looked off in the distance, probably thinking back to that fond memory.

"I remember," Rachel said. "I was there, and getting everything done in time was a real cluster. We could barely find a venue."

"But we did, and it was magical."

Rachel let out a short sigh. "Do you and Patrick still have, you know? A spark?"

"Oh my God, yes." Ashley's eyes lit up. "We have our problems, all couples do, but I swear I still get butterflies when he looks at me a certain way."

"I don't think I've ever felt butterflies for Laurel," Rachel said.

"Really? Not even in the beginning?"

"I don't know." Rachel shook her head. "Laurel is fine. Our relationship is fine. I just…" She paused, searching for her words. "I want more than fine."

"And you deserve more than fine."

"But I can't help but think I'm being too picky, you know? If things with Laurel are fine, then I should just stop overthinking. What if I say no and never find anyone?"

"Well, little sister, you have never stopped overthinking, so why would you start now?"

"Fair."

"I thought things were going well with Laurel."

"Yes and no."

"And you both seem to want the same things."

"We do." Rachel picked up her wine glass needing something to do with her hands.

"So, if things are going well and you both want the same things, when she asked you to marry her, why didn't you say yes?"

Why *didn't* she say yes? And why couldn't she explain it? "It's so hard to articulate. The best way to put it is sometimes you don't know the answer until someone asks the question."

"Tell me this, how would you feel right now if you went home and didn't hear from Laurel tonight?"

"That's ridiculous. Why wouldn't I hear from her?"

"I don't know, maybe because she asked someone to marry her and you said 'ask me again later' like some kind of Magic 8 Ball? Whatever the reason, just play along. How would you feel?"

Rachel tried to picture her apartment void of Laurel's things. They didn't live together, but traces of Laurel were scattered throughout her place. A surprising calm washed over her as she thought about never having to share the sink with her again. "Relieved," she finally answered.

Ashely gave a knowing look. "You deserve to be happy, and I think you know what you need to do."

"She's going to be so heartbroken if I break up with her."

"But you'll be heartbroken if you stay."

Rachel looked at her watch as she picked up her wineglass. Seven ten. The sign out front said live music starting at seven. The stage from the other night housed the same barstool and microphone, but there was no performer in sight. Rachel took another sip from her glass. God, it tasted delicious.

"I support you no matter what," Ashley said. "But I don't think you should marry Laurel. Now or in the future."

"You don't?" Her sister was no stranger to speaking her mind, but Rachel hadn't expected her to be so blunt. She figured she would just tell her to be happy and she was by her side always. If her sister didn't think she should marry Laurel, maybe her own thoughts weren't so far off.

"Like you said," Ashley swirled her wine, "Laurel is fine. I have watched you two for however many months, and the bottom line is, you deserve to be more than fine. And if you think that you need to marry Laurel because there is no one else out there for you, then you are not nearly as smart as I give you credit for."

A breeze tickled Rachel's arms as the front door opened and a blonde carrying a guitar case rushed into the building. She wore dark skinny jeans with high brown boots. Rachel shook her head when she caught herself staring at her ass as she stepped up onto the stage. Her tight purple T-shirt hugged her body in all the right places, and Rachel shook her head again. She was here to talk with her sister, not ogle strange women. The woman set her guitar case behind the divider, then emerged a few moments later, guitar slung over one shoulder. She propped a large black sign up against the microphone stand and Rachel read, "McKenzie McCall."

CHAPTER FOUR

The Friday night crowd was awesome. The tips were rolling in. The requests were songs Kenzie liked, and all in all this was shaping up to be a good night. Kenzie was beyond thankful for Jenni's frantic call that a singer backed out. Anything was better than staring at the blank page on her piano at home.

It didn't make sense. Songwriting was what Kenzie did. It was what she lived for, how she expressed herself. So when Global Studios approached her wanting a song for an upcoming movie, of course she said yes. It was a period piece about two lovers during World War II slated to come out in December. The studio knew it would be a contender for many Cinematic Council of America Awards, the most prestigious film award around. She technically had until August to get the song out, but nothing would come. Perhaps the crowd tonight would spark inspiration.

Kenzie finished her first hour and headed to the bar where she desperately needed the Jack Daniel's Jenni kept waiting for her. The crowd seemed into her set, not talking too loud or soft. Someday it would be bigger crowds requesting only songs she had written.

She reached over the ledge of the bar for her bottle. A small glass was placed next to it. She poured herself three fingers and took a small sip. She let out a satisfied breath as the familiar burn coated her throat.

"I didn't know they served whiskey at a wine bar," someone said from behind Kenzie.

Kenzie turned and met the woman the voice belonged. "They don't, but I'm not a big wine drinker, and Jenni takes care of me." Kenzie pointed at Jenni, who currently ran around the room attending to customers. This brown-haired woman looked familiar, but Kenzie couldn't place where she knew her from.

The woman drummed her fingers on the bar and looked around.

"I can grab you something if you want?" Kenzie offered. "It might be a minute to get Jenni's attention."

"She's got you performing and bartending?" the woman said playfully.

"I have many talents." Kenzie hopped off her barstool. "What are you drinking?"

The woman pointed to an opened bottle on the back shelf. "That pinot there. Two glasses. My sister and I are drinking the same thing."

Kenzie picked up the bottle. "This one?" Kenzie knew nothing about wine and didn't want to pour the wrong thing.

The woman nodded. "You're good, you know."

"Thanks." Kenzie took two glasses down.

"I heard you briefly at the Valentine's Day dinner. I liked you then too."

"You're little black dress woman." The words came out before she could stop them.

The woman cocked an eyebrow. "Excuse me?"

"Sorry," she said. "But you were wearing the hell out of that dress and I took notice." Kenzie set the wine down. "You were with someone."

"Yeah…"

"She requested Jewel, of all things, and then you stormed off." Kenzie thought about that moment all week. What happened that would make someone react that way? It would make a great song.

"She proposed to me."

"Oh." Why did she feel disappointed? She knew this woman was with someone. "Congratulations." Kenzie raised both glasses and set them on the bar in front of her.

"I haven't said yes yet."

Kenzie gave a questioning look.

"There's no statute of limitations on marriage proposals," the woman fired back.

"This is a story I would love to hear the end to. I have to finish my set, but is there any chance you can stick around?" Kenzie looked into her brown eyes.

The woman looked back at the table she came from. Another woman played on her phone, Kenzie assumed her sister. "Yeah. I can stick around."

"I will get you the best glass of wine in the place to make it worth your while." A small flutter ran through Kenzie's stomach.

"That's a pretty big promise for someone who doesn't like wine."

"I'm a big promise kind of girl," Kenzie said. "I'll try and make this last set quick. Any requests?"

"Yeah," the woman nodded, and her mouth formed a small smile. "You played Eric Clapton. I'd love to hear more."

Not only did little black dress woman like her playing, but she remembered what she'd played. "You got it." Kenzie headed back to the stage. What else did little black dress woman like?

Chapter Five

Rachel returned to the table with two full wine glasses. Ashley looked up as she reached for her glass. "Took you long enough."

"Sorry," Rachel said as she sat down. "It's a busy night here." Rachel couldn't help but notice McKenzie McCall as she resumed her place onstage. She admired her slender fingers as she skillfully formed them into chords on the guitar. God, her lips looked soft as she sang. *What am I doing?* She still needed to sort things out with Laurel. She didn't have space in her brain for whatever this was.

She and Ashley resumed their conversation. They talked work, family, Ashley's kids, all of the usual stuff. Rachel couldn't help but keep being drawn into McKenzie McCall's smooth voice. She wanted to listen to her sister, but each time a new song started, she found herself excited, trying to figure it out.

Rachel spun her head around when Ashley snapped her fingers at her. "What's that?" she asked, knowing full well she hadn't paid attention.

"What's gotten into you?"

"Nothing."

Ashley's gaze burned through her. "You can't lie to me, little sister." Ashley looked from McKenzie McCall to Rachel. "Is it her? Are you distracted by the cute blond singer?"

"What? No, of course not." *Yes, oh my God, yes.* She couldn't admit that out loud, and not to her sister, of all people.

"I'm going to let this go," Ashley said, "but only for now." She finished the last sip of wine in her glass and looked at her watch.

"Patrick will kill me if I don't get home soon. I'm going to head out."

"I'm going to stick around and listen to the music," Rachel said.

"Mm-hmm." Ashley nodded with a mischievous grin.

"What?"

"Oh nothing." Ashley waved her off and didn't lose the grin on her face. "Let's do this again, soon." She emphasized "soon."

Rachel pulled her into a hug. "Yes. Soon. I promise I mean soon and not a month from now."

Rachel checked her watch. McKenzie said she'd make her set quick. She'd hoped that meant it was almost done. Not that she didn't want to keep listening to her sing, but getting alone time with McKenzie excited her. She couldn't explain it. Rachel never made friends quickly, but in the brief interaction she'd had, she found McKenzie easy to talk to. It didn't hurt that she'd complimented the way she'd looked on Valentine's Day. But that didn't mean anything. Lots of straight woman could have said something like that.

McKenzie told the room good night. Rachel caught herself staring at her ass again as she bent down to put her guitar away. *Get yourself together.*

"You mind if we head to the back?" McKenzie asked once she had packed up for the night. "Closer to the drinks." McKenzie smiled and the tiniest of sparks ignited inside Rachel.

"That's great." Rachel followed her.

McKenzie pulled out a barstool for Rachel and then one for herself. "I'm Kenzie, by the way." Kenzie held out her hand.

"Not McKenzie?"

"McKenzie McCall looks better on a sign. All my friends just call me Kenzie."

Rachel took her hand. "Rachel Park."

"Rachel Park, it is fantastic to meet you." Kenzie signaled for the bartender's attention. "Jenni," Kenzie started, "I promised my new friend Rachel here a glass of your best wine. Can you help me out?"

Jenni's gaze found her. Was that a twinge of jealousy coming from her? Clearly, Kenzie and Jenni knew each other, but she had no idea in what capacity.

"Of course," Jenni finally answered. "It's the least I can do after you so graciously helped me out tonight."

Kenzie reached over the bar for her bottle of whiskey and poured herself another glass. She took a sip and her T shirt slipped, exposing her collarbone. Rachel wanted to run her fingers from the nape of Kenzie's neck to the smooth expanse of her shoulder. She needed to stop staring. Her attention redirected from Kenzie as Jenni reappeared, pushing a full glass in front of her. "Thank you," she said and Jenni took a step back. Rachel swirled the wine and pulled the glass up to her nose. This one smelled fruitier than the last. Strawberry maybe? She took a small sip and swirled it over her tongue. "This is really good."

Jenni looked proud of her selection. "I thought you'd like it. Well, I'll leave you to it."

"So." Kenzie leaned her elbow against the bar and faced Rachel. "Your date comes to request Jewel. I play an amazing rendition, if I do say so myself, and then what happens?"

Rachel swirled her wine and cleared her throat. "Laurel, my date." God, that was a weird way to refer to her girlfriend, but in Kenzie's mind, that's all she was. "She came back to the table and told me that she requested our song."

"That's your song?"

"No. At least I didn't think so. I expected Bruno Mars, but then your amazing rendition played instead. Then she pushed a box across the table, and in the middle of the ring was one of those candy hearts that says 'Marry Me.' "

Kenzie snorted. "Are you serious?"

"Yeah. She thought it was romantic or something."

Kenzie gave a laugh and then appeared to catch herself. "Was the ring nice?"

"No." She hadn't admitted out loud that she didn't like the ring. "It was the wrong kind of gold and pear-shaped."

"Pear-shaped?"

"Yeah." Rachel furrowed her brow. "Who even wants that?"

Kenzie shrugged. "So you didn't say yes?"

"I know." Rachel put her head in her hands. It was freeing to talk through her situation with a complete stranger. Talking with

Ashley helped, but her sister was biased. Kenzie knew nothing about Laurel, and that helped her find a new level of clarity.

"Why not?" Kenzie asked.

Rachel looked up and faced her. "I look at my parents," she said. "They've been married over thirty years. They are happy enough, I guess." She shrugged. "I want to be married and start a family, but I can't help but think there has to be more than happy enough. I swear my parents only had sex two times. I want stability, but I want passion. I want dancing in the hallway at midnight, you know?"

"I do."

"I want to be a mother." Again, Rachel found herself admitting more than she normally would. "I want to start a family, but I want a happy family." She paused and looked at the wine in her glass. After a moment passed, she turned to face Kenzie. "Are your parents happy?"

Kenzie gave a nervous laugh. "Well, it's a little complicated."

"I'm sorry." Rachel shook her head. "I shouldn't have asked. I barely know you, and that's a personal question." Rachel often forgot that not everyone had the simple home life that she did. Her parents had been married her whole life, and she never had even an ounce of family drama.

"No. It's okay We're being honest with each other." She locked eyes with Rachel. "It's complicated because my dad passed away."

Rachel placed her hand on Kenzie's thigh. "I'm so sorry." She pulled her hand back like she touched a hot stove. Kenzie's gaze moved to her hand. What was she thinking? Asking all of these personal questions and then touching her like that? She didn't know what had come over her, but she needed to comfort Kenzie.

"It's okay," Kenzie said reassuringly, and Rachel didn't know if she meant the question or her hand. Maybe both. "It was a long time ago," Kenzie continued. "My dad was sick, basically my whole life. Pancreatic cancer." Kenzie paused and took another sip of whiskey. "His whole goal was to see me grown." Kenzie waved her arm as she spoke. "He said he knew he couldn't be around for long, but he could at least get me to being an adult. So, I graduated high school then turned eighteen the next week. Two days later, he was gone."

"That's hardly grown," Rachel said. A small break formed in her heart for young Kenzie. What a horrible thing to have to go through.

"I know." Kenzie smiled, but it didn't reach her blue eyes. "But it's the best he could do. He fought for as long as he could."

"Thank you for sharing."

Kenzie let out a breath. "But while he was alive, my parents were extremely happy. I don't know if it's because they knew they didn't have much time together, or if they were just happy people, but they were madly in love with each other."

So such a love did exist out there.

"So much so," Kenzie said, "that my mom never remarried. Honestly, I don't think she's been with anyone since my dad."

"Wow."

"Right?" Kenzie replied. "Can you imagine almost fourteen years without sex?"

Rachel burst into laughter, caught off guard by the comment. "That's not where my mind went, but no, I can't imagine that either." At the rate she and Laurel were going, she was headed on a similar streak. Rachel took another sip of her wine. Kenzie's demeanor changed. Probably from the memories of her dad that must be flooding her brain now. Rachel hadn't meant to get so personal but couldn't help herself. She changed the subject. "You're really good, you know? You should sell your songs or something. I'm sure people would buy them."

"Thank you, but legally I can't."

Rachel cocked her head to the side. "Why's that?"

"The short story is I didn't read the fine print."

Rachel knew all about the dangers of fine print. "And the long story?"

"Do you know the singer Braxton?"

"Doesn't everyone?" She held Kenzie's gaze for a beat. Those blue eyes pulled her in. "She's only one of the most popular singers right now."

"I wrote four of the tracks on her album, and we are in the process of recording her second." Kenzie grinned.

"Shut up!" Rachel slapped her shoulder with the back of her hand. "Seriously?"

"Seriously."

McKenzie McCall was quite possibly a full-fledged rock star and here she was, drinking with her. "So, if you can write songs like that and sing as well as you can, why are you letting someone else perform? Why not do it yourself?"

"That's where the fine print comes in. When I signed with Global Recording, I didn't realize I was selling them my songs. Like, I knew they were getting my songs, I just thought that I would get to be the one performing them. Turns out, they get to pick. And they get first rights to any and all future songs."

"So you just have to watch other people perform your songs?"

"For now. I hope to get my shot someday. But it's all a business, you know? They only want so many female artists, blah blah blah." Kenzie finished her drink and refilled the glass.

"How many years are left on your contract?"

"Four, I think?"

"Is there an option to buy it out?"

"Maybe. But do you know how much money these studios have? I've never even thought to look into it. But it's okay. I love songwriting. It gives me a chance to hone my craft and play around with other genres. Then when the time is right, I'll be ready."

"So that's what you want? To be a performer like Braxton?"

"I wouldn't say I want to be exactly like her, but I absolutely want the chance to perform. When you tour like Braxton does, she's on the road nine months out of the year. That leaves next to no time for songwriting, or a family, or anything like that."

"Do you have a family?" Rachel's curiosity got the better of her. She assumed that since Kenzie was out on a Friday night, she would be single, but in all reality, she could have someone waiting for her at home.

"No." Kenzie shook her head. "Not yet. But with all the last-minute gigs and traveling, I doubt any woman would put up with me as a wife for long. I wasn't even supposed to be here tonight. But in a perfect world I'd have a wife and four or five music prodigy kids waiting at home, so I'd never have to worry about finding studio musicians again."

She'd said "wife." Excitement at this new development overtook her. Kenzie stared off in front of them. What was she thinking? "You're already putting your future kids to work?"

"Oh, I've got big plans for these future kids."

Rachel wanted to know more.

"But until then, I've got my own hopes and dreams. For now, it's nice that I can experiment musically. I can write anything I want for whoever I want, and they can take it or leave it."

"What do you mean?"

"I've been writing a lot of country songs lately."

"Country?"

"Don't knock it. There are more instruments than synthesizers in country, and it's actually been fun. But if I was a performer like Braxton and I tried to go country out of the blue, it would be difficult. Not that artists can't change genres, it's just not easy."

"You said you wrote four tracks on her first album?" Rachel eyed her expectantly.

Kenzie nodded. "I did."

"'If It Doesn't Break Your Heart' got me through my last breakup." Rachel paused. "Any chance that's a McKenzie McCall original?"

Kenzie narrowed her gaze. "Most people don't know that one."

"Oh my God. It's the best song off the whole album."

Kenzie's smile widened. "That's one of the songs I'm most proud of. We got to production late, so we missed it being a single. Then it got buried as track seven and barely saw the light of day. I actually wanted that to win song of the year, but of course 'Only You' won out. It got more airtime."

"That one was definitely overplayed, catchy, but overplayed." Rachel straightened on the stool and pointed to her rib cage. "I almost got 'We could go back. I could be unbrokenhearted, but we can never go back to how we started' as a tattoo. Right here." She ran her hand up her side.

"Damn." Kenzie reached over the bar for something. She grabbed a pen and pad of paper. "Okay," Kenzie said as she furiously scribbled something down. "I like you. I would like to get to know you better, romantically." She paused and made direct eye contact with Rachel. "But you have baggage, and I don't do fiancés, or clingy ex-girlfriends or whatever ever Laurel is, but you know she has a little bit of crazy in her eyes."

"Okay?" Rachel reached for the paper that Kenzie slid her way.

"That's my favorite gig of the whole year." Kenzie pointed to the paper. "St. Patrick's Day. It's at an Irish pub and it's basically a big singalong, and this year St. Paddy's falls on a Saturday, so it's going to be wild. It's the most fun you've had in a long time, I promise." Kenzie paused again and Rachel knew the spark that had started inside her would ignite if she held eye contact much longer. "That gives you almost a month to figure out your situation. If I see you there, then that means you want me to take you to dinner after."

Rachel wasn't used to someone being so forward with her intentions. It was refreshing. "You know, you could just give me your number and text me the info?"

"Nope." Kenzie shook her head and let out a long sigh. "Nope," she said again. "If I have your number, then I'm going to want to text you or call you or see what you've decided, and it will drive me bonkers. Plus, you need to get yourself figured out without me as a distraction."

Rachel knew she was right but also didn't know if she could wait a month to see her again.

"I know this must seem a little direct. But if there's one thing I learned from my dad, it's that life is short, and you have to be clear about what you want."

That small heartbreak opened again for a young Kenzie. How could she feel heartbroken for someone she just met?

"So." Kenzie downed the last sip in her glass. "I really hope I see you on St. Patrick's Day, but if I don't, it is always great to meet a fan and, Rachel Park, I think you will make a fantastic mother someday."

"Thank you" was all Rachel could say as Kenzie turned and made her way back to the stage to collect her things. Rachel stared at Kenzie's scrawled handwriting on the paper. She had a month to figure herself out.

CHAPTER SIX

In the weeks since Kenzie met Rachel at Pressed, she'd kicked herself on more than one occasion for not getting her number. She knew it was the right thing to do. If she had Rachel's number, she would be staring at a blank screen right now agonizing over what to text her. *Did you say no yet? How did she take it? Do you need help moving?* Did they even live together? There was so much she needed to learn about Rachel.

When Rachel admitted she almost got Kenzie's lyrics as a tattoo, it took all the willpower Kenzie had to not lean in and kiss her right there at the bar. It was a turn-on that Kenzie had never experienced before, and more than once, she found herself picturing the smooth skin of Rachel's bare rib cage. Surely Rachel had felt that charge between them too. How could she not? She shook her mind to clear those thoughts. She needed to focus. She was meeting with lawyer number three today. The law firm was only a few blocks from Pressed, so she stopped in to grab a coffee first.

The wonderful aroma of ground coffee beans consumed her as she entered. Jenni looked up from behind the counter. "Hey, Kenz," she said with a wave, and pointed to the end of the counter.

Kenzie grabbed the warm drink waiting for her. "Thanks." She fished a few one-dollar bills out of her wallet and dropped them in the tip jar.

Jenni wiped her hands on her black apron. "You look nice."

"Thanks." Kenzie blushed. Since she was in the music industry, she could get away with wearing a nice pair of jeans but had added a sky-blue blouse and black blazer to appear more professional. "I hate this part of the job."

"You mean the part where you make money?"

"I hate the steps involved to getting the money. If Cooper would just play more of my songs, I wouldn't have to resort to this."

"You just like the part where you get to write about how nasty your awesome exes are." Jenni grinned.

"Hey now." Kenzie held her hands up defensively. "That's not entirely fair."

"It's true."

"I didn't say it wasn't true, it's just not fair." Kenzie felt a little guilty about the success of her breakup songs with Jenni, but not guilty enough to stop writing them.

"Anyways, you know what they say?" Jenni sounded playful.

"What's that?"

"Third time's a charm. Speaking of, what time is your meeting?"

Kenzie furrowed her brow trying to remember. "Nine, I think? I was on a roll this morning, Jen. I might have a melody."

"Jesus, Kenz." Jenni shook her head and pointed at the clock behind her. "It's five till. You better get moving."

Damn, again. She picked up the coffee and raised it toward Jenni. "Thanks again. I'll let you know if this lawyer's a go."

"Good luck," Jenni called after her.

Kenzie was only five minutes late arriving at the large lobby of Pierce & Lloyd, the all-encompassing law firm that she had learned about from one of her producer friends. They had ties in all areas of the law, and unlike her first two meetings, Kenzie had a good feeling.

She checked in with the receptionist at a round, wooden desk in front of a marble covered wall. Hopefully, the amount of money poured into the decorations of this office was a sign they knew what they were doing.

The woman led Kenzie toward the back and told her to take a seat in the large conference room. The long, dark wooden table had seating for twenty. Kenzie couldn't imagine a meeting needing twenty people. Windows framed the walls, so Kenzie could see out into the busy office, and employees could see who was occupying the conference room. She rocked in one of the black captain's chairs and swiveled around. She caught a baby grand piano in the corner of the conference room on her third spin. Seriously? *They have a Steinway as decoration?*

Kenzie opened the top of the keyboard. She couldn't help herself. Kenzie could rarely see a piano without playing it, let alone a Steinway. She made a C chord and instantly winced. Clearly the piano hadn't been tuned since someone moved it into the room. She powered through and started playing a Braxton song. One of the less famous but still chart-topping ones. As she got through the end of the verse, someone else entered the conference room.

"I'm sorry. Was I being too loud?" She paused her playing but didn't look up.

"No. I love this song."

Kenzie knew that voice. "Rachel?"

She took a seat at the conference room table. "Keep going."

Kenzie picked up where she left off, this time thinking about her performance. It was one thing to fool around on the keyboard, it was another to try and impress someone. The music flowed out of her. The lyrics connecting in a way she hoped reached Rachel. Before the song ended, a small crowd had formed in the conference room. They gave mild applause as Kenzie finished, and she waved them off. She hoped they would disperse quickly and leave her alone with Rachel.

An older woman wearing a designer suit with chin-length blond hair entered the conference room from the other side. "Alright." She commanded the attention of the room. The bangle bracelets on her wrists clanged together as she clapped her hands for attention. "Last I checked, we have a meeting scheduled in this room. Ms. McCall, I presume?" The woman stretched out her hand.

"Yes." Kenzie took her hand. "I didn't mean to cause a scene. I just can't help myself when I see a piano."

"It's quite alright." The woman waved her off. "I'm Gail Pierce. Shall we start?"

Kenzie went back to her original chair. Rachel sat across from her, trying to contain a grin. So Rachel was a lawyer. Interesting. Another man entered the room. Gail motioned to him. "This is Greg Lloyd, and next to me is one our associates, Rachel Park."

"I get both named partners?"

Greg was much younger than Gail, possibly mid-forties. "Your business proposition is intriguing," Greg said. "We wanted both of us in this meeting so we can fully understand what exactly you are asking of our firm."

Kenzie rubbed her hands together. Business meetings always made her nervous. Now with the added pressure of Rachel staring at her, she needed to not look like a complete moron. "What would you like to know?"

"Actually," Gail flipped through some papers in front of her. "We have reviewed what you've sent us, but if you could just explain to us one more time your proposition, that would help us tremendously."

"I have access to a recording studio," Kenzie said.

"Yes," Gail said. "Band Geek Studio," she read off the papers in front of her.

Kenzie drummed her fingers on the table. "Yes. Silly name, I know, but that's not the point. Essentially, I sell time in the studio for other artists to record their work."

Greg glanced at Gail. "That seems like a pretty standard business transaction."

"Part of the studio time includes my services." Kenzie looked at Greg.

"What does that mean?" Greg narrowed his gaze.

"There are a lot of artists who want to bill themselves as singer-songwriters. If they record at my studio, I won't take any credit for any songs that come out of that time that I help them create. They can still list just themselves and the name of the studio they recorded at."

Greg leaned back and rocked in his chair. "Interesting."

"They get all rights to the song. I only ask that the studio be listed and that I receive a certain percentage of profits."

Gail flipped over the papers in front of her, quickly reading through them. "And you have laid out certain, let's call them bonuses, depending on the success of the song?"

"Exactly," Kenzie said. "The more successful the song, the more the studio gets. Where I need you guys is on the enforceability of the bonuses, as you called them, as well as keeping track of things.

It is highly likely I could help on a song this year that won't make money for another four or five. I can't keep up with that." Kenzie paused. "The other piece is discretion. Confidentiality is key. Artists aren't going to want this to get out, so we may need to change the business name, cease and desist letters. You get the idea."

Gail slid a piece of paper to Greg. He looked at it and nodded. "These are your projected figures for the studio?" Greg asked.

"Those are the projections for this year." Greg's eyes went wide. She knew she was sitting on a gold mine, but she didn't want just anyone helping with her business. Kenzie reached into her bag and pulled out her own manilla folder. She pushed it across the table to Gail. "I can't let you keep this, but if you look at the bottom of the first page, that's the total of all the clients I have lined up for the next three years."

Gail's face formed a tight smile and she passed the paper over to Greg. Rachel, who had kept quiet the entire meeting, peered over Greg's shoulder. Her eyes went wide.

"Ms. McCall," Gail said, "I think that Pierce and Lloyd would be happy to take you on as a new client."

"I was hoping you'd say that, but there are two pretty big contingencies before I can decide."

Greg turned his palms up. "Anything."

"My name can't be tied to any of these songs at all."

"We can be discreet, but guaranteeing your name won't be tied at all is extremely difficult," Rachel said.

"I'm confident you can do it." Kenzie stared into her brown eyes. Had her eyes been that brown at Pressed? She looked so different in a professional environment. Such a lawyer in her suit jacket. "I have a strict contract with Global Recording, which is owned by Global Studios, that is pretty clear they get access to all of my songs."

"We can't do anything that would conflict with Global Studios," Greg said.

"I'm not asking you to. All I'm going to do is unlock the doors to the studio I have access to, and then whatever happens happens."

"It's not impossible. Just a gray area," Rachel said.

"I knew you could do it."

"What's the second thing?" Gail asked.

"Joey, my drummer. He got so many parking tickets his license has been revoked, and it has become increasingly annoying to pick him up. If you guys can make that disappear, the business is yours."

Gail and Greg exchanged a knowing look. "I think we can handle that," Gail said smugly. "Rachel here will be your personal contact for all matters. She is one of our leading contract lawyers and one of the best in the country, if I do say so myself."

Rachel's cheeks flushed red.

Gail continued. "She will be able to help you with anything you need, and I am sure you won't regret becoming a part of the Pierce and Lloyd family."

"Actually, there's one more thing."

Gail furrowed her brow. "What's that?"

"Get that piano tuned." Kenzie motioned to the baby grand in the corner. "Something like that needs to be more than decoration."

"Of course."

Kenzie exchanged handshakes across the table.

"Ms. McCall, why don't you follow me back to my office, and we can get started on some of this paperwork," Rachel said.

Kenzie definitely had a great feeling about this law firm.

CHAPTER SEVEN

Y ou didn't tell me you were a lawyer." Kenzie shut the door to Rachel's office.

"You didn't ask."

"True. Best contract lawyer in the country, I hear." Kenzie leaned back into the chair across from Rachel's desk.

"I'm technically not a contract lawyer."

"You all really aren't helping with the 'all lawyers are liars' stereotype."

"I wasn't supposed to be in that meeting today. Our actual contract lawyer got held up in court, and they didn't want one of the first-years sitting in on a meeting that important."

As a third-year associate, Rachel could relax a little more than the first-years, but when Gail asked her to sit in a meeting, even though she was juggling three big cases of her own, she knew better than to say no. Her hope was to focus more on her actual cases and less on the interoffice politics of who had the most billable hours, but if she had any shot of making partner in the next five years, she needed Gail on her side.

"How does this all work? I mean, now that I'm an important client and all."

"First, I need to recuse myself as your lawyer and get you assigned to someone else."

"What? Why?"

"For starters, I've met you outside of work and you've asked me out."

"Right. Does this mean you've dealt with your situation and you plan to say yes to our date?" Kenzie leaned forward.

Rachel needed to end it with Laurel. She didn't know what her holdup was. The thought of breaking up with Laurel seemed overwhelming. Starting over at this stage in life. Dating again? After hearing all the horror stories from her single friends, dating was something she never wanted to do.

Besides, things with Laurel were fine. They'd looked at the cute house and she could picture herself living in it with a few kids running around. Who said that a marriage had to have a spark? In the nights since talking with Kenzie at Pressed, she couldn't stop thinking about the pull she felt toward her after just one conversation. She had to have been imagining it. Right?

"It means I haven't sorted things out yet, and it would be inappropriate for me to represent you."

"Right." Kenzie leaned back. Was she disappointed? She definitely seemed disappointed.

"I didn't know you could play the piano." Rachel wished she could have seen Kenzie's hands on the keys. She should have assumed she played, since Kenzie was a songwriter, but some musicians just stuck to one instrument. Rachel had been a Braxton fan for years. She had even seen her in concert. Yet the way Kenzie sang her song in the conference room was so much deeper, more soulful. She loved it. It was probably due to the fact that Kenzie had written the song. She had lived the words and all that went into them. Braxton had an amazing voice and fancy dance moves, but did she know about heartbreak?

"I am a woman of many talents." Kenzie winked, and Rachel's body shook. God, she could only imagine what some of the talents would be.

"Is that who I think it is?" Kenzie stood and reached for the framed picture on the top shelf behind Rachel.

"Oh. Yes. That was at a conference shortly after I graduated."

"You actually met RBG?" Kenzie ran her hands over the glass frame.

"I did, and if you look behind her—" Rachel froze. Her hand brushed against Kenzie's on the frame, sending a jolt straight to her core. How could just a mere touch have this reaction on her? She cleared her throat. "If you look behind her, you can see the Supreme Court building."

Kenzie closed the gap between them. Their shoulders brushed. "That is really cool. Sounds like it was a great trip."

"It was."

"They say never to meet your heroes, but I got to meet Carole King a few years back, and it was freaking amazing."

"I can only imagine."

Kenzie placed the picture back. Rachel held her breath as Kenzie's arm moved around her to the shelf behind them. It would be so easy to lose control. But she couldn't. Not yet. No matter how amazing Kenzie smelled or how strong her arms looked, Rachel wasn't a cheater and this wasn't right.

"This is you and Laurel?" Kenzie picked up another framed picture.

"Yeah." Rachel's throat went dry.

"You make a nice couple."

Something about the picture was all wrong. Rachel leaned against Laurel in one of her favorite blue dresses, but the smile didn't reach her eyes. It was not a picture of a couple destined to have a happy future.

"Alright. So, will someone reach out to me about who my real lawyer is?"

"Yeah."

"Not that you're not a real lawyer, but you know what I mean." Kenzie placed the picture on Rachel's desk.

"I'll get the notes over to Nina and she can start drafting a contract for you once she's out of court. You should be hearing from her shortly."

"Cool. Well, I know that this didn't work out between us." Kenzie pointed back and forth between them, and Rachel could feel the electricity in the room. "But I promise you, I can be professional, so don't worry."

"Right. Professional." Professional was the last thing on her mind right now.

"But I still might come by and ask you for help on reading the fine print. It's been known to be an issue for me."

"It's very important to read the fine print."

"I'll see you around, Rachel."

Once the door shut, Rachel sank into her office chair. Holy hell. McKenzie McCall was something else. For all of her questioning and hesitation over the last few weeks, ten minutes in Kenzie's presence and she knew exactly what she had to do. It was time to rip off the Band-Aid.

CHAPTER EIGHT

St. Patrick's Day had become Kenzie's absolute favorite gig of the year. Finn's was an Irish pub a few miles from her house, and this was their busiest night. She set up her keyboard on the makeshift stage toward the back, a few feet off the ground so that the entire bar could view her. She'd play in front of a large white projector screen that would display the lyrics so that the bar could sing along. When Finn's owner approached her with this idea five years ago, Kenzie thought that drunk group karaoke sounded like an awful idea. However, after the first few songs, she realized there was something almost magical about a group of strangers joining together, belting out lyrics to popular songs. She had grown to love it and could barely contain her excitement.

She needed to focus on the excitement of strangers because Rachel was not coming tonight. After seeing her at the law office, it was abundantly clear that Rachel would stay with Laurel. And why wouldn't she? She seemed nice and predictable and the kind of stable relationship Rachel was looking for. Besides, Kenzie didn't have time to focus on a girlfriend. She needed to be available to Global to help with other songs, and hopefully get her own chance to perform soon. What girlfriend was going to put up with that?

Chilled air wafted in as the front door opened, and Kenzie shuddered. It had been a rare sunny day, and Kenzie had chosen a green V-neck short-sleeve shirt. Once the bar filled up, she would heat up onstage, but that was still a ways away. Her hair was down again because she was working for tips tonight. She played a few chords on the keyboard, and it echoed in the mostly empty bar. The crowd started to filter in, as some folks had been drinking since ten a.m. Kenzie had learned after the first year that her keyboard lent itself better to this kind of group gig. She could add drumbeats and give the appearance of a full band. Ultimately, the more people drank, the less it mattered what she sounded like. She just needed to get the song going and the crowd would take it from there.

Satisfied that her keyboard was set up properly, she made her way to the bar for a drink. She signaled the bartender for a glass of whiskey. She held the glass up to the fluorescent bar lights. Was the glass green or the whiskey green? She couldn't tell and she wasn't sure if she cared, except how much green dye did it take to turn whiskey green? Finn's pulled out all the stops with decorations. Shamrocks and Irish flags adorned every possible surface. Apparently, the drinks needed to be festive as well.

"You ready for this?" Jenni wore tight green pants and a matching green top that would certainly help with their tips.

"I am now." Kenzie raised her glass and took another sip. She loved the feeling of whiskey warming her throat. "Thanks again for your help."

"It's no problem at all." Jenni took the seat next to her.

Kenzie did better with crowds when she wasn't alone. She had learned this after many years of being a solo performer. Tonight, she was the entertainment and she needed backup. Things would get busy with people asking for requests, and it helped to have a support person. That, and Kenzie knew her own vocal range had limits. Jenni could hit a high note like nobody's business, and she was going to need her skills at some point tonight.

"I'm thinking our usual repertoire tonight for the first songs, then we'll start with requests, if you're good with that?"

"I'm just excited to be in someone else's bar for a change. I'm good with whatever you want."

The crowd grew and Kenzie couldn't help looking for Rachel every time the door opened. No matter how many times she told herself Rachel wasn't coming tonight, part of her still hoped she would. "Shall we?"

"After you." Jenni followed Kenzie to the stage.

Kenzie's nerves subsided after the first few songs. She knew they would. The growing crowd was into it and singing louder than

Kenzie anticipated. They cycled through a few Top 40 songs to get the bar going, and it was working. Kenzie played a few chords quietly and spoke over them. "Alright, folks," she started. "Miss Jenni here is taking requests tonight." She pointed to Jenni, who held a large mason jar over her head. "So, if there is something you want to hear, write it on a five-dollar bill and Miss Jenni will make sure it gets played."

There were a few cheers and hollers as Jenni danced around the bar with the tip jar. Jenni was outgoing in a way Kenzie would never be, and it was great for nights like tonight. A mildly drunk guy placed five dollars in the jar, and Jenni shimmied her way back to the stage.

"Looks like we have our first request," Kenzie said. Jenni pulled the bill out and flashed it at Kenzie. "Okay." Kenzie tried to stifle her laughter. "Not what I was expecting you to request, sir." She found the guy in the crowd, and he raised the green beer he was drinking toward her. "And lucky for you, Jenni here can hit the high notes." Kenzie modulated the key from the riff she was playing and slowed her tempo. She motioned for Jenni to grab the microphone.

Jenni started in on the disco hit. The drunk guy in the back cheered and clapped wildly. Kenzie didn't know if he was cheering Jenni or the song itself, maybe both. It didn't matter; this was the fun part. Normally, Kenzie would try to harmonize, but in this setting, no one cared. The group sang along, and no one would hear her. She rested her voice and looked around the crowded room.

Then for the second time, the room stopped around Kenzie. Even though hordes of people sang at the top of their lungs, she heard nothing. Her eyes focused and narrowed in at the bar. Rachel. She wore jeans and a green sweater, her hair partially pulled back in a clip with the rest of it flowing down. Kenzie had never seen casual Rachel. She'd seen her dressed up on Valentine's Day, and lawyer Rachel. She liked this version of Rachel. She seemed relaxed, like she was ready for a night of fun. Rachel spoke to the woman next to her. Kenzie recognized her sister and was relieved that Rachel wasn't here alone. She didn't want her getting hit on by some drunk guy or having her feeling bored hanging around by herself.

After what seemed like hours, Rachel looked up, and Kenzie made eye contact. She tried to play it off like she hadn't been watching her every move, but didn't think she was succeeding. Rachel raised her green beer in a toast, and Kenzie wanted nothing more than to jump off stage and run to her.

"Hey," Jenni snapped at Kenzie.

The song had long ended, and they had been standing in silence for several moments. "Sorry," she mouthed to Jenni. Rather than take another request, Kenzie knew the exact song for this moment. She clicked her tablet to get the words projected behind her. She looked at Rachel, hoping she wasn't being too obvious with her song selection, but then decided she didn't care as she started in on Van Morrison's "Brown Eyed Girl."

The crowd really got into the "sha-la-la" part, and Rachel and her sister joined right in. The song ended and Kenzie spoke into her microphone. "Jenni and I are going to take a quick break, but we will be back shortly. Get your requests in and we'll make sure we get to them." With that, Kenzie stepped down off the stage. She could think of one thing and one thing only. Rachel.

CHAPTER NINE

"If it's lame, we can leave." Rachel shouted over the crowd as they crammed into Finn's.

"Are you kidding me?" Ashley said. "A night out with no kids? Even if it's lame, we're staying." She placed a hand on Rachel's shoulder and pushed her forward. "Drinks."

Rachel managed to get the bartender's attention through the crowd of green-clad people. She ordered two beers and handed one to Ashley. Kenzie was right, this was fun. Hearing the crowd of people singing along was mesmerizing. She took a long drink of her green beer, and the nerves building inside her began to settle. She found the source of the music and scanned the bar, finally seeing Kenzie onstage in the back. Her stomach did a flip as she realized Kenzie was looking right at her. Had Kenzie noticed her? Was she waiting for her to arrive? She raised her glass.

"This is fun!" Ashley shouted over the crowd. "So is that the dream girl?" She turned to face Rachel and flashed a toothy grin.

Rachel tensed. "I wouldn't say she's my dream girl."

"Well, whatever she is, I am happy that she gave you the kick in the ass you needed to finally move on from Laurel."

Rachel opened her mouth to speak, but nothing came out. What could she say in response to that anyway?

"I'm proud of you. I know that making that decision was hard. But you did what was right for you, and I'm excited to see what comes next for you."

"Yeah." Rachel nodded, still not ready to take her eyes off

Kenzie. Who was that singer with her? She looked familiar, but Rachel couldn't place her. There was an awkward silence between songs, and Rachel raised an eyebrow. Kenzie started in on the next song, and Rachel hoped Kenzie directed it at her.

The song ended and Rachel had hoped they'd keep playing. Watching Kenzie perform one song wasn't enough. The way she projected confidence while at her keyboard was what Rachel wanted to watch all night. She lost Kenzie in the crowd. She probably needed to go to the back or something. Rachel would just need to be patient. Someone brushed up against her. The bar had become increasingly crowded as people gathered for refills during the break. Then someone tapped her shoulder. She turned around to see a grinning Kenzie, and her heartbeat quickened.

"You made it." Kenzie's blue eyes lit up.

"I did."

Kenzie wrapped one arm around Rachel's middle and gave her a side hug. At almost six feet tall, it was rare for Rachel not to tower over people. Kenzie was only a few inches shorter, and Rachel liked it. She leaned her body into Kenzie's, tentatively accepting her hug. They fit perfectly. She could have held this position all night.

Kenzie pulled back quickly and motioned for Rachel to follow her. Rachel did, despite not wanting to break contact so soon. Kenzie reached her hand behind her, and Rachel grabbed it. She knew Kenzie just didn't want to lose her in the crowd, but she jumped at another chance to feel Kenzie. Rachel followed as Kenzie dodged between people and tables and led them to a seemingly open space just off the side of the stage.

Kenzie stopped and pulled Rachel in closer. They were barely six inches apart. "I'm so glad you're here," Kenzie said, and the smile had not left her face.

Rachel's face flushed. "Me too."

"So?" Kenzie looked at her expectantly.

"I am baggage free," Rachel answered, assuming she knew what Kenzie's question was.

"And you're doing okay?" Kenzie's tone changed to concern.

Of all the things for Kenzie to ask her in that moment, she hadn't imagined that. Hadn't Kenzie been rooting for her to end things with Laurel? Shouldn't she be jumping up and down? Kenzie showed genuine concern for her, someone who was still more or less a stranger. She shook her head to try to quiet the competing thoughts in her brain. "I'm doing great." It was the truth. Not being tied to Laurel, or anyone, had brought her a freedom she hadn't known in years. Yes, being single at thirty-one was in some ways terrifying, but in other ways, it was exciting.

"Good." Kenzie let out a long breath and shook her head. "I can't believe you're here."

"Why's that?"

"You're a smart and practical person, and staying with Laurel was the safe thing to do." Kenzie paused and looked Rachel in the eyes. "I am so glad you're here. And you know what this means?"

Rachel swallowed hard. She cleared her throat and stared at Kenzie's lips. "What?"

"I'm taking you to dinner tonight."

Rachel let out the air from her lungs. "That's right." Was it possible to feel disappointed and excited at the same time? She barely knew this woman. She couldn't expect her to stop what she was doing and kiss her in front of a crowded room. Rachel looked down and held the gaze of those blue eyes. If she had had any doubts about her decisions lately, all of it was gone now.

Their moment was interrupted when someone cleared her throat. "Ready?"

Kenzie turned to the woman from singing earlier. "Rachel, you remember Jenni. She owns Pressed."

"Yes, of course." It all clicked into place for Rachel. She stretched out her hand. "I'm Rachel."

"Jenni hits the high notes," Kenzie said. "She's more or less my backup," Kenzie shot Jenni a look.

"More," Jenni said. "Definitely more." She pushed a glass of whiskey into Kenzie's hand. "Here, I figured you'd need a refill."

"Thanks." Kenzie reached for the glass and took a sip.

Rachel couldn't keep her eyes off Kenzie. The way her hand gripped the glass, the way her throat moved as she swallowed.

"We're supposed to finish around eight thirty. It's a little earlier than normal, but the owner is nervous about the crowd getting rowdy. You're good to stick around?"

"Yes," Rachel answered a little too quickly. She cleared her throat. "I'm here with my sister." She motioned back to her sister at the bar. "Ashley is just happy to be out on a Saturday night, so we're good."

Kenzie looked past Rachel and Rachel followed her gaze to her sister leaning against the bar, talking to a strange man. "Great. I'll find you when we're done."

Rachel signaled the bartender for another round. The bartender put two green beers in front of her. Rachel fished around in her purse for her wallet.

He leaned in and shouted over the music, "You're covered."

"How's that?" Rachel asked, wondering which drunk guy was offering to buy her drinks.

The bartender nodded at the stage. "Kenzie said you're with her."

"Thank you." She turned around and caught Kenzie's eyes on her again. She raised both glasses and mouthed, "Thanks."

Rachel spent the next hour singing and dancing along with the increasingly drunken crowd. She remembered Kenzie saying that this would be a fun night, but she didn't know how right she had been. Rachel couldn't remember the last time she let loose and enjoyed a night like this. The final song played and as Rachel danced along to "I'm Gonna Be (500 Miles)" she found herself again disappointed and excited. Kenzie and Jenni waved the crowd good night and took down their things.

Rachel and Ashley found a high-top table and took a seat. Ashley slumped down. "Well, that was far from lame." She took a long drink of water, and sweat beaded on her forehead.

"Yeah. That was really fun."

"So, now you have a date?" Ashley's eyes went wide.

"It's just dinner."

"Mm-hmm." Ashley took another long drink of water. "You can't fool me, little sister. I know you're excited."

Rachel was. This was all she had thought about for the last several weeks. Was she putting too much pressure on a dinner?

"Hi." Kenzie finally joined them.

Rachel turned and her heart rate kicked up. "Hi." She gave a small wave.

"I'm so glad you both made it." Kenzie stuck her hand out across the table. "I'm Kenzie."

Ashley shook Kenzie's hand. "Ashley. Rachel's wiser, older sister."

"It's great to meet you," Kenzie replied.

"I was just leaving. This was a really fun night. You are really good. You should cell CDs or something."

Kenzie gave a small laugh. "Thank you."

Rachel hugged her sister goodbye.

"Behave," Ashley whispered into her ear as she left.

Would something be happening tonight where she wouldn't be behaving?

"I just need to load my keyboard, and we can head out," Kenzie said. "I know this great Mexican place if that's okay with you."

"Mexican? On St. Patrick's Day?"

"It's just around the corner and I figured it won't be too crowded, so we can, you know? Talk."

Rachel followed Kenzie out of the pub.

❖

Mariachi music played over the speakers, and brightly colored scenes of marketplaces and oceans covered the walls of the Mexican restaurant. The booth in the back was deserted, which made it much easier to talk.

Kenzie grabbed a chip from the basket in front of them and dipped it in the salsa. "I'm starving." She shoved the entire chip into her mouth and barely chewed. "So," she reached for another chip, "Tell me the whole story."

Rachel let out a long sigh. "Laurel and I met through a mutual friend. We had a lot in common and seemed to be in similar places in life." Rachel paused and looked at Kenzie. She had said to tell the whole story, might as well start at the beginning. "Things were good at first."

"Things are always good at first," Kenzie said between chips.

"True. Then, I don't know." Rachel waved a hand. "I think I've been so focused on making partner at the firm that I haven't stopped to think about any other aspect of my life. Laurel was always just there. In a lot of ways, I took her for granted."

"Second thoughts?" There was a hesitation to Kenzie's question.

"More like regrets. I should have looked at my relationship sooner. Not been so hyperfocused on work. I'd been meaning to break up with her for some time."

"Really?"

"I don't know why I kept putting it off. I guess the idea of starting all over was overwhelming." She reached for the glass of water in front of her and took a long drink. "But now that I've done it, it's kind of exciting."

A server appeared with a pad and paper. "Can I get you ladies something to drink?"

"Just water for me," Kenzie replied.

Rachel looked at Kenzie. "A margarita sounds really good."

"Go for it," Kenzie answered. "I'm driving. And we'll take a plate of your famous nachos," she said to the server. "Trust me, we need these nachos."

"Tonight was fun." Rachel didn't want to talk about Laurel.

"I'm glad you had a good time. It's seriously my favorite night of the year."

"You were really great."

"Thank you. It definitely helps to have backup in these settings." Kenzie played with her water glass.

"So, you and Jenni are close."

"Yeah. You could say that."

Rachel shot her a questioning look.

"I never understood the whole lesbians staying friends with their exes thing until Jenni."

"Oh." Rachel tensed at the thought of Jenni with Kenzie. "So, you two were together?"

"Does that bother you?"

Rachel let out a short breath. "No. I certainly understand that running into exes is some how ingrained in being a lesbian. So, what happened?"

"With Jenni?"

Rachel nodded. She didn't really want to know the answer, but also couldn't think of anything else in the moment.

"Honestly? I'm never on time."

"You broke up because you are never on time?"

Kenzie nodded. "That's the short version."

"What's the long version?"

"I can't help it. I just get caught up in things and I'm always late. Jenni thought it meant I wasn't paying her enough attention or wasn't invested in her, but honestly, I get caught in the moment and lose track of time. Songwriting isn't just my job, it's my passion. I know it's hard for some people to understand, and I never mean for it to be rude, it just happens. It's not like she was perfect either. She was hyperfocused on getting Pressed off the ground, so it was just getting too hard."

The idea of being late gave Rachel actual anxiety. She couldn't imagine someone not being on time, let alone admitting they can't be on time.

"The last time she brought it up, I just couldn't keep having the same fight. If she couldn't accept that it was part of who I am, then I wasn't going to fight to make things work. Relationships shouldn't be that hard."

"But you're still friends?"

"More or less," Kenzie said. "We don't hang out or anything, but she sings vocals at my studio and helps me on nights like tonight. She lets me play at Pressed when I want, that kind of thing."

Rachel could live with that. Not that she had a right to be making demands or anything, but it sounded harmless enough. Just because a romantic relationship was over, it didn't mean people had to stop seeing each other altogether.

The server reappeared and delivered Rachel's drink and a steaming plate of nachos. Rachel pulled the drink in with both hands and took a sip through the short straw, her mouth puckering at the sour lime taste. "That is strong."

"But good." Kenzie raised both eyebrows.

"So good."

Kenzie passed a small plate to Rachel and then took some nachos for herself. "Did you cry at the beginning of the movie *Up*?"

"The Disney movie?" The sudden topic change took Rachel by surprise.

"Yeah." Kenzie kept plating her nachos.

"Yes. Ashley had a sleepover in high school, and for some reason they were watching Disney movies. She let me join in and we all bawled our eyes out at the opening to that movie."

"Did you go to school around here?"

Rachel nodded. "West Valley."

Kenzie snapped her fingers together and pointed at Rachel. "That's it. That's where I know you from."

Rachel gave a questioning look.

"I knew you looked familiar at Pressed, but thought it was from Valentine's Day. You were the freshman phenom."

Rachel blushed. "I haven't been called that in a long time."

"I went to Central. I'd be a year ahead of you."

"I didn't peg you for a basketball fan."

"Oh, I'm not, but I was in the pep band, and I remember it was always a big deal because it was a rival game. And then when you showed up, it became an even bigger deal because you killed us every year."

Rachel had been an exceptional basketball player in high school. It was hard to believe that Kenzie knew that detail about her. "Figures you were a band geek."

"Hey now." Kenzie's posture straightened.

"Sorry. I didn't mean to offend."

Kenzie waved her off. "You jocks are all the same."

"Now who's offending?"

Kenzie shrugged and helped herself to more nachos.

"What did you play?"

"Electric bass."

"I don't know much about music, but last I checked, that's not a band instrument."

"It's not. But my dad was the band director. I was never drawn to brass or woodwinds. I don't know, there's just something about strings. I like the way they feel on my hands. My dad was so happy I was interested in music, he didn't care what I played."

Rachel hoped she hadn't struck a nerve. She took another long sip of her drink to avoid saying something else over the line. The tequila burned her throat.

"Honestly? Pep band was just an excuse to get high behind the gym."

Rachel coughed as she spit out her drink.

"You okay?" Kenzie handed her a napkin from the pile at the end of the table.

"Yeah, that just caught me off guard. I mean, obviously I know that people smoked pot in high school. That just wasn't my experience at all. Where did you even get it?"

"The band director."

"Wait." Rachel paused, thinking carefully about her words. "You said your dad was the band director?"

Kenzie shrugged. "My dad had pancreatic cancer, and I was the kid with a dying dad. People didn't ask a lot of questions."

Rachel picked up her drink and leaned back against the booth. She tried to picture a young Kenzie smoking pot with her dad behind the Central gym. She couldn't.

"You were supposed to go on and be the next Michael Johnson or whatever? What happened?"

"Michael Jordan?" Rachel said.

"I said whatever." Kenzie waved her off.

"I went on to play in college. Got a full ride to State, actually."
"Impressive."

"Well, it was, until I blew out my knee freshman year. I wasn't even supposed to play that night, but we had three upperclassmen foul out, so coach put me in. I went up at the same time as another girl, and when we came back down, she landed right on my knee. My career was over."

Kenzie snapped her fingers. "Just like that?"

"Just like that." Rachel put her now-empty glass on the table. Her eye lids grew heavy as the alcohol started catching up to her. She wasn't drunk, but a little more open than she would normally be.

Kenzie reached her hand out. "You want to get out of here?"

"Yeah." Rachel took her hand. She didn't know what Kenzie had in mind, but she wanted to find out.

CHAPTER TEN

Kenzie put her car in park and sprinted around to open the door for Rachel. She still couldn't believe that Rachel had shown up, and that she was single. Rachel slipped as she got out of the car, and Kenzie grabbed her to keep her from falling.

"Easy does it. You good?" Kenzie wrapped an arm around her waist to keep her from tripping on the curb.

"I'm good," Rachel said, but was still a little unsteady. "Where are we?"

"I want to show you my studio." Kenzie led her through the small parking lot and to a metal door. She fumbled on her key ring until she found the right one and unlocked it.

The small hallway opened to a showroom revealing various band instruments, sheet music, and other items needed to fully stock a school music room. Rachel's elbow knocked into a set of wind chimes on a drum set, and the clanging sound filled the room.

"This doesn't look like a studio." Rachel looked around.

"It's not." Kenzie stopped and steadied the chimes, dampening the sound. "You sure you're good?"

"Yeah. What is this place, anyway?"

"Mr. Summer's Music Store." Kenzie raised both arms. "He supplies most of the rentals for the local schools. He sells other instruments and music as well. He lets me use the studio here as much as I want, and I just bought the loft above the building. He was one of my dad's best friends. Mostly it's just a place for band geeks, as you call us, to hang out."

Rachel's face flushed.

"It's okay." Kenzie bumped her shoulder into Rachel's. "I would have loved a place like this in high school." Kenzie grabbed Rachel's hand and led her through the back of the store. There was something about holding her hand that felt so natural. She could do anything while holding Rachel's hand.

She pushed open another door and led Rachel into the studio. The plexiglass window in front of a large mixing board looked like any other sound studio, but this wasn't any other studio. This was Kenzie's. This was where she found most of her inspiration and the room where she would hopefully get her big break. Kenzie flipped another light, and the area behind the window illuminated to reveal a black grand piano, drum set, numerous guitars, and other stringed instruments. A large red oriental rug lay in the middle of the floor.

"Oh wow," Rachel said with wide eyes.

"This is my day job," Kenzie said. "I convinced Mr. Summer to add a recording studio to the shop. He had the space for it, and when people other than me use it, he can rent it out and make money."

"Did you record any Braxton songs here?"

"As a matter of fact, I did." She hated to name-drop, but Rachel seemed really into it. It was an odd feeling being so close to so many rock stars but not famous herself. At least not yet.

Kenzie sat at the piano. "Actually, 'If It Doesn't Break Your Heart' was recorded right here."

Rachel's eyes went wide. "No way."

"Way." Kenzie nodded and started moving her fingers across the keys. She played the piano riff that she could play in her sleep. Rachel joined her on the piano bench. It was a small seat, and Kenzie swallowed hard when Rachel's thigh bumped up next to hers. She started singing. Thankfully, she knew the words forward and backward, as her mind couldn't focus on anything other than Rachel's closeness.

Kenzie got to the chorus. She knew Rachel loved this part. She sang, "We could go back to where we started," and her mind went blank as Rachel rubbed a hand up her thigh. She knew that her mouth was still moving, and she was still singing, but she didn't know what. She hoped she sang the right words. She closed her eyes, and a small sigh escaped her mouth between verses. Did Rachel know she was driving her wild?

By the time she reached the end of the song, Rachel had her other hand wrapped around her and rubbed Kenzie's neck. Kenzie resisted the urge to end the chords abruptly and take Rachel on top of the piano. She was trying to be cool, but the way Rachel touched her sent shock waves through her body and she couldn't control herself much longer. She raised her hands from the final chord and held them just above the keys.

"That was amazing," Rachel said, barely above a whisper.

"I thought you might like that one."

"I did."

Kenzie turned her head to face Rachel. She waited expectantly. Her eyes were closed and her head tilted to one side. Kenzie leaned in. Their lips met. Rachel's lips were soft and held the faint taste of lime. The desire inside her grew deeper. Rachel let out a small groan, and Kenzie took that opportunity to move her tongue inside her mouth. She put her hands on Rachel's hips and pulled her closer. Their tongues swirled for several moments, each one of them vying for control.

Rachel moved a hand between Kenzie's thighs and held it in place. Kenzie burned red hot, and she knew Rachel could feel her wetness through her jeans. She broke the kiss and pulled back. "Not here," she said, barely above a whisper.

"Why's that?"

"We can't have sex in the studio."

"Okay," Rachel whispered into her ear. "Where can we have sex?"

"Oh God." Kenzie might melt into a puddle right on the piano bench. "Upstairs." Kenzie grabbed Rachel's hand. Holding hands was great, but Kenzie needed more. She led Rachel up the small stairway out the back of the studio and up to her loft.

"What is this place?" Rachel's words slurred, and she seemed out of breath from the walk up the stairs.

"My loft." Kenzie put her keys on the hook by the door.

Rachel stepped closer to Kenzie and playfully moved her hand up Kenzie's chest. She stroked her fingers on her shoulder. "It's impressive."

"Thanks." Kenzie tipped her head up to kiss Rachel again. The kiss was soft, and Kenzie wanted to kiss her lips all night. She moved toward the couch in the middle of the room. Gripping Rachel's hips, she guided her to the arm of the couch.

Rachel went to sit on the brown couch arm, but slid off and fell to the floor. "Whoops." Rachel burst into laughter.

"Oh shit, are you okay?" Kenzie bent to help her up.

"Yeah," Rachel said through lazy giggles. "I think that margarita is catching up to me."

Kenzie pulled her up and helped her on the couch. Rachel in turn pulled her down next to her until they were sitting thigh to thigh. "How many of those green beers did you have before that margarita?" Kenzie asked.

Rachel moved her fingers like she was counting. She finally shrugged. "Not sure. Someone else was buying, so…"

Kenzie groaned into her palms. "Goddammit."

"Did I do something wrong?" Rachel said playfully.

"No. You did nothing wrong."

Rachel moved her hand on Kenzie's thigh and held it between her legs again. "Then what's the matter?"

Kenzie clenched her jaw and looked up at the ceiling. She let out a long breath and met Rachel's brown eyes. "You are way too drunk to say yes."

"I am not." Rachel sounded offended.

"I really want to do this." Kenzie looked her in the eyes again. "But not like this." Kenzie stood. "Come on, I'll take you to bed."

"Finally," Rachel said and grabbed her hand.

Kenzie led her behind a wooden divider to her makeshift bedroom. She pulled back the white down comforter. Rachel motioned for Kenzie to join her on the bed. You're doing the right thing, she reminded herself. God, it would have been so easy to just give in. Younger Kenzie probably would not have shown such restraint. "Lie down," she said, and Rachel obliged.

Kenzie unbuttoned Rachel's jeans and Rachel dug her hands into her shoulders as she did it. "God," Rachel sighed. Kenzie slid Rachel's jeans off her, folded them, and laid them on the floor. She sat at the top of the bed next to Rachel's head and carefully stroked her hair. "Don't hate me."

Rachel propped herself up on her elbows. "Why would I hate you?"

"We aren't sleeping together tonight."

"We aren't?" Rachel whined.

"We aren't. We are going to bed. I'm going to be out on the couch, just over there." Kenzie pointed to the couch they had just been on. "The bathroom is right around the corner if you need it." Kenzie leaned in and kissed Rachel on the forehead.

Rachel lay back down and pursed her lips in a pout.

"If you still want to sleep with me tomorrow, I promise I'll blow your mind." Kenzie stroked her hair again.

"Fine." Rachel rolled over on her side, with her back toward Kenzie.

Kenzie leaned down and kissed her temple. "Good night, Rachel."

CHAPTER ELEVEN

Rachel couldn't hear anything over the pounding in her ears. Someone repeatedly beat a bass drum in her mind. Had there been a drum last night? Why would there have been a drum? She opened her eyelids, and the light shot pain to her dry eyes. She clamped her eyes back shut and rolled away from the window.

This wasn't her bed. The cloudlike down comforter was amazing, but it definitely wasn't hers. Her bad knee itched, and she scratched at the scar from her surgery. Where were her pants? Oh God, she remembered Kenzie saying she'd take her to bed. Had she slept with Kenzie? She was still wearing her shirt and her underwear. Surely she would have taken those off if she'd had sex.

Rachel couldn't remember the last time she had blacked out from drinking. If she ever had. What had gotten into her? Her stomach twisted in knots and her vison blurred. She vaguely remembered something about a bathroom being around a corner. She clamped her hand over her mouth and sprinted around the wooden divider. She found an open door and prayed it was the bathroom. She fell in front of the toilet, hitting her bad knee on the tile floor as she went down. She couldn't control herself as she emptied the contents of her stomach into the white porcelain, and panicked at the green color.

The thought of green alcohol tied her up in knots and she retched again. A warm hand rubbed circles on her back. Kenzie pulled her hair away from her face and held it behind her neck. "Easy does it."

After an unattractive display of spitting and clearing her mouth, she turned and blinked Kenzie into focus. Her face flushed as embarrassment washed over her. "I am so sorry," she managed to get out.

"It's more than okay. I swear that green dye should be illegal." Kenzie opened the medicine cabinet over the sink. She pulled out a packaged toothbrush and handed it and toothpaste to Rachel.

"Does this happen often?" Who kept unopened toothbrushes in their bathroom?

"More than you'd think. But not like that," she backtracked. "I have a lot of couch-surfing musician friends. They have no qualms about using my toothbrush, so I keep a stash handy."

Rachel took Kenzie's outstretched hand and pulled herself off the floor.

"I'll give you a minute." Kenzie left Rachel to herself.

Rachel brushed her teeth and examined herself in the mirror. She looked every bit of the hell that she felt. Her mascara had run completely over her bloodshot eyes. She couldn't keep the waves of embarrassment from crashing over her as she tried to piece together the events of the night before. She remembered having fun, but she couldn't remember a whole lot after leaving the Mexican restaurant. She rinsed her mouth out and ran water over her face.

Rachel took small steps leaving the bathroom, careful not to take on too much too fast. Kenzie waited on the couch, scrolling on her tablet. God, she looked good, even from behind. If Rachel had slept with her, it wouldn't have been the end of the world.

"I'm sorry about last night," Rachel said to her back.

Kenzie turned around. "You have nothing to be sorry for."

Rachel couldn't help but think about that blond hair and those blue eyes. Even with her hair pulled into a messy ponytail, she looked amazing. "We didn't…"

"No," Kenzie said, eyes wide. "But not for lack of trying." She looked to Rachel's bare legs. "You were persistent."

"I'm sorry." The wave of embarrassment came back.

"It's okay. Really it is." Kenzie sounded sincere.

"I didn't really get the grand tour of your place last night."

"You're looking at it. The couch here is what I call the living room." Kenzie motioned to the upright piano toward the entryway. "When I first moved in, I had big plans to add rooms and walls, but the acoustics are just too good."

"I can see that." The rustic wooden floors and vaulted ceilings would create great sound.

"Come on." Kenzie motioned for Rachel to follow her behind a large wooden divider. "This is the bedroom." It at least gave the illusion of privacy, masking the king-size bed from the rest of the loft. "I folded your jeans."

Rachel picked them up and slid into them. Kenzie opened and shut several drawers. After she had riffled through a few, she handed her a folded shirt. "Here."

Rachel stared at the Braxton shirt in her hands. "I actually have this one," she said.

"Now you have two." Kenzie turned around. "Put it on. We're going for pancakes."

Rachel found it endearing that she had turned around. It would have been fine for her to see her in just a bra. She had taken her pants off, after all. "I don't know about pancakes."

"Oh, we're getting them. You need them and you owe me."

"Owe you?" What could Rachel possibly owe her?

"That's the rule," Kenzie explained to the window. "You stay at my place, you buy pancakes. Ask any of my friends."

Rachel quickly changed shirts. "Well, I am a rule follower."

"I was counting on it."

"You can turn around now," Rachel said.

Kenzie turned around and Rachel's face flushed again.

"The shirt looks great. I can see why you already have one."

After a quick wait, they sat in a booth at a nearby diner. "The pancakes here are the best." Kenzie didn't even open the menu.

"I'm sorry about last night." Rachel couldn't think about anything else.

Kenzie reached her hand across the table and put it on top of Rachel's. "You have nothing to be sorry for."

"I don't normally get like that." Rachel looked down. God, she loved the feeling of Kenzie's hand on hers. It was strong and comforting. "I remember something about Disney movies, and a drum set, and did you sing for me?" Rachel squinted, trying to put the pieces together.

Kenzie chuckled. "All of those things are true." She pulled her hand back.

A server appeared and asked if they were ready to order. "I'll take the pancakes and a coffee," Kenzie said and handed her the menu.

"I'll do the same." Rachel hadn't even looked. She wasn't sure she could get her eyes to focus on anything long enough.

"Can I let you in on something?"

"Okay?"

"The Disney question is kind of a line."

"What do you mean?"

"It's my roundabout way of figuring out how old you are."

"Shut up."

"If I ask you if you cried at the beginning and you tell me you haven't seen it, you were either way too young when it came out, therefore probably too young for us to date, or you were too old to be watching Disney movies and probably too old for us to work out."

"What if I just don't like kids' movies?"

Kenzie clasped her chest. "Then this definitely won't work out."

"Why not just ask someone how old they are?"

"I don't know if you know this." Kenzie lowered her voice. "Women hate admitting how old they are."

"So, did I pass your test?"

"You did."

She must not have made as big a fool of herself as she thought if Kenzie still wanted to spend the morning with her after last night.

The server returned and delivered their pancakes and coffees. Rachel couldn't help but notice Kenzie's lips as she blew on her hot coffee. Another round of memories flooded her brain. Oh God, she had kissed Kenzie. A lot. She had kissed her, on a piano? She ran her hands over her face trying to put the puzzle together. "Did we kiss last night?"

"We did." Kenzie put a large bite of pancake into her mouth. She chewed a few times and swallowed. "I guess I'm not as memorable as I thought."

"No." Rachel shook her head. "I'm just…"

"It's okay," Kenzie said. "I had a really good time last night, despite the fact that you sexually harassed me at my place of work."

"Oh my God, what?" Rachel said louder than she meant to. A few people turned and looked at their table.

"Your face," she said, clutching her side with laughter. She composed herself. "Rachel." She looked her in the eyes. "I had a great time last night. Really. I am so glad you came to the show and let me take you to dinner after. I hope that will be the first of many nights where you actually let yourself let loose and have a good time."

"You do?" Rachel's heartbeat quickened at the idea of more fun nights with Kenzie.

"I can do without the you being too drunk to consent part, but every part up to that was great."

Rachel bobbed her head back and forth. "Okay."

Kenzie reached her hand across the table and put it on top of Rachel's. Rachel swallowed hard.

"I would like your phone number now," Kenzie said.

"Of course," Rachel replied.

Kenzie pulled her phone out and pushed it across the table. "You have to do it. I can barely work this thing."

Rachel happily created a new contact in Kenzie's phone.

CHAPTER TWELVE

Rachel slumped against the front door to her apartment as she shut it. It had been an especially awful day at work. The client had refused the offer on the table and insisted on moving to trial. It wasn't a case Rachel thought they could win. Yes, she would fight her hardest, but this was an uphill battle. On top of that, her monthly reminder that she was still not a mother had made an appearance two days early. She leaned her head back against the door and let out a long sigh. Her phone buzzed in her pocket. She pulled it out and was met with a quick flutter in her chest. A text from Kenzie.

Hey

She texted back. *Hey*

Bubbles appeared at the bottom of her screen. It didn't take long for Kenzie to answer. *How was your day?*

Rachel debated how she wanted to answer the question. Should she play it off and give a generic "good?" Something inside her wanted to be honest. She stopped overthinking and typed out a reply. *Not great actually. Really rough day at work.*

Just as she regretted her honesty, a reply came through.

I'm sorry to hear that

Rachel wasn't sure if that was a standard reply or if Kenzie really was sorry to hear that. She was still learning how to read Kenzie. She was about to respond with a topic change, something more lighthearted when her phone buzzed in her hand.

Want company?

She did want company. But not just anyone. She wanted Kenzie. She had had multiple bad days in the past and had wanted nothing more than to be left alone, but that was the exact opposite of what she wanted now. After typing an answer that she hoped seemed nonchalant, she sent Kenzie her address and started whirlwind cleaning her apartment. Not that she was a messy person by any means, but she had clothes strewn across her bed and this morning's dishes still in the kitchen. She had been too busy nursing her hangover Sunday to get her normal chores done and kicked herself into high gear as Kenzie said she was fifteen minutes away.

Thirty minutes later, there was a knock at the door. Rachel opened it to reveal Kenzie, pizza box in hand, on the other side. "Hi."

"Hi." Kenzie made her way inside. "I figured a rough day calls for pizza." She held up the box in her hand.

"That smells amazing. Is that what took you so long?"

"What do you mean?" Kenzie asked as she made her way to Rachel's couch. She set the pizza box on the wooden coffee table.

"Just that you said fifteen minutes, and it's been almost thirty." Rachel tried not to sound judgmental.

"Dang. Really?" Kenzie looked honestly surprised. "I swear I hurried. I had this badass chord progression that I needed to write down. I'm sorry."

"It's fine. I have a bottle of wine open. Can I get you a glass?"

"I'm not a huge wine drinker…"

"Just try this. For me?"

"I guess I can keep an open mind."

Rachel turned to the kitchen counter where she had one of her favorite Pinot Noirs open. She took a moment to get herself together. Kenzie looked amazing. Her blond hair was pulled back into a ponytail, and this was the most casual Rachel had seen her. The jeans and hoodie were relaxed but fit her perfectly. Yes, this was just the kind of distraction she needed after her sorry excuse of a day. "What are you doing?" Rachel asked hesitantly as she turned around, wine glasses in hand.

Kenzie sat on the floor, leaning against the couch with the pizza box open. "Eating?" Kenzie responded, unfazed.

"On the floor?"

"Oh, yeah. I always eat pizza on the floor. I have a history of getting cheese in places that are hard to get it out of."

"Oh, really?" Rachel set the wine glasses on the coffee table and joined Kenzie on the carpet.

"Trust me, this is much safer."

Rachel looked at the pizza Kenzie had brought—a large square divided into four distinct parts.

"I didn't know what you liked, and I was in a hurry," Kenzie said. "So, I brought a variety. There's pepperoni, of course, veggie lovers, in case you're a vegetarian, which I don't think you are, but I wasn't sure. A chicken pesto in case you don't like red sauce. And I really hope you aren't a monster who eats pineapple on pizza, but I brought Hawaiian on the off chance."

Rachel's heart swelled at the thoughtfulness that Kenzie had put into such a small gesture. "I am not a monster, I promise." She raised her right hand.

"Thank goodness." Kenzie handed her a paper plate and swirled the wine in her glass. "I don't know what this does, but I always see people do it."

Rachel smirked. "It opens it up."

"Whatever that means." Kenzie took a sip. She eyed the glass carefully. She held it up to the light and wine ran down the glass. "That is not awful."

Rachel nearly spit out her own sip. "I would hope not. This is a really good bottle."

"Then I'm glad we agree." Kenzie raised her glass in a toast.

Rachel flipped through the channels on the TV while they ate, finding some old sitcom that they both had grown up watching.

"Oh, is this the episode where they finally hook up?" Kenzie perked up.

Rachel waved her off, suckered into the old show. "No, that's the next episode." She clicked the guide button for the TV. "And we are in luck, because it's on next."

Kenzie moved herself closer to Rachel until their thighs touched, still sitting on the floor, with her legs outstretched under the coffee table. "I guess we better settle in."

Rachel liked feeling Kenzie close to her. How could she already feel so at ease with someone she had just met? In a moment of courage, she pretended to yawn and stretched her arms up to the ceiling. When she brought them back down, she wrapped one around Kenzie's shoulder. Kenzie didn't move away. Instead, she leaned herself in closer and rested her head on Rachel's shoulder.

Rachel didn't remember how it happened, but somewhere between the main characters fighting and making up, Kenzie had leaned over until she straddled Rachel on the floor. Rachel leaned up to kiss her. Kenzie's lips were soft. She remembered her being a good kisser, but details after that were a bit fuzzy. She put her hands on the small of Kenzie's back and held her in place, deepening the kiss. Kenzie grabbed Rachel's face with both hands, grasping her tightly. Rachel swirled her tongue inside Kenzie's mouth and Kenzie groaned. Kenzie was passionate, and kissing her was nothing like any other kiss before.

Kenzie moved her hands from Rachel's face, her fingers igniting her to her core. Rachel needed more. She needed to feel Kenzie. To be consumed by her. Kenzie played with the waistband of Rachel's yoga pants, lingering for just a second.

Rachel broke the kiss. "Wait."

"You okay?" Kenzie pulled back.

"I hate to do this, but it's not a good time."

"Okay?"

"Of the month, that is."

"Oh." Kenzie sat back and Rachel could see the pieces clicking in her brain.

"I know some people don't mind, but…"

"No. It's okay. I get it." Kenzie moved herself to the floor next to Rachel. She leaned her head back against the couch and let out a long sigh.

"I'm sorry." Rachel looked down.

"Don't be," Kenzie said to the ceiling. "Just give me a second to get out of the mood." She let out another long breath. "I'd tell you to say something unsexy, but I'm not sure you can."

"I understand if you want to leave."

"What?" Kenzie lifted her head up off the couch and looked Rachel in the eyes. "No. I didn't come here just to have sex with you."

"I know. But…"

"Hey. I came here because I like you and I like spending time with you. Then I saw you looking all sexy and couldn't control myself. But the main reason I came over is because when someone has a rough day, it's nice to have company."

Rachel nodded.

"Come here." Kenzie motioned with her arms. Rachel hesitated, but Kenzie insisted. "Come here."

Rachel moved over, and Kenzie wrapped her into an embrace. Rachel leaned back against Kenzie and couldn't remember the last time she felt safe in someone's arms. Kenzie squeezed her tight.

"Tell me about your day."

"Here? On the floor?" Rachel started to turn around, but Kenzie tightened her grip.

"Yes. When we have a rough day, we eat pizza on the floor and talk about it."

Rachel resigned. "Well, I've been working for weeks to get my client to accept a settlement. Then today, as they were about to settle out of court, my client backed out and now we have to go to trial." Rachel paused and Kenzie didn't say anything. Laurel would have offered a million suggestions at this point. Told her all the ways she had approached it wrong and what she could have done differently, even though she knew nothing about law. Yet Kenzie stayed quiet. "So now I have to take an unsympathetic client to a jury."

"What does that mean?"

"It means that I have to convince twelve people that the drugs my company manufactured didn't inadvertently make people sicker than they intended."

"Did they?" Kenzie didn't loosen her grip.

"That doesn't necessarily matter. Either way, out of court is always easier, and I worked really hard to get that deal in front of them."

"I'm sorry you had a rough day." Kenzie kissed Rachel's cheek.

It was a small gesture. The listening, the kiss, but it was all Rachel needed. It was a level of contentment she hadn't experienced before. "It's okay. Today isn't all bad." Was this what a relationship with Kenzie would be like? She'd never envisioned herself as an adult eating on her floor, but somehow, it was the perfect ending to the miserable day.

CHAPTER THIRTEEN

K enzie hated working on Saturdays. It was a necessary evil of her chosen profession, but that didn't make her hate it any less. If she was going to get her own album, she wanted to at least record samples herself and hope Global wouldn't interfere too much creatively. Saturday was the only day schedules all synced up. Most of the band had played late gigs on Friday night and could barely agree to a noon start.

Kenzie entered the recording studio, and much to her surprise, most of the band gathered around the small coffee table outside the recording booth yelling and laughing. It was odd for them to be so awake at this hour after a late night before. Then she saw it. The long lines of white powder they all hovered around. "Dammit, guys, we said no drugs in here." Kenzie burst into the middle of the room. "There are kids on the other side of that wall!" She motioned to the door with the music store on the other side.

Joey wiped his nostrils, his brown hair disheveled, and he looked like he hadn't slept in days. "Sorry, Kenzie. I forgot."

Kenzie pinched the bridge of her nose. "Joey, I liked it better when you couldn't drive." The band had already made a huge mess, glasses and cans strewn across the table. "Look, guys, drinking is fine, but this is too much. We're recording vocals today, for God's sake."

Jenni gathered some of the loose cans and bottles. "Sorry, Kenz."

Kenzie rubbed her hands over her face. "Look, I'm going to

go outside for like five minutes. Then when I come back, you are all going to pretend to be professionals and we will see if we can actually get some work done."

Kenzie pushed the metal door open with both hands. The sunshine burned her eyes as they adjusted. A few of the trees finally found their green leaves around the empty parking lot and it was starting to feel like spring. The urge to smoke overcame her, and she wished she had a cigarette. Not that she was a big smoker or anything, but just a moment of peace outside with nicotine sounded exactly like what she needed. She clasped her hands on top of her head and looked up to the blue sky. Drugs were a part of the music culture. She knew that. She had been a part of it in her younger years. Somehow, she had always thought that if she could control the atmosphere, she could change the dynamics. If it weren't for the fact that a teenage band kid could have seen, she wouldn't have cared so much. The sound of a familiar voice interrupted her thoughts.

"Hey." A red-faced Rachel greeted her. She wore shorts and a tight-fitting long-sleeve blue T-shirt.

"Hey."

Rachel paused the large watch on her wrist. "Did I interrupt anything?"

Kenzie shook her head. "No. I just needed some fresh air. Do you ever feel like you're the only one who takes your job seriously?"

Rachel caught her breath. "All the time."

Kenzie finally registered that Rachel had just appeared out of nowhere. "What are you doing here?"

"Oh, I was just out for a run, you know?"

Kenzie shook her head. "I don't. Was someone chasing you?"

"No. I just like to run, and it was too nice outside not to."

Kenzie knew that Rachel's apartment was several miles from her house. Maybe she had run out of her way hoping to see her. "I'm working on my album today."

"Oh? You're working on an album?"

"The studio keeps promising me they'll release one, so when that day comes, I want to have it ready."

"That's awesome."

"Well, it would be if I wasn't the only one taking it seriously. I get it. It's my album with my name, so why should anyone else care? It's just tough, you know? I have worked so damn hard for so damn long, can't these guys just give me two hours of respect?"

"Are you sure everything's okay?"

"It just feels like I'm a hamster running on a wheel sometimes. Just running and running hoping I'll get somewhere, but I never do. I don't know if I should get off or keep running. Hey, wait, that's pretty good."

"What is?"

Kenzie reached for her phone, wanting to type the exact words she had said. Not that she had a song to use them for yet, but hopefully soon inspiration would strike. "You want to come in and watch for a little bit?"

Rachel looked at her watch.

"Unless you have to finish whatever this is."

"I could use a little break, actually."

"Great." Kenzie pulled open the metal door for Rachel. The group had found their way into the recording booth, and the mess from earlier was more or less cleaned up. "Bill, this is Rachel." Kenzie motioned to a younger man sitting at a large sound board. He had his headphones on but barely over one ear and nodded a hello.

Kenzie pulled out a chair for Rachel. "You can sit here. Or stand, or there's a couch behind us."

"This is great." Rachel sat in the black swivel chair.

"It's several originals I'm working on today, so you'll have to let me know what you think."

"I can't wait," Rachel replied.

Kenzie blushed. "I'll just be over there." She pointed to the piano behind the glass.

"I'll be right here," Rachel said playfully.

Butterflies went wild in Kenzie's stomach as she sat at the piano. She never got nervous recording, but today she did. Rachel had heard her sing before, so why was this any different? "Okay, you all ready?" The band nodded. Joey beat his drumsticks four times over his head, and the music started.

Kenzie had the song all but memorized. Her fingers just knew what to do. She almost missed her cue to come in. Rachel in the other room was so distracting. But she got her mind back into it. The song finished, and she turned to the group. "Let's take that one again. It was a little pitchy in the middle, so tighten it up." Joey hit the drumsticks over his head again.

CHAPTER FOURTEEN

Rachel welcomed the chance to rest. She'd misjudged how far Kenzie's place was from hers and had clocked just over five miles. She worked out often, but that was a lot of running for her. She had caught Kenzie at just the right moment. They kept missing each other over the past few weeks. Rachel was buried in trial preparation, and she had learned that one downside to Kenzie was that she kept her phone off anytime she was working. It made her next to impossible to get hold of. Her best chance of seeing her was coming over herself, but a run seemed like the most subtle way to do that.

"So, you and Kenzie, huh?" a voice said from behind Rachel.

Rachel turned around and recognized Jenni. "I don't know what you mean."

"Just be careful," Jenni said, barely above a whisper.

"Excuse me?"

"Kenz makes her living writing breakup songs. She hangs on just long enough to get a new take and then she's gone."

"Is that what happened with you two?"

"It was certainly part of it. I don't know if we would have worked out in the long run, but she wrote a few songs about me after we broke up."

Which McKenzie McCall originals were about Jenni? "Does Kenzie date a lot of women?"

"How long do you have to be with someone to consider it dating?"

"What do you mean?"

"I've known Kenzie a while, you know we have a history. I've never known her to have a long-term relationship. I'm not saying she can't, she just puts songwriting above everything and everyone else. So just know what you're getting into."

"Thanks for the advice." In their short time together, Kenzie had been late because of songwriting, and she'd admitted that was part of why she and Jenni didn't work out. Was Kenzie ready for a relationship? Could she even commit to one?

The band played the same song multiple times. Rachel didn't tire of hearing it, which surprised her. Hearing the same song repeatedly on the radio would drive her nuts, but seeing the process like this, up close, was fascinating. She could have watched Kenzie work all day. The band paused for a break.

"This is going to take a while." Kenzie sounded defeated as she approached her. "The vocals sound like shit, and it's going to be a bit until we get something we can actually use."

"I think it sounds great."

"Thank you. But it's not going to cut it. So unfortunately, I'm stuck here a while. Is there any chance you're free tomorrow? I can take you to dinner?"

"No."

"Damn." Kenzie's shoulders fell.

"Because I am taking you."

"So it's like that, huh?"

"It is. I'll pick you up at five forty-five?"

Kenzie raised one eyebrow. "Are you doing that thing where you tell me you'll pick me up fifteen minutes early so that I'm actually on time?"

Rachel shrugged. "That depends. Is it working?"

"Well, not now that I know that's what you're doing."

"Be ready at five forty-five and you'll find out if I'm doing that thing or not."

"I'll do my best. When you get here tomorrow, come to the side door here and I'll buzz you in."

"I'll see you tomorrow." Rachel pushed a few buttons on her GPS watch to wake it back up.

"Are you seriously running back home?"

"I'll see you tomorrow." Rachel headed outside. The run home was exactly what she needed to sort through the cluster of thoughts in her brain. Kenzie was fun and things were easy, but they were also so casual. Rachel was ready for more. She was ready for a serious relationship. One where her partner answered the phone when it rang and it didn't automatically go to voicemail. While she was enjoying her time with Kenzie, was there enough here to build a real relationship on, or was she just going to end up another one of McKenzie McCall's songs?

CHAPTER FIFTEEN

K enzie stared at the blank page on the piano. She had never had writer's block for this long. She didn't even have her normal crumpled pile of papers in the wastebasket nearby. She just had nothing. She banged the keys and let the dissonance resonate in the apartment. "I have nothing," she sang to no tune in particular. "Blah blah blah love song." She put her head in her hands and let her elbows hit the keys. The intercom buzzed, waking her from her pity party. Shit. She fumbled for her phone. It was off. Of course. Wait? Why was it off? She would have welcomed a distraction. She tried to power it on and the flashing red charging signal greeted her. Dammit. How had her phone died again? She squinted at the microwave clock and the green numbers flashed 12:00. She had no idea what time it was, and wasn't even close to ready.

She sprinted to the intercom. "It's unlocked. Come on up." She dashed behind the wooden divider, shedding her clothes as she moved. She found a pair of dark jeans and pulled them on as quickly as possible. Hanging in her closet, she found a white linen shirt with a deep V-neck. She rushed it over her head.

Kenzie composed herself and opened the door, trying to seem casual. "Hi," she said as she opened the door.

"Hi." Rachel waved.

"I'm ready." Kenzie went to grab her purse hanging on the hook by the door.

Rachel raised her eyebrows and then stared directly at Kenzie's bare feet.

"Right." Kenzie bowed her head in defeat. "Please come in."

"We actually have fifteen minutes if you aren't ready."

"So, you did do that thing." Kenzie would have been offended, but she wasn't ready.

"I hate being late."

Kenzie shuffled through her drawers until she found two socks that matched. She grabbed a pair of tall brown leather boots and pulled them on. "Okay." Kenzie took a breath to compose herself. "Now I'm ready." Rachel made a show of looking at her from head to toe.

"I'm just making sure you're ready." Rachel raised her palms in innocence.

"Let's go." Kenzie ushered her out of the apartment.

After dinner, Kenzie invited Rachel up to her apartment, and was thankful when she agreed. Kenzie didn't know how much longer she could go without touching Rachel. She had already kissed her lips and had spent many nights falling asleep thinking of her touch. She knew that Rachel was feeling the same way. She kept touching her throughout dinner. She'd run her fingers playfully across the back of her hand on top of the table. At one point, Rachel reached over to tuck a stray strand of hair behind Kenzie's ear, and Kenzie thought she might explode right at the booth of the restaurant.

Kenzie hurried up the stairs with Rachel right on her heels. She opened the door as quickly as possible and motioned Rachel inside. She hung her purse on the hook by the door, took Rachel's hand, and led her to the couch. She wasn't wasting any more time. At this point, she knew the attraction was there, and it was time to act on it.

Kenzie took Rachel to the couch. "I can't go any longer without kissing you," Kenzie said.

"And you shouldn't have to." Rachel leaned her head in.

Kenzie met her lips, and they kissed. Kenzie applied more pressure, and Rachel followed her lead. Kenzie pulled Rachel on top of her until Rachel's knees were on the couch, straddling her. Kenzie leaned her head back to continue the kiss. She pulled Rachel in, needing to close the space between them.

Rachel grabbed Kenzie's shirt at the bottom and pulled it over her head in one motion, revealing Kenzie in her nude bra. Kenzie looked up to Rachel's eyes raking over her. "What?"

Rachel shook her head. "I haven't seen you undressed yet. I've only pictured it."

"You've been picturing me, huh?"

Rachel leaned down and wrapped her arms around Kenzie's back. She whispered in her ear, "You have no idea." Rachel started to find the clasp of Kenzie's bra. Something buzzed against her thigh. She patted her pocket trying to figure out which phone it was. It buzzed again.

"Dammit." Rachel pulled her phone out of her back pocket and studied the screen.

"Don't answer it."

"It's work." She sighed. "I have to answer it." Rachel clicked the green button. "Rachel Park."

The expressions on Rachel's face moved from concern to annoyance, and Kenzie's night slipped further and further away the longer Rachel stayed on the phone.

"Okay. I'm on my way." Rachel hung up. "I have to go."

"On a Sunday night?" Kenzie knew she had an untraditional work schedule but assumed that lawyers didn't.

"Yeah. There's an issue with the client and we have trial in the morning, so they're calling us into the office now." She leaned her head down until their foreheads touched. "I'm really sorry."

Kenzie swallowed. "It's okay. It's not your fault."

Rachel kissed Kenzie on the forehead. "Rain check for later this week?"

"Sounds good. Call me." Kenzie never worked this hard for a woman's attention before. Not that she hadn't ever cared or tried before, but never like this. There was never this much preamble before the bedroom. Rachel Park was something else, and Kenzie wanted to find out if she was worth the wait.

CHAPTER SIXTEEN

There was not enough coffee to get Rachel through the morning. She'd stayed at the office well after midnight preparing for the case today and had barely slept once she got home. Just when she thought she could quiet her mind from all the problems with taking her client to trial, Kenzie would pop into her mind. Getting to know her had been fun, but if they didn't get things to the next level soon, Rachel might actually explode. She had to find a way to get uninterrupted time with Kenzie. One of the young ladies at the reception desk greeted her before she could sneak into her office, large thermos in hand.

"Ms. Park?" the receptionist stopped Rachel at the front desk.

"Yes?"

"Ms. Pierce asked to see you as soon as you got in."

Rachel looked at her watch. "I have to leave for the courthouse in twenty minutes."

"She said it was urgent and it couldn't wait."

"Please tell her I'm on my way." Rachel knew better than to argue with one of the named partners. She would make sure the meeting ended quickly so that she and the other lawyers could get to the courthouse in time. Whatever Gail had to say, surely it couldn't take twenty minutes.

Rachel didn't even stop at her office as she made her way down the long hallway. She figured if she still had her bag over her shoulder, Gail would get the message that she was tight for time. She stood at the doorway to the large corner office and waited to be invited in.

"Rachel, come in, please." Gail waved her hand enthusiastically.

"Good morning," Rachel said.

"I wanted to be the first to congratulate you." Gail didn't stand up from her large desk.

"Thank you," Rachel said, unsure of what Gail was referring to. She didn't want to risk seeming out of touch but thought better than to just go along with it. "Can I ask what for?"

"The settlement," Gail said.

"Settlement?"

"I just got off the phone with the drug company you've been representing. Turns out, they had a change of heart after last night and have decided to settle out of court."

"Really?" Rachel tried to contain her excitement, but this was a huge win, not only for her but for the firm. While it meant that her client had to pay, it would still lead to billable hours for the firm. "I thought after last night they'd want to go to trial for sure. This is great."

"It is," Gail said. "Plus, they informed me that they will be bringing all of their business exclusively to Pierce & Lloyd. It's close to fifteen million a year. Don't think the partners don't know who put this all together. Great work."

"Thank you." Excitement and relief hit Rachel at the same time. The thought of taking this case to trial had kept her up all night.

"Keep up the good work, Rachel. These are the kinds of wins we need. A new client came in this morning, and I'd like you to join the meeting."

"Of course."

"Head into the conference room and someone will get you up to speed."

One meeting turned into three, and before Rachel knew it, late afternoon hit and she'd barely stopped to come up for air. Her stomach growled but if she ate something now, it would ruin her appetite for dinner. Speaking of... She dialed Kenzie, hoping to make good on her raincheck.

"Hey, you." Kenzie answered after a few rings.

"Guess who was a totally kick-ass lawyer today?" Rachel swiveled in her office chair.

"Does this mean you were a real lawyer today?"

"And then some."

"That's great! What did you do that was so ass-kicking?"

"I got the drug company to take a settlement out of court, and I've just been assigned to a huge case at the firm. Possibly the biggest of the year."

"You are definitely a real lawyer."

"I was hoping you would help me celebrate."

"Hell yeah."

Relief flooded Rachel. Not that Kenzie would say no, but they were still figuring out what they were. Were they dating? Were they exclusive? At some point they might need to have a conversation about this. "Dinner tonight? My treat?"

"Damn. I can't tonight. I'm in Nashville."

"Nashville? You didn't mention you were going out of town." Not that Kenzie owed her an itinerary or anything, but didn't people share when they had big trips coming up?

"I just found out today. We actually just landed."

"What?"

"Cooper called this morning saying he had two artists he wanted me to work with, so here I am."

"Who's Cooper?" One of the many questions Rachel had right now.

"I guess you could say he's my boss. He's the producer I work with."

"Does this happen often?"

"A few times a month, I'd say. Sometimes people just need that McKenzie McCall magic."

"When will you be back?" Rachel tried not to sound needy. She wasn't prepared to not see Kenzie yet. Nashville seemed worlds away.

"Coop, when will we head back?" Kenzie unsuccessfully covered the phone as she yelled. "He doesn't know."

"You left this morning and you don't know when you're coming back?" It was way too soon for Rachel to feel sad that she didn't know when she'd see Kenzie next.

"My best guess is a week. What do you say we celebrate your world-class lawyering once I get back?"

"I'd like that."

"Cooper's glaring at me. I have to go. Can I call you later?"

"I'd like that too." What was happening? The range of emotions Kenzie brought out in Rachel was jarring. Confusion to sadness to happiness, all in the course of a single phone conversation. Very little about her growing attraction made sense to her, but for whatever reason, she couldn't resist the pull.

CHAPTER SEVENTEEN

Nashville was awesome. Exhausting but awesome. Kenzie met two artists she otherwise wouldn't have, and they collaborated on some great songs, if she did say so herself. Now only if that could translate into her own song. Just one song. That was all she needed. One song, and maybe the doors to this industry she wanted so much to be a part of would be opened to her.

Kenzie preferred writing breakup songs. The language and feelings associated with a breakup held much more interest to her than simply falling in love. She'd managed to get three songs out of her breakup with Jenni. She denied it, but when Jenni heard the lyrics "You walked out and I didn't fight you," Kenzie admitted she might have used their relationship as motivation. Now she needed a song about love during the time of war, and she needed it to be good. She put her elbows on the keys and her head in her hands. "Think," she said out loud. "If I was off to war, what would I write my girl back home?" She rubbed her face in her hands. "Nothing, because this is dumb."

She played an E chord and let it echo in her apartment. "Deadlines are dumb," she said to no one. Her phone buzzed on top of the piano and she hurried to answer it, welcoming the distraction. A picture of Rachel flashed across the screen, and her heartbeat kicked up a notch.

"Hey." She tried to sound cool.

"Hi." Rachel's voice was light and breezy. God, she missed her. "Any update on when you'll be back in town?"

"Got in late last night, actually. I didn't text you because I didn't want to wake you up. I was going to call you later this morning."

"Oh." Rachel sounded off. Not her upbeat self she was a few moments ago. "You wouldn't have woken me."

"I didn't peg you for a hard sleeper."

"No. My phone. When it's in sleep mode, texts don't go through."

"Really? That's a thing?" Kenzie was lucky most days when she could figure out how to turn her phone back on.

"It is. A very helpful one when too many clients have your phone number."

"You're going to have to show me how to do that." Silence stretched on between them.

"Good trip?"

"Productive trip." Kenzie formed chords on the keyboard but didn't push the keys. Now if she could only have her own productive day. "I was hoping I might be able to cash in that rain check today."

"I can't do it today, I'm afraid."

"Oh?"

"I just left the office, and it's only long enough to go watch my niece and nephew play soccer, then I'm headed right back in."

"Damn. On a Saturday?"

"This case is all hands on deck."

"It's nice they let you out for the soccer game."

"I haven't missed one yet."

"They are lucky to have Aunt Rachel cheering for them." Kenzie hadn't seen youth sports since her pep band days. "Maybe we can meet up later this week, then?" Kenzie wanted to see Rachel again. She needed to. The few interactions so far hadn't been enough.

"I hope so. I'm going to be pretty tied up, but I might be able to sneak away."

"I hope that's true."

"I'm glad you're home, Kenz."

Her heart warmed. Whatever was growing between them was definitely mutual. "Me too. Let me know when you are free this week. I'd love to see you."

"I will. Enjoy your Saturday."

"You too." She banged her head against the keys. The notes clashed, and she grimaced. That wasn't helping anything.

CHAPTER EIGHTEEN

All hands on deck quickly morphed into every waking hour needed to be spent at the law firm. The payoff for the partners would be huge, making it more than worth their time. It would only be worth Rachel's if it led to her own partner track. All she could do was put her head down and work. After the drug company settlement, she'd garnered positive attention from the voting members at the firm. She just needed to keep riding that momentum.

"You wouldn't have a minute to help me read some fine print, would you?" Kenzie stood in the doorway of Rachel's office.

"Kenzie. What are you doing here?"

"I have this rain check I can't seem to figure out how to use."

"Is that so?"

"Any chance you know how they work?" Kenzie took a seat across from Rachel.

"This week has been a little nuts."

"I get it."

Laurel never got it. But Kenzie wasn't Laurel, and Rachel wasn't dating her. She didn't know what they were. It could certainly be called dating, but anything more than that would be too difficult to label right now. "It's not that I don't want to make good on our date." She really did. There just weren't enough hours in the day for everything she wanted right now.

"Any chance you've had lunch yet today?"

"I don't have time to leave for lunch." Rachel didn't know if she'd ever had time to leave for lunch.

"That's not what I asked."

"I haven't. No."

Kenzie pulled a brown paper sack from her shoulder bag. "Here. Jenni makes the best sandwiches. I assumed you'd be too busy to stop and eat."

"Thank you." She unwrapped the sandwich and took a bite. "Holy crap, that's good. Is that pesto?"

"She refuses to give me the secret ingredient."

"If I had a recipe this good, I would too." It might have been the hunger, it might have been that the sandwich was that good—either way, Rachel didn't care. "This was very thoughtful. Thank you."

"I know you are busy with work, I just really want to find a way to spend more time together. The moments we have don't feel like enough."

They didn't. It was never enough. "I'll be here late at least every night this week. Any chance you're free Saturday night?"

"I'm playing in Eugene this weekend and then heading to LA next week."

"Do you always travel this much?"

"It comes and goes. Depends on the opportunity. I don't suppose you're up for a trip down to Eugene this weekend?"

"I can't head out of town. I told my niece and nephew I'd be at their soccer game Saturday, and I have family dinner on Sunday."

"If you ever figure out how a rain check works, you be sure and let me know." Kenzie got up. "But when we finally get our time alone together, I know it's going to be worth it."

Rachel's breath hitched. What would it take to finally get alone time? "Wait. You said you're going to LA next week?"

Kenzie sat down on the edge of the office chair. "I am."

"How far will you be from Long Beach?"

Kenzie pulled out her phone. "Forty-five minutes. We stay at this huge resort-type house. The recording studio is on-site, but there's also a pool and a bar and the best view of the Pacific Ocean you've ever seen."

"Does this fancy place have Wi-Fi?"

"Why, yes it does. What are you thinking over there?"

"One of our clients is in Long Beach. If I went down next week to see him as a work trip, I could potentially work remote the rest of the week."

"Really?"

"Potentially."

Kenzie shot up in excitement. "This is great. Send me where you're staying. I'll have Damon come pick you up. I can't believe you're coming."

"Slow down. I'm joining you on my *work* trip. You send me the address of where you're staying and I'll let you know when my client meeting ends. Who's Damon?"

"Only a godsend. You'll see when you meet him. Whatever you want to call this trip, it's fantastic." Kenzie crossed to the other side of Rachel's desk and pulled her out of her chair. "If we weren't in your office I would kiss you so hard right now."

Butterflies swirled in Rachel's stomach. Goddammit for being in her office right now. "I hope you still feel the same way next week."

"I can assure you that I will." Kenzie placed a kiss on Rachel's cheek before she left. Rachel's hand touched where Kenzie's mouth just was. Next week could not come fast enough.

CHAPTER NINETEEN

"L et's go, people." Cooper made a circling motion with his hands. Kenzie loved working with Cooper. He was direct and to the point, and after several years of recording with him, she had a sense of what he was looking for in sessions like this. It was a bond that could take decades to form. The lights reflected off Cooper's bald head, that already housed beads of sweat. Not a great sign if he was already sweating and they'd barely started.

Kenzie was thankful for the large glass window separating the musicians from the rest of the production. Black leather couches popped against the bright red carpet, and Kenzie couldn't wait until Rachel occupied one of them. How long would her client meeting go again? Posters of all the famous artists the studio represented lined the seating area.

"Cooper said we just needed to get a few tracks today, so maybe you could try not to take forever," Kenzie joked as Braxton fiddled with her headphones at the music stand behind her.

"Oh, I'm feeling good today. I bet we can get it in three takes or less." Braxton's hair glistened under the fake studio lights. Even when there wasn't a real audience, Braxton still dressed like there could be one at any minute. "Now if the rest of you could keep up, that would be nice." She made a sweeping motion to the rest of the band. They groaned and laughed along to humor her.

Kenzie played a few scales to remember how the studio piano would respond. After a few seconds, she gave Cooper a thumbs-up.

"Okay, Kenz." He pushed a button that allowed them to hear

him from behind the glass. "I want just piano and vocals on this track. Whenever you're ready."

Kenzie breathed in through her nose and exhaled. She made eye contact with Braxton. "Two, three, four," she counted out and then started playing the keys. Her vocals mattered today. She didn't always end up on the final tracks, but for many of the songs on this record she would be. What would Rachel think of that? She couldn't wait to see her in person again. The texting and phone calls were great, but they weren't enough. It was never enough. To think, tonight she would finally get her in person. "Fuck." Kenzie grimaced as her fingers hit the wrong keys. "Sorry."

Cooper spoke to the room. "It was good up until that point. Take it from the top again."

Kenzie counted them in and started the song over. Her eyes wandered, searching for a clock. Had Rachel said it was a morning or afternoon meeting? Kenzie thought she said she'd be here in the afternoon. That would be any minute, right? Kenzie missed the chord again, but powered through, hoping that no one else would notice.

"Cut!" Cooper's voice infiltrated the booth.

Shit. It had not gone unnoticed.

"Let's try a different track, yeah? Skip to track eight."

Track eight started with a guitar solo, giving Kenzie a much-needed break. She needed to get her act together. She wrote most of these songs, she should be able to play them in her sleep. Rachel would be here any minute and it would be fine. She just had to hang on until then.

When was it going to be her turn in this booth, recording her songs? Recording with Braxton was amazing, but it just wasn't the same. She wanted her chance. She wanted to be the one that was the center of attention. She'd certainly worked hard enough for it.

"Cut!" Cooper said again.

Shit. What had gone wrong now?

"Kenzie. Let's take a walk."

Fuck. Cooper took band members for walks when he needed to get through to them. When their guitar player couldn't stop getting speeding tickets, Cooper took him for a walk. When Braxton couldn't hit the high note on her last album, Cooper took her for a walk. Braxton came back to the booth teary eyed, but hit every note perfectly after that. Kenzie didn't know what was said but had hoped to never have that kind of meeting with Cooper.

"Good luck, Kenz," Braxton said as Kenzie left the studio.

"Want to tell me what the fuck that was about?" Cooper asked once they got outside.

Kenzie's eyes adjusted to the bright California sunshine. "What what was about?"

"Oh, I don't know, maybe why you can't hit the chords to the songs you wrote? What's gotten into you?"

"Coop, I love Braxton, you know I do. I don't have siblings, but I imagine this is a lot like what it feels like to watch your younger sister be successful off your hard work."

"Are you serious? That's what this is?"

"What?"

"You're messing up in there because you can't stand to be second fiddle?"

"It's not just that, Cooper. I've been working really hard and I just need to know that it's going somewhere."

"And going toward award-winning albums isn't enough?"

"You know what I mean." It wasn't enough. They weren't *her* albums.

"Kenz. We've been over this. It's all about timing. You know I love your work, but we have to get everything just right."

"I've been sending you lots of songs, are you telling me you can't use any of them?"

"Is this about money? Do you need me to ask the studio about an advance?"

"No. I mean yes." An advance would help take the pressure of some things, but that wasn't the whole point. "But back to the songs."

"I'm waiting for the right artist."

"I could be the right artist." Kenzie pointed to her chest. What was he not understanding? She had the talent. She had the drive. What was the hold up?

Cooper rubbed both hands over his bald head. "We have to get the timing right. You deliver a slam dunk on this new movie soundtrack, and that's our ticket in. The studio knows who you are right now, but you aren't big enough. You deliver a song for pop star turned movie star Braxton to sing the crap out of, and then it's our time to strike. Got it?"

Kenzie's mind started spinning. She didn't even have an inkling of what that song would be yet and now had the added pressure of it needing to be the biggest hit she'd ever written. "If I deliver a big hit, you'll give me my chance?"

"You deliver a hit, and I'll talk to the studio. That's the best I can promise. Okay?"

It wasn't anything Kenzie could take to the bank, but it was more of a timeline than she'd ever had before. "Okay."

Cooper wrapped a strong arm around her. "Now get out of your head and help make your little sister famous."

❖

Braxton bounced in the booth, showing Rachel her sheet music as Kenzie came back down the stairs. Wait. Rachel? Kenzie burst into the studio. "Rachel!"

"Hi." Rachel met her with a hug.

Kenzie wrapped her arms around her, squeezing her tight and relishing the feel of finally having her in her arms.

"Damon brought me down here. I heard you were on a walk."

"Yeah."

"Everything okay?" Braxton asked.

"I think so." If Kenzie could write that damn song it would be.

"Don't worry, I played a good hostess to Rachel while you were gone and introduced her to everyone."

"Right. I'm so sorry."

"Braxton has been great." Rachel still looked starstruck. It would take a while for that to wear off, Kenzie had learned from experience.

"Rachel!" Cooper called from the soundboard.

Rachel turned around and stared.

"You can sit here if you want." He pointed to the open chair next to him.

"Really?"

"Get over here." He waved her over and pulled the chair out.

"That's Cooper. He's our main producer. You don't mind just hanging out?"

"Mind? This is awesome!" Rachel gave her a peck on the cheek as she exited the booth.

Kenzie wanted it to last longer. She wanted a kiss on the lips, but this was work. She needed to get the work part out of the way and get to the more exciting part of her night.

"So, she's cute," Braxton said as soon as the door was shut.

"She is." Kenzie blushed. She knew Rachel couldn't hear them, but she looked in her direction nevertheless. Cooper had her full attention showing her all the different controls.

"And you two aren't…"

"Not yet. I'm trying to impress her, so let's try and get a few good takes in."

Five takes later, Cooper said he had what they needed and could break for the day. She and Braxton left the recording booth and met Rachel on the other side.

"I insist you have dinner with me." Braxton spoke fast.

"Um." Rachel looked like a deer in the headlights.

"We would love to," Kenzie responded. "If that's okay?" She made eye contact with Rachel, who merely nodded.

"Great. I'll meet you poolside in two hours."

"We would have had more time if you could have gotten it in three takes," Kenzie joked.

"Whatever." Braxton dismissed her comment as she left.

"That was amazing." Rachel finally found words.

"She's very good," Kenzie said.

"Yes, but not just her. All of it." Rachel made a sweeping motion with her arms. "The whole process. This is amazing."

"Come on. I'll show you our room." She led her up the stairs and back to the main floor. The marble staircase opened into a long hallway.

"How many rooms is this place?" Rachel looked all around.

"Honestly? I don't know. We've had as many as seven band members here before. I don't think anyone has ever had to share a room." Kenzie pulled a key card out of her back pocket and unlocked the door in front of them. "They had locks installed a few years ago. Trust me, it's a good thing."

"I just can't believe places like this exist."

Their bags were in the entryway. Damon must have dropped them off earlier. The room opened to a sitting room with a plush brown couch in front of a TV. "The bedroom is just this way." Kenzie pointed to a door just inside the room. "I always stay in this room. I guess I didn't think to see if we needed a bigger one."

"Bigger one? No, this will be plenty big enough." She stepped forward and pulled Kenzie in toward her by her hips. "And which way was the bedroom?" she asked suggestively.

Kenzie nodded with her head toward the bedroom door. Rachel leaned her head in, and Kenzie met her lips. The air between them electrified. Rachel's hands on her hips, her lips on hers. She couldn't believe that she finally had Rachel alone. The fact that she was even here meant that there was something between them, even if Rachel was playing it off as a work trip, she still put in the effort.

Kenzie's phone buzzed, and she reached for her back pocket. Rachel put her hand on hers, stopping her from pulling it out. "Don't answer it," she whispered.

Kenzie groaned and reluctantly pulled her phone out. She checked the screen. "Ugh, it's work."

Rachel raised an eyebrow.

"Cooper, I just saw you and I'm kind of in the middle of something." She held Rachel's gaze.

"Kenz, I just had a breakthrough. I need you." He sounded panicked.

"Okay?"

"Can you come back downstairs? I want to do that track again but just guitar instead of piano. I want to get it now before I lose this idea."

"Of course. I'm on my way." She hung up and ran her hands over her face. "I need to go back downstairs."

"I'm glad I'm not the only one that gets urgent work calls," Rachel said.

"Better now than at three a.m. That's been known to happen."

"I'm going to shower and get settled in," Rachel said.

"You sure you're good?"

"Of course. Plus, I have Damon's number if I need anything."

"I'm sorry." Kenzie couldn't believe Cooper's insistence that this happen now.

"It's fine." Rachel pushed her toward the door. "It *is* a work trip."

"Okay. I'll try and make this quick, and I'll meet you by the pool for dinner at six."

Rachel reached for Kenzie's hand and pulled her back just as she started to leave. She pulled her in and kissed her on the cheek. "I'll see you soon."

Kenzie had to tear herself out of the room. She would have much rather stayed to see if there was any more to that kiss, but this was a work trip and she needed to put that first.

CHAPTER TWENTY

Kenzie practically ran up the two flights of stairs once they finished recording. Cooper had been right. The track sounded much better with just guitar. She didn't mind the retaping, but it was sometimes annoying to spend hours recording a song one way just to have a producer want it done completely different.

"I am so sorry about that." She looked around and found no sign of Rachel. Her bag had been moved and unpacked. It was a great sign that Rachel felt comfortable enough to be out on the property and didn't confine herself to the room, but that didn't mean Kenzie hadn't hoped she'd find her alone to pick up where they left off.

She figured she had a few minutes until dinner, and a shower sounded amazing. They weren't necessarily going out for dinner, but she still wanted to look nice. She showered quickly and pulled her hair back in a loose ponytail. She found her black capris pants and pulled them on. The sun remained out, but it wasn't quite shorts weather just yet. Her blue tank top was just dressy enough without trying too hard.

Kenzie joined the group on the pool deck, and as she got closer, she saw Rachel and Braxton chatting and laughing like old friends.

"Hi," Kenzie said as she got within speaking distance.

"Hey there." Rachel looked up from the bar. She looked stunning. She had changed into a yellow sundress, and her brown hair hung in loose curls just below her shoulders. If Kenzie didn't know any better, she would have thought she had dressed up for her.

"Well, it's about damn time." Braxton slapped a hand on the bar. "Didn't we agree on six?" She dramatically looked at her watch.

"How late am I?" Kenzie asked. She had hurried to get ready and thought for sure she hadn't taken thirty minutes.

"Only ten minutes." Rachel crinkled her nose at her.

"Damn." Kenzie approached the bar. "I need a drink." She signaled the bartender, and he poured a glass of whiskey.

Rachel eyed the drink. "Come here often enough that he knows your drink?"

"Yes." Kenzie raised the glass. "But he's new. If I had to guess, Damon tipped him off."

"That kid is good," Rachel said.

"He's the best."

Braxton chimed in. "Can we eat, please? I'm starving."

"After you." Kenzie motioned to a table in the corner.

"So..." Braxton settled into her chair. "I'm sure Kenzie has told you all about the exciting project she's working on."

"I'm afraid she hasn't." Rachel shot Kenzie a confused look.

Kenzie raised her palms. "There's not much to talk about."

Braxton put her hands on the table, and the silverware rattled. "Don't even tell me you haven't started."

"Uh..."

Braxton rubbed her hands over her face. "Dammit, Kenzie."

"What's going on?" Rachel hadn't lost the look of confusion.

"Kenzie here is supposed to be writing a major song for only the biggest movie of the year." Braxton motioned to Kenzie across the table. "But apparently she hasn't started yet."

Kenzie held her hands up in defense. "Trust me, it's not for lack of trying."

"Do you have anything?" Braxton asked.

Kenzie sighed and shook her head. "No."

Rachel cut in. "I'm sorry. I'm still not following." She turned her attention to Kenzie.

"There's a big war movie coming out in December. It's projected to win all kinds of awards. I am writing the love song to accompany it and Braxton is going to perform it. It's a really big deal. It's just not coming together."

"They are giving me an acting role in exchange for me singing the song." Braxton perked up. "But if there's no song, there's no role, Kenzie." She dragged out her name. "They will cut my scenes if you don't come through! Tell me you have a lyric or a chord progression or something."

"It'll happen," Kenzie said. "I know I'm not good at showing up on time, but I've never missed a deadline. You know that."

"No, but you've come real damn close." Braxton held her thumb and forefinger together.

"But I've never missed. Don't act like there isn't anything riding on this for me either."

"Is that what you and Cooper talked about on your walk?" Braxton asked.

"Do you two always speak in code?" Rachel looked between them.

"I'm sorry," Kenzie said. "But yes. It was part of what Cooper and I talked about today. He said that if the song does well enough, that will be a great time for me to branch off on my own."

"Kenzie, that's great!" Braxton clapped her hands together. "Just make sure whatever you do, you don't become more famous than me."

"That is not part of the plan, I assure you."

❖

Once the plates had been cleared, Kenzie pushed her chair back from the table. "Well, Braxton, this has been a pleasure, but if you don't mind, I'm going to steal Rachel for myself."

"I see how it is," Braxton said playfully. "Don't stay out too late. We're starting early tomorrow."

"How early is early?" Rachel asked.

"Early for Braxton is ten a.m.," Kenzie said. "So, with any luck, we'll be ready to go by eleven."

"Oh whatever. You two have fun." Braxton waved them off.

Kenzie held her hand out for Rachel. "I was thinking we could take a quick stroll on the beach and watch the sunset."

"Sounds amazing." Rachel took her hand and followed her past the infinity pool and down the staircase to the beach.

"We can leave our shoes here." Kenzie kicked off her sandals and left them at the top of the stone stairs. Rachel did the same. Kenzie reached for her hand again and led her down the path. The sand still held the sun's warmth from the day and squished between Kenzie's toes. The tide was coming in and left only a few feet of beach.

"I have to feel the ocean," Rachel said.

"Okay." Kenzie shrugged and followed her closer to the water. Kenzie put her toes in first. "Ooh. It's colder than it looks."

Rachel dipped her feet in and jumped back. "It sure is. But I just had to feel it."

Kenzie took advantage of their closeness and put an arm around Rachel's back. She pointed down the beach. "There's a spot just up here."

Their shoulders brushed and their steps fell into stride until they came just around a sandy inlet.

"What's all this?" Rachel asked as she looked at a blanket that had been laid out for them.

"I thought we could watch the sunset." Kenzie sat down and Rachel followed suit. She reached for the open bottle of wine at the head of the beach blanket.

"And wine?" Rachel looked from the bottle to Kenzie.

"This is the one you like, right?" Kenzie had a moment of panic. She hoped she hadn't remembered wrong.

"It is."

Kenzie handed her an oversized wine glass. "I'm going to let you pour so that I don't embarrass myself."

She poured two glasses and handed one to Kenzie. She swirled the wine in her glass and held it up to the setting sun. "Braxton is really nice. Not at all what I was expecting."

"Yeah, she's great. Way more down-to-earth than people think."

"How did you two meet?"

"Through Cooper." Kenzie looked at the wine in her own glass. "I met Cooper a few years ago playing gigs in bars."

"You did?"

"Yeah." Kenzie looked off into the ocean. "I've been at this a long time. Playing dive bars, any gig I can get, really. Thankfully one night, Cooper was in the audience. He got me hooked up opening for a few people. Then I did a county fair tour one summer."

"How was that?" She waggled her eyebrows.

"A lot of fun. But you spend most of your time on a bus, and there's really no time for songwriting. I told Cooper I want to find the right balance. I want to have my work out there and perform without living on a bus or van nine months out of the year. He introduced me to Braxton, and we've been working together ever since."

"You and Braxton seem to have a good thing going."

"We do," Kenzie said. "She is by far my favorite artist to work with. We collaborate well, and she has this way of taking what I write and pushing it to the next level. But it's not quite what I want. Don't get me wrong, I'm happy for her and proud of her, but I can't wait until I get to be the one making my songs famous."

Rachel turned and looked Kenzie in the eyes. Kenzie looked into Rachel's eyes, and a small smile came across her lips. Rachel shook her head.

"What?" Kenzie asked.

"Kenzie McCall, you are exactly what I needed." Rachel raised her glass and took a drink.

"I'll drink to that." Kenzie raised her glass in return. "But what do you mean?"

Rachel turned from Kenzie to the sunset. "If you would have told me two months ago that I would be having dinner with Braxton on a work night, of all nights, and then watching a romantic sunset, I would have told you you were delusional."

"Yet here we are." Kenzie waved her arm. It made her happy Rachel had called the gesture romantic. It's what she was going for, but she didn't want to seem like she was trying too hard to impress her, even though she was.

Rachel rested her elbow on her knee and put her cheek in her palm. She turned and looked at Kenzie. "Thank you. This is quite possibly the best work trip I've ever been on."

"I should hope so. Now, come here so we don't miss it." Kenzie moved her body closer to Rachel's and put one hand around her waist until they were hip to hip. Rachel raised her arm and put it around Kenzie's shoulder. "No fake yawn this time?" Kenzie said.

"I have always wanted to try that," Rachel said.

Kenzie turned her head and looked up at Rachel. She was still getting used to the fact that Rachel was taller than her. It wasn't something she had ever experienced in a romantic partner. "Anything else you've always wanted to try?"

"I can think of a few things." Rachel pushed her chin until she was facing the sliver of the sun left above the ocean. The orange and purple hues popped against the few clouds left in the sky. Rachel took another sip of her wine and set it in the sand behind them. When she turned around, Kenzie reached out her hand and brought Rachel's face toward hers.

Rachel grabbed Kenzie's face and held her with both hands. Their lips met. Soft and slow at first, but their passion grew. Fast. They had been waiting for this moment long enough. Kenzie laid Rachel down until she was on top of her, careful to not break the kiss. She propped herself up with one elbow, leaving one arm free. Rachel let out a small moan and Kenzie pushed her tongue inside, pulsing in her mouth.

Kenzie needed more. Kissing felt amazing, but she had been thinking—no, dreaming about Rachel and the feel of her body for weeks now. She didn't care where they were or if it was a semi-public place, she couldn't wait any longer. She ran her hand down Rachel's body and paused when she got to her bare knee. She stroked up the outside of her thigh and caressed Rachel's silky smooth legs. She had shaved for tonight, and that thought gave Kenzie the confidence she needed to keep going. She kept running her hand up and down Rachel's leg. Rachel grabbed the back of Kenzie's neck, applying pressure and holding her close.

"I need to touch you," Kenzie whispered.

"Mm-hmm." Rachel nodded.

Kenzie moved to Rachel's inner thigh. With her thumb, she moved under Rachel's panties, and heat radiated off her. She gently moved her thumb, taking in all of Rachel's wetness. She paused when she got to her hood and Rachel let out a sharp breath. Rachel bucked her hips and Kenzie ran her thumb back and forth as Rachel's desire built under her touch.

Kenzie kept exploring Rachel, going slow in some places and faster in others. She could have stayed here all night and been perfectly happy. She could feel the pressure building in Rachel and wanted to push her over the edge. She moved her thumb to her warm opening and quickly inserted herself.

Rachel let out a gasp and dug her fingernails into the back of Kenzie's neck. Kenzie took her thumb back out, but not quite all the way, relishing Rachel's warmth and wetness. As she quickened her pace, a cold rush flooded her feet. "Shit." She looked over her shoulder. The incoming tide soaked the bottom of the blanket.

She started to sit up but Rachel dug her hand into her neck and pulled her back down. "Don't stop. Please," she said through shallow breaths.

"Okay." She picked up her pace and Rachel's inner walls tightened around her. She kept going, making long thrusts with her hand.

"Right there."

Kenzie kept going as another cold wave crashed against her feet. This time it came up past her ankles, and she could feel the cold ocean sinking into her capris. She kept going. Rachel's breathing picked up.

"Right there," Rachel said again and clamped her eyes shut.

Kenzie didn't let up. She pushed her right over the edge as a third wave came crashing at their feet again.

Rachel moaned and opened her eyes. Kenzie propped herself up on her elbows, and grinned at the beautiful woman underneath her. She withdrew her hand and brought it back from under her dress.

Rachel eyed the now-drenched blanket. "Sorry. I couldn't take another start and stop."

"Don't be." Kenzie leaned down to kiss Rachel on the lips.

"Why don't we head back to the room and try this with a little less sand?"

Kenzie couldn't stand up fast enough. She reached a hand out and helped Rachel to her feet. Rachel reached for the blanket. "Oh, it's fine." Kenzie waved her off. "Damon will get it in the morning. Let's go."

Rachel hesitantly took her hand as they started back. "This isn't a move or something, is it?"

Kenzie turned to face Rachel. "Move?"

"Like this is how you pick up girls or something? You bring them to this amazing place and then seduce them on the beach?"

"This is not a move. I've never brought anyone with me on one of these trips."

"Okay." Rachel nodded, and the answer seemed to alleviate whatever nervousness was there.

"I mean it," Kenzie said. "I know I hang around some characters, but the whole party scene isn't me at all."

"Okay."

"Are you having second thoughts?"

"No." Rachel shook her head. "It would be a good move if it was one, but I don't want to be just another one of your girls."

"Trust me, you're not."

"And I don't want to hear a song on the radio about sex on the beach," Rachel said.

"I can't make that kind of promise."

Rachel playfully slapped her shoulder. "Well, you will if you want this night to keep going." She arched an eyebrow.

"Oh, really?"

"Mm-hmm." Rachel nodded.

"Then I guess I have no choice." Kenzie shrugged. "No songs about sex on the beach."

Chapter Twenty-One

Rachel lay in her black cover-up on a lounge chair by the pool. It wasn't quite hot enough to get in the water yet, but the rising sun warmed her skin. She'd packed a bag full of briefs to read, knowing that working remote could mean catching up by the pool. The client meeting had gone well. Better than expected, even. She could almost relax for the next two days. Almost.

She couldn't focus on the paper in front of her as her mind kept replaying the day before. Had she really had dinner with Braxton? Then on top of that, she finally slept with Kenzie. The woman she had been dreaming about for months now. Her life was so different now than it had been before Kenzie. It was exciting and terrifying at the same time. On the one hand, the prospect of a new relationship thrilled her. Kenzie was fun, and things were fresh. Relationships were always good at the beginning.

On the other hand, if things didn't go anywhere with Kenzie, that put her that much further behind in her goal of starting her own family. She tried to push that thought to the back of her head. She needed to not put too much pressure on this. Kenzie was good. Things were good. She needed to sit by the pool and try to enjoy a few moments of fresh air.

Rachel had attempted to read the first sentence on her brief five times when she was interrupted.

"Hi." Kenzie waved from the end of the lounge chair.

Rachel looked at her smartwatch. It was barely noon. "Hey," she said with a hint of confusion.

Kenzie found the lounge chair across from Rachel. She leaned her elbows on her knees. "I'm on time-out."

"Okay?" Rachel wasn't aware that adults could be put in time-out.

"Cooper said I am grinning too much. We are supposed to be recording sad songs, and he said I had the grin of someone, who, and I quote, just got fucked by her hot girlfriend." Kenzie paused. "So, now I'm supposed to think of sad things and come back when I can stop grinning."

She smiled. "I see."

Kenzie ran a hand over her head, trying to tame the loose strands of her ponytail. "Do you have any sad things for me to think about?" Kenzie couldn't even get the words out with a straight face.

"I'm not sure I can help you there," Rachel said.

"Well, shoot." Kenzie pretended to snap her fingers. "Guess I'm stuck in time-out with you. Not that you're my girlfriend or anything. It's way too soon to be talking about that."

It was. But that didn't mean it wasn't the direction they were headed. "You could think about that big deadline you have coming up. What's that all about anyway?"

"Ugh." Kenzie put her legs up and lay back on the lounge chair. She put her hands over her face. "Now, that is a sad thought."

Rachel propped herself up and gave Kenzie her full attention. "What do you think is going on?"

"I don't write on command." Kenzie made a sweeping motion with her hands.

"But you write for albums all the time."

"Yes, but this is different. I write songs and then Cooper finds an artist to sing them. I write whatever I want to write. I've never written anything because someone asked me to. Or paid me to, for that matter." Kenzie lay on the lounge chair looking at the sky.

"Do you think it has anything to do with the fact that it isn't a breakup song?"

Kenzie sat straight up and looked at Rachel. "What are you talking about?"

"It's nothing." Rachel waved it off.

"No," Kenzie said. "There was something behind that."

"It's just that… Never mind. It really is nothing."

Kenzie swung her feet to the ground and faced Rachel. "Seriously? Just out with it."

"Jenni tried to warn me about you."

"Jenni? When?" Kenzie squinted her eyes.

"When I stopped by your studio. She told me that you like to write breakup songs and you only stay in relationships long enough to get a new take on a breakup."

Kenzie ran her hands over her head. "Are you kidding me? She actually said that to you?"

"She did." Rachel nodded tentatively.

"It's not true." Kenzie glared down at Rachel.

"Okay." Rachel shrugged.

Kenzie sat back down. "Do you think it's true?"

"I shouldn't have said anything."

Kenzie rubbed her head in her hands. "So you do think it's true?"

"Of course I don't think it's true." She should have kept her mouth shut. She wished she could have gone back in time for just a few minutes and taken the words back. She didn't even know if she believed anything Jenni had to say. "Clearly I struck a nerve here. You write a lot of breakup songs. I'm not saying I believe Jenni. I'm just saying, from what I know, most of your songs are breakup songs, and now you're being asked to write something different."

Kenzie looked up. "Because breakup songs sell." She flailed her arms. "Breakup songs are what people want to blare at the top of their lungs with windows rolled down."

"I'm sorry," Rachel said.

"It's not you." Kenzie shook her head.

"I definitely hit on something more than just the song, so for that I'm sorry." Rachel had been half joking with her comment, and it had set them down this path.

"The deadline is stressing me out, and the fact that Jenni said something to you is pissing me off. She had no right."

Rachel shrugged.

"I wrote three songs shortly after Jenni and I broke up. She thinks I was only with her so I could get my next few singles."

Rachel nodded.

"But I wasn't. It was just the timing of it. I would never use someone like that."

Rachel sat next to Kenzie. She couldn't be this far apart from her any longer. She put her arm around her and pulled her in. "I know." Rachel pulled her in close.

Kenzie let out a long sigh. "Well, I guess I'm ready to go sing sad songs now." She started to stand up and Rachel held her in place.

Rachel couldn't let her go yet, not like this. Not that this was a fight by any means, but she didn't like the energy between them. "No more grinning from being fucked by your hot girlfriend?" She made sure that this comment came across as a joke.

"Well, that depends, I guess."

"On?"

Kenzie turned to face Rachel. "Well, it's a little soon to talk about titles, and you just ended a serious relationship and I'm not asking for anything serious, but I would like to see you exclusively. We don't have to call it anything. I just only want to be with you. I'm hoping that you would only like to be with me."

Rachel looked into Kenzie's blue eyes and swallowed, hard. "I would."

"And maybe if you're not doing anything later, there's a few more moves we can try up in the room."

Rachel's face flushed. Even though she had started the flirting back and forth, it still made her stomach do a flip to have it reciprocated.

"I am definitely not doing anything later."

Kenzie leaned in until her mouth brushed Rachel's ear. "That's good, because I intend to fuck your brains out. Exclusively."

Rachel's stomach clenched. Tonight could not come fast enough. How was she going to focus on any work knowing what would be waiting for her? Kenzie leaned her head forward and Rachel met her lips. Rachel was desperate for her. She didn't care that they were in public. Her body wanted Kenzie more than anything in that moment. She grabbed Kenzie's face with both hands and deepened their kiss.

"Hey!" Cooper shouted at them. "What the fuck, Kenz? You are supposed to be thinking about sad things, not up here doing exactly what got you in time-out in the first place! Jesus." He stormed across the pool deck.

"I guess I better go." Kenzie leaned in and gave Rachel one last kiss.

"Rachel, I like you, I really do," Cooper said approaching them. "But you're going to have to break up with her right here if she can't come downstairs and get her shit together."

"I'm good, Coop." Kenzie nodded. "I got this."

Rachel couldn't help but smile as Kenzie disappeared across the pool deck and into the dark stairwell inside. Yes, it might be too soon to jump into anything again, but there was something about Kenzie she couldn't say no to.

CHAPTER TWENTY-TWO

K enzie didn't sleep naked often but loved the feel of the soft sheets against her bare skin. She opened her eyes and sunlight poured through the window, greeting her. Waves crashed against the sand outside, and she remembered how much she loved California in the mornings. She reached her arm out to feel Rachel. Memories of the night before came flooding back. Rachel under her. Rachel on top of her. Rachel on her side. Kenzie wasn't inexperienced by any means, but Rachel had had a long list of things she wanted to try, and who was Kenzie to say no?

Kenzie looked around when she realized she couldn't feel Rachel in the bed. She held the covers up over her chest as she blinked the room into focus. "Rachel?" she called out. She reached for the bedside table and picked up her phone. The display read eight a.m. It was still somewhat early. Rachel was probably the type to get up before the sun, no matter what. Not only would Kenzie never be a morning person, she would never so much as understand morning people. A door slammed shut. "Rachel?" she called again.

Rachel held a coffee cup in each hand. "Oh good. You're up." She sat at the side of the bed next to Kenzie and handed her a warm cup.

Kenzie noted her messy ponytail and her flushed cheeks. Rachel wore athletic shorts and a fitted black tank top. "Did you go for a run or something?"

"I did." Rachel nodded proudly. "I couldn't resist a beach run this early in the day. It was amazing."

"If you say so." Kenzie rolled her eyes. This was a hobby she did not understand. She brought the coffee cup to her lips. The warm air filled her nostrils, and she could actually feel the caffeine kick in just as it touched her lips. "Thank you for the coffee."

"You're welcome. I wanted to make sure you were awake."

"I'm not much of a morning person."

"I ran into Cooper getting coffee." Rachel took a sip of her own drink. "He said Braxton had a bit of a late night and that he didn't need you until eleven."

"Oh?" Kenzie reached for her phone. Sure enough, three unread texts from Cooper saying exactly what Rachel had just relayed.

"So that means I get you for another..." Rachel paused and looked at her watch. "Two hours and fifty minutes."

Kenzie took a sip of her coffee.

"I'm not kidding." Rachel's expression changed as she reached for Kenzie's coffee cup and put it on the nightstand next to her own. She moved her hands to the base of her tank top and pulled it over her head.

Kenzie took in Rachel in her sports bra on the bed. She had a line of sweat along the vee of her cleavage, and the tight bra pushed her breasts together.

Rachel pulled the sports bra over her head and, in one motion, took off her running shorts and underwear. She climbed under the covers and snuggled up close.

"You're sweaty." Her damp skin rested against Kenzie's.

"You're about to be," Rachel said, as she climbed on top of Kenzie.

Rachel was commanding in a way she wasn't used to. It was more than a turn-on, and even though they had spent hours together the night before, Kenzie could not get enough. A sharp breath left her body as Rachel took a nipple in her mouth. Her nipple hardened under Rachel's touch and chills covered her body. Rachel took her thumb and forefinger and began rolling Kenzie's other nipple between them. The mix of pleasure and pain working her body up.

Rachel kissed down Kenzie's body. She paused at her navel, licking it, and continued her path down. She ran her hand from her breast down her body. She pushed her arms under Kenzie's thighs and propped her up, exposing her. Kenzie winced as Rachel placed her mouth at her clit.

Rachel looked up. "Everything okay?"

"Yes." Kenzie nodded. "I'm just..." She paused, thinking of the right words. "A little out of practice." Kenzie wasn't sure how long it had been since she'd had sex. Jenni was probably her last, but she didn't know how long that had been. She had certainly never had this much sex in one night, and she was sore. Yet she didn't want Rachel to stop.

Rachel laughed playfully. "I guess we better fix that." She resumed her position between Kenzie's thighs and took her in her mouth. She sucked and licked, and Kenzie's orgasm built inside her.

Kenzie leaned her head into the pillow and arched her back as Rachel pushed a finger inside her. She put her hands on Rachel's shoulder blades, wanting to touch her and feel her warm skin.

Rachel picked up her pace and inserted another finger. The pressure mounted inside Kenzie. She placed her hands harder on Rachel's shoulders. She arched her back even higher and her whole body relaxed. She trembled under Rachel's touch. A few aftershocks overcame her and she couldn't control her body's motions. She lay back down on the bed, chest heaving.

Rachel crawled back up and brushed a few stray hairs out of Kenzie's face. "I told you I'd get you sweaty."

Beads of moisture formed on Kenzie's hairline. "I never doubted you," she said, still catching her breath. Kenzie stroked her hands along Rachel's shoulders, feeling the connection between them. "I love lying here with you."

Rachel squeezed her arms around Kenzie's middle. "It feels so nice. I can hear your heart beat in your chest."

Kenzie tried to slow her heart rate to its normal rhythm.

"I wish we didn't have to go home," Rachel said.

"What if we stayed the weekend?"

Rachel lifted her head. "We can't do that."

"We could. I know Cooper would let us stay, and I can make sure Damon gets us a flight back Sunday night. I can have you home just in time to get enough sleep for work Monday."

"That does sound nice."

"Just think. A few extra nights listening to the ocean. A few extra nights of this." Kenzie kissed Rachel's cheek and playfully bit her earlobe. Rachel shuddered under her. She had her right where she wanted her. It was way too soon to go back to the real world. She wanted to live in this fantasy just a few days longer.

"I have plans tomorrow."

"Oh." And just like that, the fantasy was over.

"I promised River and Ash I'd be at their soccer game."

"That's your niece and nephew?"

"Yeah."

"A freezing soccer field in April sounds terrible. Skip it and stay here with me." Kenzie tried to wrap Rachel in a hug, but she pulled away.

"It's not terrible. They're my family, and when I tell them I'm going to do something, I do it."

"But they have other games. Right? Couldn't you miss this one?"

"That's not the point." Rachel untangled herself and moved to the other side of the bed.

"Hey. I'm sorry. Come back here." Kenzie didn't need this wedge between them.

"It doesn't matter how many games they have. The point is, I told them I'd be at this one." Rachel crossed her arms and stayed on her side.

"I don't have siblings or nieces or nephews. I'm not used to family plans or soccer being important."

"What about if your own kids play soccer some day?"

"Damn. I hadn't thought of that. I always assumed they'd only be into music. I guess I'll have to get into dumb things like soccer."

"Soccer isn't dumb."

"You can't tell me you actually enjoy watching kids' soccer."

"You're missing the point. I'm going to go shower. My flight is later this morning, and I should get packing."

"Rachel, wait. I'm sorry." Kenzie's apology went to the bathroom door. Clearly soccer games for nieces and nephews were high on the list of priorities. If Kenzie had any shot of making things work with Rachel, she was going to have to learn what else was on this list.

CHAPTER TWENTY-THREE

Water soaked Rachel's toes within three steps of walking onto the soccer field. She regretted wearing tennis shoes instead of galoshes. Ashley sat with two folding chairs and a backpack full of snacks as Rachel approached, took her chair off her shoulder, and set it next to Ashley's. "Where's Patrick?" Rachel pointed to the empty chair next to her.

"Pacing."

"Pacing?"

"He gets so worked up on game days. Ash is on this field first, then River plays on the field behind us in an hour. He's pacing back and forth between them."

"He does know that this is youth soccer, right?"

Ashley waved both hands in the air. "This is not the hill I'm dying on. Someday you'll be married, and you'll understand."

Rachel stifled a yawn as she settled into her chair.

"Long night?" Ashely waggled her eyebrows.

"Yeah. My flight got delayed and I didn't get home until after midnight." She'd spent the afternoon at LAX. Once she knew the flight was delayed due to mechanical issues, she could have spent the afternoon with Kenzie, but they were out of rhythm since the morning. How could Kenzie not understand she was going to put her family first? She couldn't just bail on them.

"You're off jet-setting now?"

"Kind of. I had a work meeting in Long Beach and then met up with Kenzie. She was recording an album last week."

"Oh my God, really? That's so exciting! Did you see anyone famous? Did you go on a date? Did you finally sleep together?"

Rachel couldn't hide her smile. "Yes, yes, and yes."

"Okay. Back up. Which famous person?"

"Braxton."

"Damn."

"That's the album Kenzie was working on. We had dinner with her and everything."

"And your date?"

"We took a romantic walk on the beach and then watched the sunset. She had a blanket and a great bottle of wine laid out and everything."

"Wow. Talk about trying to impress you."

"I know. It was almost too good to be true."

"And the other stuff?" Ashley lowered her voice and looked around for any nosy parents.

Rachel blushed. "Also on the beach."

"Seriously?"

"What can I say? I got caught up in the moment."

Ashley clapped as the kids took the field. Rachel found Ash in the crowd and yelled encouragement.

"So now what?" Ashley asked.

"What do you mean?"

"When are you going to see her next? Are you dating?"

"We haven't talked about it."

"Which part?"

"Either part."

"You haven't talked about when you're going to see each other next?"

"Things didn't end so great yesterday."

"She pulls off a romantic date and things don't end well?"

"She wanted me to stay the weekend."

"And you didn't?" A few parents looked their way as Ashley raised her voice. She regained her composure. "Why didn't you?"

"Because I told River and Ash I'd be here."

"What the hell is wrong with you?"

Rachel bristled. "What are you talking about?"

"A beautiful, smart, fun woman asks you to stay the weekend, and you'd rather freeze your ass off at soccer?"

"It's not a matter of what the temperature is. I made a commitment."

"And I get that, really I do. I love how much you support my kids. It means the world to me, but you get to have your own life too. It would have been okay if you wanted to stay the weekend with Kenzie."

Part of Rachel had wanted to stay. A big part. But that was also a big step. A weekend alone together. Were things moving too fast? Yes, she needed things to move fast if she wanted to start a family, but was Kenzie the right person to start her family with? Had she used her niece and nephew as an excuse to slow things down? God, why were relationships so messy?

"I love you no matter what, you know that. I think Kenzie is great. You should see where things go with her."

"You do?" Ashley had never been this honest about anyone Rachel was seeing.

"I do. Even if that means you miss a few soccer games here and there."

"Who's missing soccer games?" Rachel's dad appeared and set up his own chair next to Rachel.

"Hi, Dad." Ashley greeted him. "No one yet, but Rachel here might if things with her new girlfriend take off."

"New girlfriend, huh?"

"Where's Mom?" Rachel looked around and saw no sign of their mother anywhere. She desperately needed a subject change. Not only was she not at the girlfriend stage with Kenzie, she was not at the discussing it with her father stage.

"She has decided she is too old to put up with wet socks. She loves these kids to death, but will not trudge through wet grass for them." He slumped down in his chair.

"So, she just didn't come?" Rachel didn't think her mother would miss a chance to see the grandkids for anything. Was it okay to just not come to soccer now? Maybe she should have stayed in LA.

"Oh, no." Her dad waved to the car in the parking lot. He had somehow angled the SUV in such a way that her mother had the perfect view of both fields and could see all the action. "We came up with a compromise."

Compromise. It was small. It was silly, but it worked. Maybe there was a way that Rachel could make this work with Kenzie.

CHAPTER TWENTY-FOUR

Monday morning came entirely too fast. A stack of manila folders full of new cases welcomed Rachel back to work. She stared out the window, thinking back to how she'd left things with Kenzie. She should have texted her yesterday, but she just couldn't quite bring herself to do it. Kenzie was fun. She was easy to talk to. Hanging out with Kenzie was simple and good, and she couldn't deny their chemistry. So why hadn't she texted or called her yet? Why was she waiting for Kenzie to be the one to reach out?

"Well, you're looking tan." Gail's voice interrupted her daydream. "Did you get any work done down there?"

Rachel looked at her arm. Her skin had turned an unseasonable shade of olive. "I can be quite productive."

"I'm sure you can. Which is a good thing because a lot of things happened while you were out. I see you've found the case files." Gail nodded at the unruly stack on Rachel's desk.

"Yes. I'll get right on these."

"Good. We're expecting you to bring more of that magic that you brought to the last settlement." Gail tapped the metal doorframe as she left.

Rachel picked up the first folder and leaned back into her chair. It was going to take all the focus she had to not let her mind drift back to the beach.

She made it through the first round of briefs on her desk when the sound of her phone buzzing startled her. "Kenzie McCall." She clicked the green button to answer. "Hi there." She tried not to sound overly excited.

"Hi," Kenzie answered, slightly timid.

"You make it back okay?"

"I did. Got in last night. How was soccer?"

"I think my socks are still wet. But good. The kids did great."

"That's good to hear. Look I'm sorry about what I said. I don't feel great about how we left things."

"I think I might have overreacted a bit."

"I don't have family other than my mom,, and she's on a commune in New Mexico, so I literally know nothing about making plans with family."

"I appreciate you saying something. I had a good talk with my sister, and I think I might be able to miss a few games in the future."

"I really want to see you again."

"I want to see you too. I miss you."

"That's perfect. I was hoping you'd say that."

"Okay?"

"Jenni called me."

Rachel clenched her jaw. She knew that Kenzie and Jenni were friends, but she didn't have to like it. She wasn't necessarily jealous; she just didn't like it.

"She's in a bind again and needs someone to perform over the lunch hour. I'm not doing much today, so I agreed, and I was wondering if maybe you could sneak away."

"Don't you have a song to be writing?" Rachel sounded more scolding than she meant. Kenzie's job was her business, but it was eating at her that she had a deadline she seemed to ignore.

Kenzie sighed. "I have been staring at a blank page all morning. I need to get out of the house. Plus, sometimes an audience inspires me. If you're busy at work, I get it. I just thought you might need a cup of coffee or something."

"I definitely need or something," Rachel said. "I would love to see you."

"Great. I'll see you soon."

"See you soon." Rachel hung up and smiled. She was going to see Kenzie.

❖

Rachel ordered a latte and took a seat at a center table. She'd never been much of a lunch eater, but coffee was a necessity if she was going to get through the rest of the case files waiting for her. Kenzie unpacked her guitar on the small stage, so Rachel took a seat rather than distract her.

Kenzie sat on the stool, guitar in hand, and her eyes went wide. "Hi." She looked right at Rachel.

Rachel gave a small wave. "Hi." Pressed wasn't packed, but there was a small lunch crowd hovering around.

"Alright, folks, I'm McKenzie McCall. I'll be here to help you get through the lunch hour and back to your day." Kenzie started in on some of her normal set songs, and Rachel took it all in.

"Here you go, Rachel." Jenni delivered a steaming hot latte in a white mug to Rachel's table.

"Oh, thank you." She took the coffee.

"I'm glad you could make it," Jenni said. Rachel took a sip of the hot drink, and her brain instantly awoke as the coffee hit her lips. *Damn, she can make a good latte.*

"Rachel?" Laurel's unmistakable voice filled Rachel's ears as she looked up from the table.

"Hi," she said hesitantly, as Laurel approached her table.

"What are you doing here?" Laurel took a seat in the empty chair.

"I decided I needed a break." She pointed to the coffee on the table.

Laurel raised one eyebrow. "Since when do you need breaks?"

Rachel shrugged. "It's a new thing I'm trying."

Rachel looked to the stage as Kenzie laughed. She swiped at something on her tablet and started her next song. Rachel had no idea what was so funny. She vaguely recognized the song, but she couldn't place it. She noticed Kenzie looking everywhere but in her direction and she wondered if she had seen Laurel. It would be hard to miss, but maybe she was caught up in the moment.

"Rachel, I've been thinking." Laurel broke the silence between them. "Actually, I can't stop thinking. You're all I think about. What do we need to do to give this another go?"

"Laurel—"

Rachel was cut off by Laurel holding up a hand. She braced

herself for whatever came next. "Just hear me out. We were good together. We should still be good together. I can give you the life that you want."

"What are you talking about?"

"I know you want to settle down and have a family. I can give that to you. I know it wasn't fair of me to spring the proposal on you. We should have talked about it first. Let's talk about it now."

Rachel did want to have that life, but no matter how hard she pictured it, she couldn't see Laurel there.

"What do I need to do?"

Then Rachel heard it. The lyrics to the song, and she knew exactly why Kenzie was laughing. She flared her nostrils and tried to give Kenzie the best glare she could muster as she got to the chorus and Kenzie sang about never ever getting back with an ex. Of all the songs for her to possibly play in that moment.

"Rachel? Are you okay?"

Rachel's cheeks flushed. "Laurel, there's someone else. I'm sorry, but it's the truth." Rachel decided the direct approach was best. She didn't want to string her along and give her false hope. Or give her an "it's not you, it's me" kind of speech.

"Oh," Laurel said. "Someone else? We haven't been apart that long."

"I know." Rachel let her words hang.

"So, after our time together, there's just someone else?" Laurel made a sweeping motion with her hands.

"Laurel, this isn't how I wanted you to find out." The song was officially driving Rachel crazy. She pinched the bridge of her nose.

"Who is it?"

"No one you know," Rachel answered.

"Were you—?"

Rachel cut her off. "No. I was never with anyone when I was with you. It just kind of happened." She shot Kenzie another look, hoping she would end the song early.

"Wait?" Laurel looked between Rachel and Kenzie. "Her?"

Rachel nodded. There wasn't anything more to say.

"You left me for the bar singer?"

"No." Rachel tried to keep her voice even. The last thing she needed was a blow-up argument in a public place. "I left you because we weren't good together. Then I happened to meet Kenzie. They were not related." It was more or less true. Yes, Kenzie had been the push she needed to leave Laurel, but she certainly wasn't the only reason.

"And you expect me to believe that? Does she even have a real job?"

"Yes, she has a real job." Not that she needed to explain any of this to Laurel. The genie was out of the bottle, and Rachel knew she couldn't put her back in. Laurel had a heck of a temper, and once she made up her mind on something, it was difficult to reason with her. She didn't want to hurt her, at least not any more than she already had, but at the same time, it wasn't her job to make her feel better. Not anymore. "It's the truth," Rachel finally said.

"Okay." Laurel pushed herself back quickly from the chair. "I thought I knew what you wanted, but clearly was I wrong. I don't know what kind of life you think she can give you, but it won't be anything like what you pictured. Good luck, Rachel."

Rachel cringed as Laurel approached the small stage. A confrontation in public wasn't high on her list of wants. Rachel couldn't make out what Laurel yelled before she stormed out of the restaurant. Rachel pushed herself back from her chair and followed her out. She didn't want to be with Laurel romantically, but she couldn't end things like this. By the time she reached the sidewalk out front, there was no sign of Laurel anywhere.

CHAPTER TWENTY-FIVE

As Kenzie finished the song, Jenni sent the next one to her tablet. She laughed out loud as she made eye contact with Jenni. She shook her head, but Jenni gave her a look that meant she better play it. That was their deal, after all, and it was funny.

When Rachel glared at her, she knew she had crossed a line. A small lunch crowd had gathered and seemed to be into the song. If she could have just ended it abruptly, she would have. Singing about never getting back together while Laurel was clearly groveling was a joke gone wrong. She didn't have to finish. She could just end at the next chorus and move on to something else quickly. As she thought through the transition in her mind, Laurel pushed herself back from the table.

Laurel went in Kenzie's direction instead of out the door. She approached with clenched fists and moved with heavy footsteps. "Here's a tip!" Laurel yelled three feet from the stage. "Don't fuck other people's girlfriends!"

Kenzie didn't realize she had stopped playing until the sound of the front door slamming echoed throughout the space. Rachel chased after her. Why would Rachel chase after her?

"I'll be right back," Kenzie said into the microphone and followed Rachel out into the street.

"What the hell was that?" Rachel glared at her as she joined her on the sidewalk.

"I'm sorry." Kenzie moved closer. "A bad joke."

"Really bad." Rachel fumed.

"Jenni sends the songs and I play them, and it seemed like it would be funny."

"Oh? So, you just do whatever Jenni tells you?"

"No." Kenzie tried to take it back. "No, not like that. I'm sorry."

"You come running whenever Jenni calls and I'm supposed to just be okay with it, but then when I try to have a conversation with Laurel, you lose it? It doesn't make any sense."

"What?" Kenzie's head spun. What did Jenni have to do with any of this?

"You and Jenni." Rachel pointed to her. "I'm supposed to be okay with you being friends, but you can't give me the same respect?"

"You have nothing to worry about with me and Jenni." The idea that Rachel would be threatened by Jenni made Kenzie want to vomit.

"And you have nothing to worry about with Laurel."

"Okay. Point taken."

"I know she's my ex and all, but I don't want to be on bad terms with her." Rachel rubbed her hands over her face.

"I don't know what came over me. I saw you two and I just. I don't know…"

"What do you mean, you don't know?" Rachel furrowed her brow.

"I'm not a jealous person. I'm not competitive or threatened, and stuff like that…" She motioned with her head to Pressed. "Normally wouldn't faze me."

"But it did just now?"

Kenzie took a step closer, trying to close the gap between them. "I don't want to write breakup songs about you."

"I thought that wasn't something you did." Rachel held firm.

"I didn't want to admit it was something I did." She shook her head. "But when I think about it, yes. I write a lot of breakup songs. And for the first time, I don't want to write one about someone."

"So, what? That's supposed to make things all better? That's supposed to excuse what just happened?"

"No." Kenzie took another step in and reached for Rachel's hand. She breathed in relief when Rachel took it. "I think I got jealous."

Rachel shook her head. "You have nothing to be jealous about. I ended things with her, remember?"

"No, I know. I'm not explaining this well."

"You're really not."

"It's like, with you, things finally make sense."

Rachel cracked a smile, and Kenzie's tension started to melt away.

"I don't see an end and I don't want to see an end. I want happily ever after, forever, kids, all of it." Kenzie paused and looked at Rachel's face. She wanted to make sure she wasn't scaring her away with her admission. She knew Rachel was looking for long-term, but they were still so new. Rachel didn't say anything but kept the smile on her face. "I want to get past forever with you."

"Past forever?"

"It's like there's now, then there's forever, then there's the other side of forever. I want to get to the other side of forever with you. Wait." Kenzie snapped her fingers. "That's it. Let me write that down. That's good."

"Way to ruin the moment." Rachel playfully nudged her shoulder while Kenzie frantically looked for her phone or anything to jot a note down with.

"No, don't you see?" Kenzie paused and put her free hand on Rachel's chest. "This is the moment."

Rachel grasped Kenzie's hand over her chest and squeezed it tight. "I like that explanation better."

"I really am sorry about what just happened. I promise I won't let it happen again." Kenzie tried to hold on to this moment. She didn't want it to slip away.

"I promise you have nothing to be worried about with Laurel or anyone. I only want to be with you. To get to the other side of forever, or whatever it was you just said."

Kenzie leaned in and pressed her lips softly to Rachel's, sealing her apology. She pulled back. "Okay, I really have to go jot that down. I think I'm finally ready to write that song."

CHAPTER TWENTY-SIX

Chilled air met Rachel as she turned the lights on to her office to start her Monday. The heat hadn't kicked on yet, and the November air had all weekend to cool the building. She rolled her eyes at 200 unread emails. It astonished her that she could work so hard to get her inbox to zero just to have it build back up over the weekend.

Things with Kenzie were going great. They had settled into a rhythm, spending most nights and weekends together over the past several months. Yes, Rachel was ready for things to move faster, but Kenzie had been so tied up with the studio with her pending song release, and Rachel had been so busy with all the cases Gail kept assigning her, that their relationship was moving as fast as it could.

Rachel put her headphones in, her playlist on shuffle, and attacked her inbox. She kept her door shut as she worked. While she liked the banter with her coworkers, the closed door would allow her to focus and get the week off to the right start. After several songs, an old Braxton hit came across her playlist. She had always loved Braxton, but meeting her in person and meeting the woman behind all of her songs gave them such a deeper meaning. Something seemed off. Were her headphones dying? It seemed like the song was playing in surround sound, but a beat off. She took her headphones out of her ears and looked at them. The song kept playing. Louder now than before.

Rachel opened her door. The sound echoed from down the hall. She followed it and paused at the entryway to the main conference room. Kenzie plucked away at the keys. She loved to watch and hear her play and rarely got to do it without her noticing. Kenzie hummed along but didn't fully sing, and Rachel wished she'd sing it herself. She waited a beat longer and a grin formed on Kenzie's face.

She stalked her long enough and joined her. "Hey," she said softly.

Kenzie looked up, but didn't stop playing. "Hi. I came by your office, but your door was shut."

Rachel took the spot next to Kenzie on the piano bench. "I needed to focus. I didn't know you were coming by today."

Kenzie stopped playing and put her hands in her lap. "I wasn't. It was a last-minute thing that came up."

"Oh?"

"Yes. I'm hoping it's good news."

"Is that why you were smiling just now?" Rachel nudged her with her shoulder.

"Oh. No." Kenzie shook her head.

"What?"

"C-sharp minor," Kenzie replied.

"I'm not following."

"I always have a hard time playing C-sharp minor. It's a chord. Like this." Kenzie took her right hand and played three keys on the piano. "For some reason, the C-sharp always gets me. I don't know why."

"I find it hard to believe that after all these years, there are still chords you have a hard time with."

"Right? But for whatever reason, it gets me. So, when I can hit it without thinking about it, I smile."

"Why would you write a song with chords you have a hard time playing?"

Kenzie shook her head. "Unfortunately, it doesn't work like that. It just so happens that this is a great key for Braxton, so I end up writing a lot of songs with this chord."

"Like your new one?"

"Maybe."

"Am I ever going to get to hear it?" Rachel pouted. "Or find out anything about it, for that matter?"

Their banter was interrupted by Nina announcing herself from the doorway. "Good morning, Kenzie."

Kenzie looked up. "If it isn't my favorite lawyer."

"Are you ready?" Nina asked as she took a seat at the conference table.

"Yes." Kenzie shook her head. "Can I come by your office after this?"

"Of course." Rachel squeezed her thigh as she left. She wanted to lean in and kiss her but didn't think it was appropriate with Nina right there. Even though she had just seen Kenzie a few hours earlier, she yearned to be close to her.

Rachel thought through all the possible reasons for a last-minute meeting. Kenzie had been working hard at her studio all summer and had taken on many new clients. It had to be something along those lines. Not that it really mattered. Kenzie was successful and seemed to make a good living, Rachel just couldn't help but be nosy about how it all worked.

Twenty minutes later, there was a soft knock at her office door. Rachel looked up and motioned Kenzie in.

"Are you coming over tonight?" Kenzie took a seat across the desk.

"Yes?" Rachel furrowed her brow. She had been coming over after work for basically the last month. Why would tonight be any different? "Should I not?"

"No." Kenzie shook her head. "I want you to come over tonight. I was just making sure is all."

"What's going on?"

"We really need to figure this living situation out." Kenzie looked out the window. "Move in with me."

"No."

"What do you mean, no? I thought we were heading that direction."

"We are. But, babe, the next place I move is going to be a family place. You know, a house with a real kitchen and rooms with walls. Maybe even a yard for the kids to play in. Not a loft above a music store."

"My commute is really short."

"Except for the weeks when your commute is to Nashville."

"Fair point."

"Can we get back to why you're here, please? Or is it to talk about our living situation?"

"Oh, right." Kenzie shook her head like she was finding her thoughts. "The song premieres tonight."

"What?"

"Nina just got the call this morning. There was a scheduling issue, so we got bumped up. It's going live on one of those entertainment shows tonight. Seven p.m."

"That's great!" Rachel still hadn't heard the song Kenzie had been working so hard on. Kenzie had wanted to keep it a surprise.

"So, I needed to make sure you're coming over tonight so you can finally hear it."

"Of course. I wouldn't miss it. But there *is* something we need to talk about?"

"What's that?" Kenzie asked.

"I thought I was your favorite lawyer?"

"Technically, you're not my lawyer," Kenzie pointed out. "You recused yourself. Remember?"

"No. But I am a lawyer. And I certainly hope I'm your favorite."

"It's pointless to argue with you."

"It is." Rachel gave a satisfied nod. "I'll see you tonight."

❖

Rachel couldn't focus the rest of the day. She knew that the movie premiere would be soon, which meant the song would be released soon, she just hadn't expected it to be today. Finally being able to hear what Kenzie had been working on all summer seemed surreal. She had a brief moment of panic thinking how she would react if she didn't like the song, but she pushed that to the back of her mind. She had listened to almost everything Kenzie had written and could honestly say she liked it all.

When Rachel got to Kenzie's apartment after work, she was greeted by her pacing back and forth. "You okay?"

Kenzie clapped her hands together. "I don't know why I'm so nervous."

"Because this is a big premiere and you've never been a part of a movie before. This is a big deal."

Kenzie resumed her pacing. "No. That's not it."

Rachel set her bag behind the couch. "Then what is it?"

Kenzie paused. She looked Rachel in the eyes. "I think I'm nervous for you to hear it."

"Really?"

"I've never felt like this before. Ever."

Rachel grabbed both her hands and squeezed. "I'm sure I'll love it."

"I think I've been pushing this off because there's only one person I care about liking this song, and that's you." She looked into Rachel's eyes. "Now the moment is here, and I just…"

Rachel put her hands on Kenzie's face and pulled her in close. She kissed her lips as a means of settling her nerves. She pulled back and kept her hands firmly on Kenzie's cheeks. "The song will be great. You will be great. The movie will be wildly successful. It's all going to work out."

"Thank you."

Seven p.m. finally rolled around, and they sat next to each other on the couch, eyes glued to the TV. They had to sit through a few segments about celebrities in the news and other gossip until the C-list host announced that after the break would be the world premiere of "The Other Side of Forever." Rachel squeezed her hand on Kenzie's thigh to steady it from bouncing up and down. "Does this song have one of those C-whatevers?" She tried to keep her tone light.

"You mean C-sharp minor?" Kenzie asked.

"Yes."

"Actually, it does."

"I don't understand why you would put something in that you don't like playing."

"It isn't always up to me." Kenzie shrugged. "Besides, I'll probably never perform it, and I can have as many takes as I want in the studio. There have been many tracks we've had to piece together."

"It amazes me that there is this whole world that you live in that I know nothing about."

The show came back from commercial break and cut to the music video. Soft piano played in the background as it panned to Braxton standing on a beach. "Are you playing piano in this?" Rachel asked.

Kenzie nodded. "Piano is all me. But no vocals. That's all Braxton and studio musicians."

"That's too bad." Rachel turned to look at Kenzie.

Kenzie playfully touched her cheek and pushed her face back to the TV. "Watch."

Rachel could feel her heart beating in her chest. The anticipation of the moment caught up to her. She tried to listen closely to the lyrics, but it was hard to catch them all. It often took her four to five listens to any song before she could pick out all the words. The video imposed scenes of Braxton against scenes of the main characters in the movie. It was expertly done, and Rachel could tell from the first minute that it was going to be a hit. The song was slow, yet upbeat, and she knew it would be a chart topper.

The song ended, and Kenzie stayed silent. Rachel turned to her. "I love it."

"Yeah?" Kenzie was hesitant.

"Yes." She nodded.

"You're not just saying that?"

"I'm not." Rachel shook her head. "I love it and I can't wait to hear it a hundred times on the radio."

"I know I wrote it for the movie, but I wrote it for you."

Rachel leaned in and kissed her again. She broke the kiss. "Don't think I didn't hear the lyrics about waves crashing on the sand. I thought you weren't going to write about that."

"Yeah, well…" Kenzie's phone rang, and she reached for it.

"Saved by the bell," Rachel said.

Kenzie answered the phone to screaming on the other side. "Hang on, let me put you on speaker." Kenzie clicked the button, and Rachel could make out the "Oh my Gods" coming from the other end. "Braxton, I have you on speaker with Rachel."

"Oh my God, Rachel. Hi! Did you hear it? What did you think? It looked so good." Braxton was speaking fast in a pitch higher than Rachel was used to hearing.

"It was great. I loved it," Rachel answered.

"Oh my God, I know. The video was so good. And, Kenzie, you nailed it. I knew it was going to be good when we recorded it. But that was…that was…I can't explain it."

"It was great, Braxton," Kenzie said.

"Okay, well, I'll let you get back to having sex or whatever you were about to do to celebrate. But I just had to call someone. That was amazing."

"I'll talk to you tomorrow." Kenzie shook her head at the phone as she hit the red button. "She always gets excited when songs are released."

Rachel reached for Kenzie's hand. "Come on. I think we were about to have sex."

"I think you're right."

❖

The next morning, Rachel woke, showered, and got ready before Kenzie had even stirred. It was still weird to her that Kenzie didn't have a set start time to her day. She poured two cups of coffee, adding an ungodly amount of sugar to Kenzie's, and took them back to bed. She sat at the end of the bed and Kenzie kept the covers over her naked body.

She squinted her eyes awake. "Good morning," she said through a yawn.

"Morning." Rachel handed her the mug of coffee.

Kenzie took the mug in both hands and took a sip. "You bringing me coffee in bed might be one of the best things about dating you."

"Oh, really?" Rachel raised an eyebrow. "I can think of some pretty good things you were saying last night."

"I didn't say the best," Kenzie said. "Just one of the best."

"So, I talked to my parents, and they were thinking we would eat around two on Thursday. I hope that works."

"Thursday? What's Thursday?"

"Thanksgiving," Rachel said, confused. How did Kenzie not know a major holiday was coming up?

"Shit. That's this Thursday?"

"Yes."

"I'm sorry. I can't. I have to work."

"You have to work?" Rachel wasn't following. Kenzie didn't have a set schedule. How would she have to work on a holiday?

"I swear I told you. With the movie premiere. That was part of what Nina was going over with me yesterday."

"I think I would have remembered you telling me you have to work on Thanksgiving."

"They want us to go to New York for the parade."

"You're going to be in the parade?"

"Maybe."

"You're missing Thanksgiving to maybe be in a parade?"

"Braxton is singing for sure. They are still working out the logistics. I don't think she's on a float. It's likely she'll just be at the main stage, and there's a good chance I'll get to accompany her. This is a huge shot for me."

"It is." Rachel couldn't help the disappointment. Yes, it could be Kenzie's big break, but going all that way for just a chance still stung.

"I'm sorry. You're upset."

"No. It's okay." Rachel tried to shake it off. "I shouldn't have assumed. I just thought it would be a great chance for you to finally meet my parents."

Kenzie reached a hand out and placed it on Rachel's arm. "And I want to meet them. I do. I just can't this week."

"I understand." Rachel looked at her smartwatch. "I have to get going."

"No. Wait." Kenzie reached for her phone.

"I'm going to be late for work."

"This won't take long. What's the plan for Christmas?"

"What are you talking about?"

"We have established that you are a part of a family that does things, and I know nothing about family things, so let's get everything in the calendar now. I'm not going to miss another important holiday with you."

The gesture warmed Rachel's heart. It would suck not having Kenzie at Thanksgiving, but at least it was a scheduling issue and not because she didn't want to be there. "I don't know the plan exactly, but can you at least block out Christmas Eve and Christmas Day so that we can spend them together?"

Kenzie swiped at her phone. "Done. Those days are all yours. Whatever holiday traditions you have up your sleeve, I'm in."

Rachel leaned in and kissed her. Kenzie set her coffee and phone down and pulled Rachel into bed. She grasped at her shoulders and deepened their kiss.

"If you start that now, I'm going to be late for work."

"Yes, and?" Kenzie playfully bit her bottom lip.

Rachel pushed herself back. "And today is not a day I can afford to be late. Now I really have to get going. When do you leave for New York?"

"Tomorrow morning."

"Then tonight, we are going to pick up where this left off."

CHAPTER TWENTY-SEVEN

Thanksgiving in New York City could only be described as cold. Kenzie blew on her fingers to keep the blood circulating. She danced back and forth, as her toes were barely surviving their third hour of standing in Times Square.

"Can you believe it, Kenz!" Braxton found warmth and energy Kenzie never would. "This is so amazing."

"I've always watched the parade on TV, but I never knew this many people actually showed up for it."

"And it's almost our turn."

"Alright, ladies." Cooper put an arm around Braxton and Kenzie, and she appreciated his warmth. "Braxton, you're up after the next commercial break. That float is going to come pause on that big 'X,' and you'll take the song from the chorus. Got it?"

"Got it!" Braxton bounced to her place.

"What about me, Cooper?"

"Look, Kenz." He looked at his feet. Kenzie's stomach soured. No good news ever came after that. "The window is too tight. They're going with the studio musician. If we just had a little longer, we could get you in there, but the parade is running behind."

"Got it." She kept her head held high. There was no sense in fighting with him. Nothing could be done about it now.

"But later tonight, I want you to come out to dinner with me and some of the Global execs. It will be great for them to put a face to the name of the gal that's about to make them boatloads of money."

"Sure, Cooper. Just text me the details." Kenzie left for the hotel. There was no point freezing any longer. Braxton had the adoration of every other fan in New York and wouldn't even notice that Kenzie had left.

Public transportation was out of the question between the crowds and the road closures. Thankfully, the hotel wasn't far. Kenzie fought her way upstream against the mobs of people and made it to the hotel. A few minutes inside and her fingers were in full working condition again.

Her phone vibrated in her back pocket. Rachel. As much as she didn't want to talk to anyone right now, the last thing she could do was decline Rachel's call. "Hi." She flopped onto the hotel bed.

"Hi. How's New York?"

"Cold."

Rachel laughed on the other end. "I just watched Braxton sing."

Then that means she watched who wasn't performing. "How'd she sound?"

"Great. It's a really amazing song. It's even better live."

It'd be even better with the right pianist. "How's your family? I got your text at the ungodly hour this morning that the turkey was going in the oven." Kenzie needed to change the subject. She couldn't talk anymore about her performance, or lack thereof.

"You have to get up early to put the turkey in. It's tradition."

"I'll take your word for it."

"You'll see next year."

That was a nice thought. Much nicer than sitting alone in a hotel room three thousand miles away from home. "What else do you have planned for the day?" Kenzie couldn't focus as Rachel spoke about aunts and uncles and other family members joining them for lunch. Today had been too much of a disaster. She would have other chances, she knew it, but this one stung so much. She had been right there. Right on the edge of playing on national television, but couldn't get thirty extra seconds to get on screen. Frustration, exhaustion, numbness—it all caught up to her. She sniffled as she kept the tears that pricked at her eyes from falling.

"Babe? Are you listening?"

"Yeah. I'm right here. Sorry." She sniffled louder, but tried to muffle herself from the phone.

"Are you okay?"

"Yeah. Sorry."

"Are you crying? What's going on?"

She did not want to cry on the phone with Rachel. She dabbed the tears at her eyes, willing them to go away. "No. It's just allergies or something."

"Allergies. In New York. In November. You expect me to believe that?"

"I think there's mold in my hotel room or something." Kenzie wiped the tear from her eye.

"Mold at the Ritz-Carlton?"

"You know how these old hotels are. Basically impossible to keep clean."

"Why don't we switch to video and you can show me this mold?"

"It's too disgusting. It will ruin your appetite, and you didn't get up at an ungodly hour to make a turkey you can't eat." The request for a video call came anyway. Kenzie could fight it. She could hang up and hide from Rachel altogether, but as nice as hiding under a rock sounded, she didn't want to keep herself away. Her red eyes filled the screen, and she quickly minimized herself.

Rachel's face shown with concern. "Babe, what's wrong?"

"Today sucks." Kenzie could barely get the words out before more tears streaked down her face. With her free hand she covered her eyes and let the tears fall.

"It's okay, sweetheart. Talk to me. What's going on?"

Words wouldn't come. She kept picturing the long nights, the dive bars, the grueling recording sessions. What was the point? What was all of her hard work leading toward? She swallowed the lump in her throat as she composed herself. Rachel's concerned face still covered her phone screen after several minutes.

"Where are you?" Kenzie asked.

"I moved to my bedroom. More privacy."

"Where are you sitting?"

"On the floor. When we have a bad day, we sit on the floor and we talk about it."

Kenzie slid to the floor and slammed her head back against the mattress.

"Now, talk to me."

"I came all this way and it wasn't even worth it. I knew it was a gamble, but I had a good feeling that I would finally get a chance to show the studio execs what I can do. Instead I froze my ass off for hours, didn't get to play, and you're upset with me for not being there for Thanksgiving."

"I'm not upset with you."

"You don't have to lie."

"I don't know that upset is the right word, but yes, I would have rather you been here with me than so far away on Thanksgiving. Especially for something that wasn't a sure thing."

"I should have just stayed home."

"Was that an option?"

Kenzie wiped at her face. "It's always an option. I'm just so close. Part of me wants to give it up and just resign myself to the fact that I'll only ever be a studio musician."

"What would that mean?"

"It would mean writing songs for other people and living a life in the background."

"And what would be so bad about that?"

"If I give up now, then what has been the point of all of this? The long nights. The crappy shows. I could have stayed at home and written songs all along. I'm so close to breaking through, I can taste it. I just need my shot. I really really thought today was going to be the day." Kenzie kept that darn lump in her throat down. She did not need another breakdown on the phone.

"I'm sorry that it wasn't."

"And I wish my dad was here." Kenzie hadn't been much for holidays ever since her dad died. Her mom had left almost instantly, and Kenzie spent every holiday alone for the last fourteen years. She could usually block the world out and forget it was Thanksgiving, but being in the thick of the largest parade in the country made that impossible.

The cartoon turkeys brought back distant memories of her father. Kenzie pictured him in the kitchen, new electric knife in hand, ready to make a mess of the family turkey. Every year, he purchased the latest and greatest knife in an attempt to carve the perfect bird, and every year it was an epic disaster.

"My dad would have absolutely loved this cold-ass parade."

"Oh yeah?"

"At one point one of the wranglers lost one of Snoopy's ropes and he almost got away. My dad would have found that hilarious."

Rachel laughed on her own end of the phone. "I can imagine that was a sight to see."

"Thank you for sitting on the floor with me."

"It is what we do when we have a bad day."

"It is. I'm sure your family is going to start wondering where you are, though. You should get back to them."

"Are you sure you're going to be okay?"

"Yeah. Cooper wants me to go meet him and some bigwigs for dinner. I'll get my act together by then."

"Do you know when you'll be home yet?"

Kenzie could hear the hesitation in Rachel's voice. She was trying her best to be understanding, but the fact that Kenzie left home with a one-way ticket more often than not made it difficult for a planner like Rachel. "I'm hoping tomorrow. I'll let you know as soon as I do. It'll be too late to text when I get back tonight, but I'll call you in the morning."

"It won't be too late to text, or call. Just call me tonight once you get back."

Kenzie was still getting used to having someone to text or call her whereabouts. Not that she hadn't dated before, it had just been a long time since it had gotten to this stage. "Okay. I'll call you when I get back. Now go enjoy family time and wish me luck."

"Good luck. Your song is amazing, and you will do great."

The song was pretty amazing. Now if she could just convince the studio the same could be said about her.

CHAPTER TWENTY-EIGHT

Rachel waited at Ashley's kitchen island as Ashley put the finishing touches on the casserole before placing it in the oven. "Are you nervous for her to meet Mom and Dad?" Ashley asked.

"A little." Rachel drummed her fingers on the countertop. It was Ashley's turn to host family dinner, and schedules had finally aligned so that Kenzie could join.

"Just a little?"

"Maybe more than a little." Kenzie had been recording in California all week with Cooper. The session went long into the weekend, but Kenzie had assured her she would be home in time for Sunday dinner. She should be pulling in any minute. Rachel checked her phone again for any form of communication. With Kenzie in the booth all day and then on the airplane, she knew a text was a long shot, but couldn't help herself from checking anyway.

"Kenzie is great. They are going to love her."

"She is great. She's just so different than my last girlfriends."

"And that's what makes her great!"

"Come on now."

"I'm serious. She's fun, she's cute, and you actually have started to let loose since being around her. It's nice to see."

Rachel had started to relax slightly since Kenzie came into her life. Life with Kenzie was spontaneous and unpredictable. Not everything had to be so regimented and planned out. Rachel was learning that this was okay. "She's just not as traditional as Dad is used to, and I hope he doesn't come down too hard on her."

"Traditional?"

"You know? She doesn't have a nine-to-five job and probably won't talk about the stock exchange with him."

"Oh my God, listening to him and Laurel talk about international bond indexes is two hours of my life I will never get back."

Rachel had never dated anyone her parents hadn't approved of. Her dad absolutely adored Laurel. He took it harder than she did when they broke up. Rachel didn't need to worry. Kenzie was charismatic and likable, and she had yet to meet a single person who she couldn't charm. Rachel's phone vibrated on the countertop. Ashley grabbed it.

"Hey! Don't do that." Rachel reached for her phone and Ashley held it just out of arm's reach.

"Ooh, it's your girlfriend." Ashley waved the phone back and forth.

"Would you stop that and give it back?" Rachel jumped off her stool and swatted at her sister.

"Hey now! Don't let the kids see you hitting. I've been trying to teach them that we don't use violence." Ashley pushed Rachel away.

"Then don't let them see you stealing my phone." God, would sisters ever stop doing childish things?

Ashley answered the phone and put it on speaker. "Hey, Kenzie!" She dragged out her name.

"Hi? Why does it sound like something weird happened to your voice?"

"Because my sister is weird!" Rachel tried to snatch the phone, but Ashley turned and ran to the other side of the counter.

"Ah. Okay. I have interrupted some weird sister thing. Got it."

"Are you almost here? I need backup." Rachel yelled.

"About that."

Ashley stopped her playing and set the phone on the countertop. "I'm still in San Francisco."

"You're what?" Rachel ran to the other side of the counter and stared at Kenzie's picture on her screen.

"Cooper had us recording all day, and we couldn't get anything right. No phones were allowed in the booth, and I had no way of telling you. I'm so sorry, but we literally just finished. I called you as soon as I could."

"Oh." Rachel's stomach dropped. Kenzie wasn't coming. Kenzie wouldn't be meeting her parents at Sunday dinner tonight. Just like Kenzie hadn't been able to meet her parents at any of the other Sunday dinners. Something always came up. Ashley put a comforting hand on her back.

"But I think I know how I can make it up to you." Kenzie sounded hopeful.

"Let's hear it."

"I was able to sweet-talk my way into two tickets for the premiere of *To Hell and Back*. It's in two weeks. I'm hoping you'll go with me."

"You what?" Ashley squealed.

"The movie premiere. They're giving me a ticket and a plus-one. I want it to be you."

"If she doesn't say yes, I will!" Ashley yelled.

"You said it's in two weeks?" Rachel pulled up the calendar app on her phone.

"Don't even make some lame excuse like work or soccer," Ashley said. "You can get the day off, and the kids will have hundreds of other games. She's going."

"Yeah?" Kenzie asked.

"She's going," Ashley said louder.

"I'd kind of like to hear it from her, since I'm trying to make up for not being there tonight and all."

"I'd love to go." She felt like Cinderella getting an invitation to the ball.

"Great. I've already got the stylist booked, and the studio is going to put us up in an amazing hotel. The weekend is going to blow your mind."

"Stylist?"

"You know? So we can look great in all the pictures."

This was certainly going to be a weekend to remember. The lights, the movie stars, the red carpet, it all sounded like a magical fantasy.

"I really am sorry about tonight."

"I'm still not sure we're fully square," Ashley said.

"Oh?" Rachel asked.

"Mom and Dad still aren't convinced Kenzie exists," Ashley said.

"Seriously?" Kenzie said.

"To be fair, they haven't met you, and we've been together for months."

"I think you should make her go to the party," Ashley said.

"That's too mean. I couldn't do that to her. She's already agreed to be there for Christmas."

"Yes, I have! It's in my calendar and everything."

"She said she needs to make it up it you. Fancy movie tickets are a start, but if she really wants to prove it, she should go to the party."

"Why are you making a party sound like a punishment?" Kenzie asked.

"Because it is," they answered in unison.

"Will one of you please explain why I'm being punished with a party?"

"Every year our parents host a Christmas party on the twenty-third. It's their annual tradition. We go out for the party, then stay the night Christmas Eve and come home on Christmas Day," Rachel explained.

"I'm still not following," Kenzie said.

"It is the lamest, most boring party you will ever go to. I honestly don't know why they do it still. I think they think it will get less lame, and yet somehow it gets worse," Ashley said.

"So if I go to the lame party and meet your parents, you'll forgive me for not being able to make it tonight?"

"We'll have to stay in separate rooms," Rachel said.

"What?

"They aren't against the gay thing, you just aren't married. So you have to sleep in separate beds," Ashley explained.

"They do know we sleep in the same bed most nights?"

Rachel shook her head. "I don't think they do."

"Seriously?"

"I don't think they think Patrick and I have sex, and we have two kids."

"But there will be drinks?"

"Yes." Rachel nodded. "That's a necessity."

"I would love to go," Kenzie said.

"Great. Then we just have one more issue to solve," Ashley said.

Rachel didn't realize this was going to turn into a group conversation with her girlfriend.

"Okay?" Kenzie hadn't realized it either.

"How are you going to make this up to me?"

Rachel laughed. "Seriously?"

"You aren't the only victim here. Now I have to deal with a moping sister and hosting family dinner."

"Ashley, I'll tell you what, next time Braxton is in town, I can get two tickets with your name on them."

"Yup. That will work. Consider ourselves even."

"Damn, you can be bought easily," Rachel said.

"Rach, I hate to do this, but I have to go. They are loading up and I need to get in the van to catch the plane."

"You'll call me when you get home?"

"I will." Kenzie ended the call.

"So you get a fancy movie premiere, I get Braxton tickets, and we both get someone new to talk to at Mom and Dad's Christmas party. Maybe Kenzie should miss out on things more often." Ashley went to check dinner in the oven. Their parents would be arriving at any moment. How could Kenzie miss out on things *more* often? She was already pulled away so often trying to catch her big break. Not that Rachel didn't understand, but when would it end? When would she just be able to have a normal family dinner with her girlfriend at her side?

CHAPTER TWENTY-NINE

The door to the hotel suite opened and a short, curly-haired man wearing rose-colored sunglasses and what Rachel thought was a dark purple poncho entered. Or was it a cape? Whatever it was, he looked like a wizard. He was significantly shorter than Kenzie, even with the platform shoes he had on.

"McKenzie." He opened his arms and brought Kenzie into a hug. "My dear, it is so good to see you."

Rachel was not expecting the strong French accent, but it all made sense once he spoke.

"Charles." Kenzie returned the hug. "Thank you for making time for us. I know you are busy styling all the major celebrities, and I really appreciate this."

"Oh, of course." He surveyed the room. A parade of girls carrying garment bags and makeup containers followed right behind him.

"Charles, this is Rachel." Kenzie motioned to her.

Charles pushed the sunglasses down on his nose and studied Rachel. He pushed the glasses back on his face. "At last." He clapped his hands together. "You have brought me something I can work with."

Rachel furrowed her brow. "Thank you?"

He asked her to spin around. Rachel did.

"Ah, these cheekbones are magnificent." He slid his hand up one of Rachel's cheeks and she blushed. "And this hair." He picked up a long strand and examined. "This color is exquisite. What is it?"

"Brown?"

Charles let out a long laugh. "Oh, and she's funny." She turned to Kenzie, and they shared a look. "But really, dear, who does it?"

"It's natural," Rachel said.

"Oh, my God. Just when I thought I couldn't love you more." He clapped his hands together. "Okay, here is my vision." He held his hands out in front of him as if uncovering a masterpiece. "McKenzie, you will be the brilliant rock star. Long flowing hair"— he pretended to throw a long strand over his shoulder—"exquisite dress, flowing, wonderful. And you, Rachel..." His accent made her name sound like "Rochelle," and for whatever reason, Rachel loved it. "You will be her, how you say? Arm candy."

Kenzie waved her arms back and forth. "No. We are not doing that. We are going to be two women attending a movie, and you need to make sure we look nice."

Charles slouched and pretended to pout.

"Actually," Rachel cut in, and Charles raised his head expectantly, "I wouldn't mind being your arm candy."

Charles clapped his hands together. "I knew I liked her."

"Are you serious?" Kenzie tilted her head to one side.

"It sounds fun," Rachel admitted. She liked the idea of just being the pretty woman next to Kenzie.

"Okay." Kenzie sighed. "You heard her. That's what we're doing."

Charles wrapped his arm around Rachel's waist and took her into the bedroom. "You are going to love the options I brought for you."

Rachel didn't know that getting ready for a red carpet event would be so exhausting. After trying on a dozen dresses, they had settled on a dark maroon one. It ran down her body with a tasteful slit up her right side to show off just the right amount of leg. The strapless top showed off her "goddess-like arms," as Charles had called them.

He told her to take in her last big breath of the night and practically sewed her in place. The maroon dress brought out her olive-toned skin. Her hair was down with a slight wave to it. She wore more makeup than she would have normally, but not too much. She looked like an airbrushed version of herself.

"Okay, Rachel." Charles clapped from the main room. "Let's see."

Charles's vision came to life. Kenzie looked like a rock star. Multicolored flowers covered her long white dress. Daisies maybe? It had long sleeves and fringe under her arms with maroon stitching outlining the patterns. They complemented each other perfectly. Kenzie's hair was down and in large barrel curls, and Rachel knew it would drive her crazy all night, but it looked great.

"You look amazing," Kenzie said before Rachel could get all the way in the room.

"You're not so bad yourself," Rachel replied.

Charles reached his hand out for Rachel. "Spin."

She made a dramatic twirl and Charles applauded her. "Okay," he said. "Let's practice getting your picture taken. Hand me your phone." He looked at Kenzie, and she handed hers over.

"Practice?" Rachel had pictures taken her whole life. What was to practice?

"Trust me." Kenzie stepped close and put a hand around her waist. "Well, hello," Kenzie said to Rachel's chest, which was noticeably more endowed than normal. "What's going on here?" she said.

"Just trying to play the part."

Kenzie reached for Rachel's arm. "Okay, I'll put my hand here and you put yours like this." Kenzie's arm rested at her lower back. "Then you turn into me slightly." Rachel turned like she was posing for a prom photo. "Now, the trick is, don't smile."

"What do you mean, don't smile?"

"There are going to be cameras all over the place, so if you smile like you're posing, you'll get a lot of bad angles. So, stand here, close to me, and every so often, look like you've just seen a friend you haven't seen in ages. Like this."

Kenzie feigned surprise and then softened her face.

"But not like your best friend," Kenzie clarified. "Someone you haven't seen, and you are like, oh hi, we should catch up."

Rachel held Kenzie, and did her best to pose, but not too much while Charles took pictures from all angles. "Where did you learn all this?"

"Braxton," Kenzie admitted. "She found pictures after my first award show and told me that if I was going to work with her, I needed to look better on camera." Kenzie rolled her eyes.

"Okay. We got it," he finally said. He brought the phone over and showed them the best one. "You two are..." He made a chef's kiss with his hand.

"That looks really good." She looked like a movie star. "Let me send that to my mom."

There was no red carpet at the theater, and Rachel was relieved and dissatisfied at the same time. While it would have been fun, she would have been a nervous wreck, unsure of where to look and what to do with her hands.

The crowd gathered in the large area outside the theater before the doors opened. Rachel couldn't believe she walked among A-list celebrities. She kept waiting for security to ask her to leave. "Oh, my God. That's—" She slapped Kenzie's shoulder and pointed, unable to make words.

Kenzie followed her arm, and then quickly pushed it to her side. "Yes, that's Marissa Tomlinson. She's in the movie. Please don't point."

Rachel shook her head to snap out of it. "You're right. Sorry. Oh my God, that's—" Her mouth fell open as Bronson Spencer, her teenage heartthrob, walked mere inches in front of her. She had seen everything he had been in and went so far as to hang his poster on her wall after he starred in a series of teen romance movies.

Kenzie leaned into Rachel's ear. "Sweetheart, I'm glad you're having a good time, but I need you to act like these are just people."

"Okay. Okay. I'm good." She smoothed her dress, hoping that would smooth her excitement as well.

"Oh My God, Kenzie!" Braxton skipped up to them and enveloped them both in a hug. "Rachel! Hi!" She pulled back and eyed them both. "You look so good."

"So do you," Kenzie said reflexively.

Braxton put a hand over her chest. "Oh, thank you for saying that. It means so much. Can you believe we're here?"

"I really can't," Kenzie replied.

A gong sounded, signaling that the doors were open, and

people filed inside. Rachel noticed the theater wasn't as full as she expected. "Why are there so many open seats?" she whispered in Kenzie's ear during the opening credits.

"Most of the big names don't stick around," Kenzie whispered back. "Don't like seeing themselves on the big screen or something."

Rachel had always assumed that actors stayed for the actual movie, but she supposed once the pictures made it online, it was just as well for people to go home. With Kenzie looking as good as she did next to her, she wrestled with whether she wanted to watch the movie or head home herself.

CHAPTER THIRTY

Kenzie pulled Rachel in close to keep her warm as they waited for the car. God, she fit so perfectly. She loved the way they molded to each other. She nestled her head into Rachel's neck. "I had no idea that's what the movie was about."

"Seriously?" Rachel clung to Kenzie.

"Seriously. I knew it was a war movie. But that's it. It was really good."

"How can you write a song that fits so well and have no idea what the movie is about?"

"That's easy. I didn't write it for the movie."

"You literally had a contract to write a song for the movie."

"Yes." Kenzie squeezed her tighter. "But I wrote it for you. I would have written that song, contract or not. It just so happens I had a deadline this time."

The car pulled up and Kenzie opened the door for Rachel, not wanting to wait any longer to get Rachel inside and warm.

Kenzie slid in next to Rachel, resting her hand on her thigh. "Tonight did not suck," Kenzie said and let her head fall back against the seat.

Rachel took Kenzie's hand on her thigh. "No, it did not."

Kenzie rolled her head to face her. "This is the part of my job I hate. The awards and openings and milling about with famous people and studio executives. But tonight, with you, it was almost fun."

"Only almost?" Rachel played with her fingers on top of Kenzie's hand.

"Mm-hmm." Kenzie nodded.

Rachel moved her hand to Kenzie's thigh and slid it down, resting on her knee.

Kenzie's arousal that had been growing all night quickly turned into a flame. Rachel looked to die for in that dress. The fabric hugged her form, leaving little to the imagination. Not that Kenzie had to imagine—she was going to get to see the real thing soon enough. It was endearing how excited she was to be at the movie opening. Even though Kenzie had to continually remind her to stop staring, pointing, or gawking, she secretly loved how into it she was. She imagined that's what it would feel like to be a parent on Christmas morning. Watching your kids wide-eyed as they opened all the presents they'd been dreaming of.

Rachel leaned in, her lips inches from Kenzie's. "How about we make it all the way fun?"

Kenzie moved her head forward to meet Rachel's lips when she pulled back suddenly, frantically searching for something. "What?" Kenzie asked, concerned.

"I can hear my phone buzzing." Rachel fished around the back seat, trying to find the source. She found the clutch at her feet and unzipped it. "It's my mom."

"Answer it." Kenzie resigned herself to the fact that the moment was gone. But she knew there would be more soon.

"Hi, Mom…Yes, we just finished…Oh, you saw the pictures?"

Kenzie half listened as Rachel painstakingly rattled off every famous person they had seen, what they were wearing, who their date was, if so-and-so were still together and if they still looked in love. Kenzie couldn't keep track, nor would she try. She rested her head against the seat, taking Rachel in. She loved the animated way she talked with her mom. The way her eyes lit up telling the stories. The gentle smile she gave when she caught her staring. That burning inside her grew just watching Rachel talk on the phone.

The car came to a stop. "Okay, Mom. We're at the hotel and I have to go…Yes, I'll tell her hi…Yes, we will be there in two weeks…Yes, Mom, she is real. You literally just saw pictures of her. I love you too…We will." Rachel hung up and put the phone back in her clutch.

The driver opened the door, and Kenzie stepped out onto the

well-lit hotel driveway. She reached her hand out, and Rachel took it, careful not to catch her heel on anything. "Do you want a drink or anything?" Kenzie pointed to the hotel bar.

"No." Rachel shook her head. She leaned into Kenzie's ear. "I want to get upstairs and have you get this dress off me."

The burn inside overtook Kenzie, and she walked faster toward the elevator. She cursed the fact that they were on the thirtieth floor and the elevator seemed to stop every two levels. The number of illuminated buttons was entirely too large, and she willed the elevator to move faster.

The hotel room door clicked shut, and Kenzie led Rachel by the hand to the bed. She was wasting no time. She grabbed her by the hips and pulled her into her. Their kiss was passionate and held an urgency to it. This wasn't a slow, subtle kiss. Kenzie needed to feel Rachel's naked body next to hers. She needed to run her hands on each curve and every fold, feeling the body she had come to learn so well. She turned Rachel around, and Rachel rested her arms on the bed, her back slightly arched.

"Holy shit."

Rachel turned her head over her shoulder. "What?"

"You are so sexy." Kenzie put her hands on Rachel's hips and ran them up the length of her dress. She rested her hands on Rachel's bare shoulders. She kissed her cheek and then down her neck.

"The dress." Rachel sighed.

Kenzie bit her earlobe. "What about it?"

Rachel threw her head back. "Take it off. Please."

Kenzie paused her kissing. She grasped Rachel's back, looking for a zipper or clasp. A button. Anything. After running her hands up and down a few times, Rachel's back arched underneath her.

"Stop teasing and take it off," Rachel let out.

"I'm not," Kenzie said.

"Mm-hmm." Rachel's breathing turned shallow.

"Was there a clasp or anything? Maybe on the side?"

Rachel turned her head over her shoulder. "I don't think so. He definitely did something on the back."

"Don't move. I need to turn the light on." Kenzie backed away and flipped the switch. She got closer to the back of the dress, admiring Charles's handiwork. "He sewed you in. I'll be right back."

Kenzie returned several moments later from the bathroom with a nail file. "This is the best I could find."

"Are you serious?" Rachel said, eyes wide. "Won't that ruin it?"

"I'm sure Charles has someone who can fix it." Kenzie brushed her off. "Now, stay still. I don't want to slip." She found the fabric at the top of the garment where a zipper should have ended, took the nail file to the start of a maroon thread, and sawed back and forth, trying to do as little damage as possible. Finally, a thread broke free, and she pulled it, unraveling the back of the dress to reveal Rachel's smooth skin waiting for her. She moved faster, ripping the seam like she was frantically opening a present.

"Easy now. We don't want to tear it," Rachel said.

"That is the least of our concerns right now." Kenzie opened the back of Rachel's dress completely. She touched her bare hips and ran her hands up her sides. She slipped her hands onto her breasts, cupping one in each hand.

Rachel moaned and peeled the front of the dress off her. She slid it the rest of the way down and stepped out of it, then turned around, sitting on the end of the bed, Kenzie standing above her. She grasped Kenzie's head with both her hands and pulled her in for a kiss. "Your turn," she said as she turned Kenzie around. She reached for the zipper and pulled it down. "Why were you not sewn in, like me?"

"Easy," Kenzie said. She slipped the sleeves off her arms and stepped out of the dress. She turned around and faced Rachel. "I wasn't the arm candy." She put a hand on each of Rachel's shoulders and pushed her onto the bed. She climbed on top of her, unclasping her own bra, then sliding her panties off as she did. There was no waiting any longer. Once she was fully undressed, she slid her thumbs under Rachel's thong and pulled it off. She reached for her bra and Rachel moved, giving her access. She unclasped it on the first try, pleased with herself for being so smooth.

Rachel lay back down and Kenzie nudged her thighs open wider. She pushed against her legs and buried her face in her. She licked her, making lazy circles around her clit. Rachel bucked at the touch. "You even taste sweet," Kenzie said as she continued to lavish attention on Rachel. She took her in her mouth and sucked hard. Rachel ground her hips and Kenzie grabbed her thighs, holding her in place, not letting her move.

"Wait," Rachel panted.

Kenzie knew she was close and continued sucking.

"Wait, I'm going to come," Rachel panted. She pushed Kenzie's head off her and pulled her up. "Not yet," she said and planted her lips on Kenzie's. "I'm not ready yet." She put her knees up for Kenzie to lean back against.

"Okay." Kenzie sighed.

Rachel ran her hands up Kenzie's thighs and pushed them open. Kenzie's legs stretched uncomfortably wide. Her knees dug into the sheets of the bed. Rachel ran a finger over her wetness, and Kenzie thought she might come just from that touch. The whole night, the way she looked, the way she stayed right by her side, all of those moments were leading up to this. Rachel stopped the teasing and drove two fingers inside. Kenzie put her hands on her knees and leaned forward, driving herself on Rachel's hand.

"God, you're so wet," Rachel said. She picked up her pace, moving in and out to match Kenzie's.

Sweat beaded on Kenzie's forehead and a small drop fell onto Rachel's chest. "Sorry," she said between breaths.

"Don't be." Rachel's voice turned low, a husky tone reserved for moments like this. She continued pushing herself inside, not breaking her rhythm.

"Right there." Kenzie clamped her eyes shut. She focused on nothing else. Only the beautiful woman underneath her, inside her, pushing her to the edge. She let go and allowed herself to fall over the cliff, moaning as she came and collapsing on top of Rachel.

With her free hand, Rachel stroked Kenzie's back. Kenzie had never been much for cuddling until Rachel. There was something about sex with her. It was so much more than physical. She found herself wanting to be held by her, comforted by her. There was a closeness that she longed for and craved.

Rachel exited her and squeezed her tight, holding her close for a long moment. Kenzie's breathing synced to Rachel's and she savored this afterglow. "I love you," Kenzie finally said.

Rachel stroked the top of her head. "Did you just say what I think you did?"

Kenzie didn't know she was going to say those three words tonight, but they just came out. The moment of it all caught up to her, and it seemed too perfect. "I love you. I was serious when I said I wrote that song for you. I meant every word. I love you, Rachel. I know I've written a lot of love songs, but it's never felt like this."

"I love you too."

Kenzie shifted so she faced Rachel. She needed to look her in the eyes. She needed to see her love reflected back.

"The song was amazing. You are amazing. I still can't believe any of tonight was real."

"Well it was. And after tonight, I never want to go to another award show, event, premiere, or anything without you as my arm candy."

Rachel playfully swatted her shoulder. "Just your arm candy?"

"Much more. More like the woman I love."

"I can definitely get on board with that." Rachel gipped her face with both hands and captured her in a searing kiss.

CHAPTER THIRTY-ONE

This is the lamest party I have ever been to." Kenzie's warm breath tickled as she whispered into Rachel's ear.

"I tried to warn you," she whispered back.

The Park family went all out for Christmas. A tree stood in every room, each with its own theme. Rachel loved this about her mother. She took pride in her decorating. However, no amount of decorations could make up for the party's lack of anything interesting. Rachel's neighbors had been boring people her entire life, and tonight was no exception.

Rachel finished the last sip of red wine in her glass. Kenzie's glass was down to melted ice. "Should we get another drink?"

"I don't see another option."

Rachel grabbed her hand and led her into the next room where the bar was set up. Rachel's parents had hired a catering company, just like they did each year. It was one less thing for her mother to worry about.

"Rachel, it is so good to see you." Mrs. Hildebrandt, her long-time neighbor, turned around from the bar as they approached.

"Oh, hi, Mrs. Hildebrandt." Rachel gave her a hug.

"And this must be your movie star girlfriend." Mrs. Hildebrandt gave an approving nod. She wore her gray hair pulled back halfway with a clip. Rachel thought Mrs. Hildebrandt was wearing an ugly sweater, but she thought better about commenting in case Mrs. Hildebrandt didn't think so.

"I don't know about that." Kenzie's cheeks flushed. "I'm Kenzie."

Mrs. Hildebrandt waved her off. "I've heard all about you. Your mother wouldn't stop sharing the pictures of you two at the movie premiere. You looked so wonderful."

"Thank you," Rachel said.

Mrs. Hildebrandt fanned herself with her hand. "I've never been around anyone famous before."

"I'm afraid you still haven't." Kenzie's sarcasm came across more than she probably intended.

"That's not how I'm going to tell it to the girls at bridge." Mrs. Hildebrandt grabbed her drink from the bar and took off.

Kenzie rubbed her hand over her face. "Your mom knows I'm not actually in the movie, right?"

"I'm not sure she does," Rachel said. "You are the most exciting thing this party has ever seen. It's all doctors and lawyers, you know, us boring types."

"You are far from boring." Kenzie placed a kiss on her cheek.

Rachel needed to change the subject. Kenzie's gaze raked across her, and every fiber of her being wanted to rip off her red dress. "I do think my mother likes you."

Kenzie looked Rachel in the eyes. "You think? We haven't had a whole lot of interaction."

"Well, we got here a little late and she was in hostess mode. Trust me, you'll get plenty of attention later."

"Is it good or bad that I'm nervous?"

"Why are you nervous?"

"I've actually never met a girlfriend's parents before," Kenzie admitted.

"Really? Not even Jenni's parents?"

Kenzie bounced her head back and forth. "I met her parents after we were done dating. And they hate me."

"Why would they hate you?"

"The ex-girlfriend really doesn't get to tell her side of the story, so all they know is what Jenni told them. Anyway, the point is, I'm new at this."

"So far, you're doing great." Rachel reached for her wineglass off the bar. The vaulted ceilings made the living room difficult to have conversations in, but it didn't matter because no one was talking. People milled about, but there was no interacting with one another.

Rachel's niece and nephew came barreling into the room and Mrs. Hildebrandt scolded them for running inside and almost knocking all the decorations off the baby grand piano in the corner.

"That actually gives me an idea." Kenzie broke the silence.

"What's that?"

"What are your niece's and nephew's names again?"

"River and Ash," Rachel replied and shook her head. She had never understood what her sister was thinking with those names, but she loved being an aunt nonetheless.

"Which one's which?"

"River is my niece and Ash is my nephew."

"Okay, got it." Kenzie snapped her fingers in the direction of the kids and they caught their attention. "Psst," she whisper-yelled and motioned for them to meet her.

Kenzie met the kids halfway and put her hands on her knees to bend down and talk to them. Rachel had no idea what Kenzie was up to, and it warmed her heart to watch her with them. Kenzie was a natural around the kids. Rachel had been meaning to bring the topic of their own children up, but with the movie premiere, and her own work, there didn't seem to be the right time.

Kenzie pulled out the piano bench. The wooden key cover creaked as she unveiled the ivory keys. She played a few short chords, and the attention in the room turned to her.

Kenzie turned to River and Ash, who were standing in front of the piano. "Are you ready?" Both kids nodded enthusiastically.

Kenzie counted out "two, three, four," then started playing the introduction to "Rudolph the Red-nose Reindeer." Both kids sang along loudly and acted out motions whenever possible. Their infectious voices filled the room. Rachel felt Ashley beside her, cell phone out and taking pictures. "This is a fun surprise." She nudged Rachel's arm.

"Yeah." Rachel nodded.

"You put her up to this?"

"No. I told her we'd be standing alone in the corner all night, just like every other year."

"I don't know why they keep doing this."

"Tradition," Rachel said in her best impression of their mother's voice, and they burst into laughter.

The song ended, and River jumped up and down. "Can we do Frosty next?"

"You got it." Kenzie started in on the next song, and the kids happily sang along.

The kids kept requesting songs and Kenzie kept obliging. It was impressive how many she knew from memory. She loved what a good sport she was being. River and Ash could be exhausting. The Christmas carols breathed life into the party, and the group congregated in the main room, happy to watch the kids perform.

Kenzie motioned with her head for Rachel to come over, and she did.

"You're pretty good, you know." Rachel joined Kenzie on the bench.

"Thanks," Kenzie said as she played the second verse to "Jingle Bells."

"How do you know all of these?"

"My dad." Kenzie paused as her fingers moved skillfully across the keyboard. "Every year, he would dress up like Santa and I would play songs. It was kind of his thing."

Kenzie hadn't opened up any more about her father, and Rachel was happy for anything she was willing to share. She couldn't imagine the pain she carried with her. Rachel loved watching Kenzie's hands on the keyboard. Her stomach did a small flip as she pictured what those hands might be doing later. She shook her head and composed herself.

"In fact, I hope it's something that I'll be able to do with my own kids someday."

"Oh yeah?"

"I don't have a lot of family traditions, but this is one of them."

"What else do you hope to do with your kids some day?"

Mrs. Hildebrandt approached the piano. "Alright, kids"—she shooed River and Ash away—"it's my turn." Rachel's moment with Kenzie was gone, and as much as she wanted to hear more about what Kenzie envisioned for her kids, she knew now wasn't the time.

A look of shock came across Kenzie's face. "What's your song?"

"'Santa Baby,' key of E," Mrs. Hildebrandt said with confidence.

"A woman who knows what she wants, I like it." Kenzie still had the look of surprise on her face as she started the song.

"You're a good sport," Rachel said.

"Thanks." Kenzie motioned with her head to an older gentleman leaning in the large doorframe. "Any chance that's Mr. Hildebrandt?"

Rachel whipped her head around. "Oh, God." She put her head in her hands. "That's Mr. McQueary. He's been our neighbor for years."

Mrs. Hildebrandt suggestively sang in his direction like they were the only two people in the room. "There is definitely something going on there," Kenzie said. Her hands moved quickly over the keyboard. "Wait for it." She turned to Rachel.

"Okay?"

She exaggerated her hands on the next chord and smiled. "Nailed it." She looked smug.

"C-sharp minor?"

"You know it."

Rachel's stomach did that flip again. There was something incredibly sexy about Kenzie at the piano. She commanded this room with such confidence. Mrs. Hildebrandt finished, and Mr. McQueary pointed to the mistletoe directly above him and motioned her over.

"Definitely something going on there." Kenzie turned to Rachel. "Any requests?"

"Any chance you know 'Silver Bells'? I love that one."

"Of course I know 'Silver Bells.'"

There was that confidence again. Rachel leaned her head on Kenzie's shoulder as she started on the song. This was nice. It was comfortable. Rachel sat up when she thought she caught something out of the corner of her eye. She leaned her head back. Through the doorway, she watched her parents slow-dancing in the hallway, all alone. She tried to grab Ashley's attention. She motioned to their parents, and Ashley put her hand on her chest. Rachel placed her hand on Kenzie's thigh and kissed her cheek.

"You got my parents to dance," she whispered, not wanting to throw off Kenzie's rhythm.

Kenzie winked in response and kept playing. The song ended and Rachel's parents entered the main room. "Alright, Mrs. Park." Kenzie caught her attention. "Grand finale. Bring us home. What's your song?"

"Oh, no thank you." Rachel's mom blushed. She was never one for the spotlight, even though she loved hosting parties. She had dressed in a festive green sweater and fitted black trousers.

"How about I start, and then you come in in the middle?" Kenzie started playing a few chords to a recognizable song.

"I couldn't possibly." She shook her head.

Kenzie started "Jingle Bell Rock," and the remaining guests joined in where they knew the words. At this point most people were a few drinks in and enjoying the moment. "This part is all you." Kenzie prodded Rachel's mom.

Rachel was taken aback when her mom actually started belting out the bridge, even hitting some of the difficult high notes. Rachel didn't think her mom could sing and was pleasantly surprised at her voice. She looked happy, content.

"Way to go, Mrs. Park." Kenzie gave her encouragement, and Rachel's mom kept singing.

Kenzie ran her fingers all the way down the keys, drawing out the end of the song, then hammered down on the final chord. She released her hands. "And that's my time," she said to Rachel.

"That was amazing." Rachel nudged her with her shoulder. "You got my parents to dance, and my mom to sing, and this party to not suck." Rachel still couldn't believe the way the night was turning out.

"I don't know that I did that."

"Don't be modest."

"Okay." Kenzie looked her in the eyes. "Then I did all of that. You're welcome."

The remaining guests filtered out until it was only Rachel, Kenzie, and Ashley in the living room, sitting on the oversized brown leather couches.

Their mother started picking up glasses strewn around the room.

"Great party, Mom." Ashley looked up from the couch.

Her mother paused her cleaning. "It was, wasn't it?"

"Yes," Rachel said.

"Let me help you with that," Ashley said.

She waved her off. "I'm just grabbing these few. We can save the rest for the morning."

"Really?" Ashley didn't sound convinced. It was not like their mother to leave anything for the morning.

"All of this fun has me worn out. I'm going to turn in. You girls don't stay up too late. We have a big day tomorrow." She left for the kitchen.

"Big day tomorrow?" Kenzie asked.

Rachel and Ashley both burst into laughter. "My mom likes to cram a lot of traditions into a small amount of time," Rachel explained.

"What does that mean?"

"It means a lot of baking," Ashley said.

"Oh." A look of relief washed over Kenzie's face. "I can handle that."

"Baking that starts at six a.m."

"Seriously?"

Rachel rubbed her elbow. "Don't worry. You don't have to be up that early. You can sleep in."

"Since you'll be sleeping alone in the basement," Ashley joked. "We'll try to keep the stomping to a minimum."

"Thanks." Kenzie turned to Rachel. "I can be up. I'm here to do the whole family thing, remember?"

"I do."

"Okay." Ashley pushed her hands on her thighs and stood. "That's it for me. I will see you both in the morning."

"Actually, I'm right behind you." Rachel reached for Kenzie's hand and led her to the bottom of the stairs. She leaned in, inches from Kenzie's ear. "Be up in my bedroom in ten minutes."

Kenzie nodded.

"Do not keep me waiting," Rachel said in a husky tone.

CHAPTER THIRTY-TWO

Kenzie stared at Rachel's ass as she made her way up the staircase. The tight black cocktail dress hugged her frame. Rachel turned her head over her shoulder and gave a knowing glance. Kenzie had been caught. She didn't care. Her girlfriend was sexy as hell, and ten minutes couldn't pass quickly enough for her to have her way with her.

She rounded the corner, out of sight, and Kenzie let out a long breath. She had done it. She'd met Rachel's family. She seemed to have made a good first impression, and that party hadn't been so bad after all. Kenzie turned into the open study off the main hallway. A small lamp lit the collection of vinyl records lining the wall. She thumbed through them, and an Eric Clapton cover caught her eye.

"One of Rachel's favorites," a low voice said behind her.

Startled, Kenzie put the record back. "Sorry."

"Don't be." Rachel's dad entered the study. "I've always thought vinyl had a better sound. Shall we?" He pointed to the record player in the corner.

Kenzie took the record out of the sleeve and placed in on the turntable. She turned the machine on and carefully placed the needle on the right notch.

"I'm impressed you know how to use one of those."

"My dad also thought vinyl sounded better." Kenzie's dad kept one of the largest vinyl collections she'd ever seen in their basement.

"I know you're a whiskey girl. I have a great single malt scotch here, fancy a nightcap?" He pointed to a glass decanter on the table.

"That'd be great. Thank you, Mr. Park."

"Please, call me Mike." He handed her a glass and motioned for her to take a seat.

"Thanks, Mike." Kenzie flinched at the informality. She swirled the drink in her glass, admiring the amber color. She took a sip. The familiar burn filled her throat and then subsided. "Wow, that is smooth."

"I told you it was good." He closed his eyes and leaned back in his chair, his head bobbing to the music. After several moments, he looked at Kenzie. "My family means the world to me."

"And you have a lovely family." Kenzie raised her glass.

"I do." Mike raised his glass in return. "Tonight was a lot of fun. I think this is how my wife always envisioned these things going, they just never do. So, thank you for that."

Kenzie thought about protesting, but then remembered Rachel's comments from earlier. She took the compliment. "You're welcome."

"Rachel wants to start a family of her own." Mike changed his tone, more serious than before.

"Yes." Kenzie nodded.

"And that's something you two have talked about?"

"Somewhat." Kenzie nodded again. She wasn't sure where this conversation was going. She knew she was being sized up, but didn't know how she was coming across. She knew Rachel wanted to settle down, but they had yet to actually talk what the specifics would look like.

"Is that something you can provide for her?" He narrowed his eyes.

"If you're asking if I have a job, yes, I do." Kenzie was sick of people not understanding what she did for a living. She could certainly provide for herself.

"That's not what I'm asking."

"I'm not sure I'm following." A tightness formed in Kenzie's chest. Rachel's family was one of her top priorities. If she couldn't connect with her father, surely that would be a deal-breaker. The only reason she was entertaining his questioning in the first place was to try to break through with him. Her mind wandered to thoughts of Rachel upstairs. It had probably been more than ten minutes already. She needed to find a way out of this room and upstairs.

"My daughter is a successful lawyer. I have no concerns whatsoever about her being able to make money. Are you going to be able to be her family?"

Kenzie didn't answer. She looked back at him, sitting in his chair. If he was trying to intimidate her, it wasn't working. She took another sip of her drink and remained silent.

"Are you going to be able to be there for her? Rachel needs stability. Someone she can count on. Is that you?"

Was that her? Kenzie wanted it to be, but she didn't always know where she was going to be day to day. She could provide emotional stability, but if Cooper called and wanted her in another city tomorrow, she would drop everything and go.

"Your silence isn't instilling a lot of confidence in me."

"I care for your daughter very much."

"That's not what I'm asking."

"You didn't let me finish. I'm at a pretty big crossroads with my career. With my last song doing so well, I should be able to get my own album recorded soon. I don't know what that's going to do to my work hours. I will always be there for Rachel, but as far as stability in regard to what you're thinking, if I got a call that I was needed in Europe tomorrow, I would probably take it."

"You would pick your job over my daughter."

"I wouldn't view it as picking. But sir, Mike," she corrected herself, "I have worked entirely too hard for the last decade to give up now. I very much want to be there for Rachel and I want her by my side, but I also can't give up on my dream when I'm so close."

"That's not exactly what a father wants to hear."

"I plan on providing your daughter with whatever she wants."

"Do you intend to marry her?"

"What?" Kenzie hadn't thought that far. Did Rachel want to get married? She knew Rachel wanted to be a mother, but did that mean marriage? They had talked about a future together, but not in that much detail.

"Not today, or tomorrow, but eventually," Mike clarified.

"I'm not sure." Kenzie finally managed to form words. Her mouth went dry. She took the final sip from her glass, then regretted it as it did nothing for her parched mouth.

"You're going to start a family out of wedlock?"

"Is that a problem?" What year was it? Was he really implying they needed a piece of paper to start a family.

"I don't know if I'd say it's a problem, but it's certainly not traditional. Look, I like you. I like the two of you together. But I think my daughter has more traditional plans for her life."

"What are you saying?"

"I don't know how well this is going to work out. Family is everything to us, and you are barely around." Mike set his empty glass on the side table. "You haven't shown up to a single Sunday dinner, soccer game or holiday before today. It is important to my wife and important to my daughter, and you need to do a better job of showing up. My daughter deserves someone who will be there with her."

A sucker punch to the gut would have been nicer than this. Kenzie hadn't realized how much her absence from these events had been noticed. "I will," she said.

"I'm serious."

"So am I." Kenzie made a mental note to do better. Yes, her job often took her away at the last minute, but she would work to be present when she was home. And if it was as important to Rachel as Mike made it seem, she would do anything. She pictured Rachel alone upstairs. She faked a yawn. "I think I'm going to turn in."

"Good idea." Mike checked his watch. "We have a big day tomorrow."

"Thanks again for the drink." She handed him the empty glass.

"Thanks for the chat."

❖

Kenzie tiptoed up the stairs, knowing that Rachel's father wouldn't be far behind her. She took the stairs two at a time and gasped for breath as she reached Rachel's bedroom. She slowly turned the knob and opened the door.

Rachel lay on the bed, reading her phone, wearing nothing but a black bra and underwear. She put down her phone and turned to Kenzie.

"Damn." Kenzie couldn't speak as she took in Rachel's body, lying on the bed, waiting for her.

"You seriously have to learn how to tell time. It's been forty-five minutes." Her tone was short, bordering on mad.

Kenzie raised both palms. "It wasn't my fault this time. I swear."

"Get your ass over here." She motioned with her head to the spot on the bed next to her.

Kenzie didn't need to be told twice. Rachel grabbed her by her shoulders and pulled her close. Her mouth enveloped hers and she pulled her on top. Kenzie inhaled and took in her floral scent.

Rachel broke the kiss and moved her mouth to Kenzie's ear. "I'm going to make you wear a watch if you ever keep me waiting like that again."

Her warm breath teased the skin on her neck. "I told you it wasn't my fault."

"Mm-hmm." Rachel nibbled Kenzie's ear lobe.

"I swear."

Rachel moved her head and created some space between them. "Okay, then whose fault is it that you kept me hot and bothered for forty-five minutes?"

"Your father's."

"What?"

Kenzie knew the heat of the moment was gone and crawled off of Rachel and onto her side. She propped her head up on her elbow and took in Rachel again. The reading lamp cast small shadows on her lean body.

"My eyes are up here." Rachel snapped her fingers.

"Your dad and I were having a drink. I couldn't very well leave and say I had to get upstairs to screw his daughter, now could I?"

Rachel narrowed her gaze. "What did you two talk about?"

"He wanted to know what my intentions with his daughter were."

"Seriously?"

Kenzie nodded. She reached her hand out and rubbed Rachel's hip. Her skin was soft and smooth to the touch.

"And you said?"

"That I intend to go upstairs and fuck your brains out."

Rachel stiffened. "You didn't."

"Of course I didn't."

Rachel lay back down. They faced each other. "What did you say?"

"That I wanted to provide you with everything you wanted." Kenzie couldn't clearly make out Rachel's face in the light but knew she was smiling.

"And what did he say?"

Kenzie brushed a piece of Rachel's hair back from her face and stroked her cheek. "He said I needed to do a better job of coming around more. He does not like me much."

"He said that?"

Kenzie decided to leave out the part about him grilling her and saying they need to get married to start a family. "He did not explicitly say he doesn't like me, but the vibe was clear. He's not wrong on the part about me showing up for family events," she said.

"He shouldn't have said that to you."

Kenzie found Rachel's defensiveness endearing. "It's okay." She took her chin in her hand and looked her in the eyes. "He cares about you a lot and told me that I needed to make sure I was more involved and around more. It was a good conversation, I promise." That was an exaggeration, but she didn't need Rachel thinking her dad hated her any more than he did.

"It was certainly a long conversation." Rachel rolled her eyes.

"About that." Kenzie moved her hand down Rachel's body and laced her thumb under the band of her underwear. "I have kept you waiting entirely too long."

Rachel rolled onto her back and pulled Kenzie on top of her. "You have."

"And I intend to make up for it."

Rachel reached behind Kenzie and found the zipper to her dress. She pulled it down, and the straps loosened around Kenzie's body. "Make it up to me naked," Rachel said.

Kenzie slid her shoulders out of the straps and wiggled the rest of the dress down over her hips. She carefully kicked it to the floor and laid herself on top of Rachel, their warm skin coming into contact with one another.

Rachel reached both arms behind Kenzie's back and unclasped her bra. She pulled it off her and tossed it to the floor.

"You weren't messing around," Kenzie said.

"I have been thinking about your hands for the last three hours," Rachel replied. "Wait." Rachel looked at Kenzie's body. "Do you mean to tell me you went all night without wearing underwear?"

"I didn't want to have lines."

"It is a good thing I didn't know that. I could barely contain myself thinking about just your hands." Rachel lay back down hard, and her head bounced against the pillow.

Kenzie ran her hands down Rachel's body. She paused when she got to her black lace bra. She took a breast in each hand and squeezed. "These hands?" she said playfully.

Rachel bit her bottom lip and nodded.

"Sit up," Kenzie whispered. Rachel obliged, and Kenzie took one hand behind her back, supporting her weight. She reached for her bra and unclasped it. She lay her back down and tossed her bra to the side of the bed. She took a nipple in her mouth and it hardened as she swirled her tongue across the top.

Kenzie shifted her body to the side and ran her hand down Rachel's body. Still sucking the nipple, she ran circles around her navel with her fingertips. She slid her hand under her waistband and held it there. She looked up. "Are these the hands you were thinking about?"

"Mm-hmm." Rachel nodded. Her eyes clamped shut.

Kenzie increased the pressure on her hand. "What were you thinking about?"

"Please," Rachel let out.

Kenzie drove her hand down farther until she met her wet opening. "Please what?" She knew she had Rachel right on the edge. Her release would be that much better if she made her work for it a little.

Rachel looked at her. "Fuck me," she said, just above a whisper.

At those words, Kenzie drove two fingers inside her. "Is this what you were thinking about?"

Rachel clamped her eyes shut and leaned her head back. "Harder."

Kenzie drove her fingers in as far as they would go and quickly moved herself in and out. She established a quick rhythm, and Rachel's breathing picked up. "Is this what you were thinking about while I was playing piano?"

"Mm-hmm." Rachel moaned.

"You were thinking dirty thoughts while I was just trying to play Christmas songs?"

"Mm-hmm." Rachel moaned again.

Kenzie could tell Rachel was close and wanted to tease her just a little longer. Experience had taught her Rachel liked her orgasms drawn out. She kept the pressure building but slowed down.

Rachel reached her hand on top of Kenzie's. "Don't stop," she begged.

Kenzie took her cue and picked her pace up again, slamming herself in and out of her, her hand moving easily through her wetness. Rachel arched her back and bit her index finger to keep from screaming out. Kenzie loved it when she was loud in bed but knew that with her parents' room so close by, that wasn't in the cards tonight.

Rachel eased herself back down to the mattress, and Kenzie felt her release around her fingers. She exited her, careful around her now sensitive area. Rachel put her hands on top of her head, and her breasts rose as she caught her breath. Kenzie ran her fingers in circles around her navel again.

Rachel turned her head and looked up at Kenzie. "I needed that."

"I can tell."

"It's not my fault."

"Oh?"

"Yeah." She nodded. "You're the one that had to be all sexy with your piano playing and actually getting my family to have a fun time. I couldn't help it."

Kenzie shook her head and leaned down to place a kiss on her forehead.

"You were wonderful tonight," Rachel said. "From start to finish."

"I better get downstairs."

"I wish you didn't have to go."

"Me too. But if I stay much longer, we'll fall asleep, and I'm guessing your mom is the type that still likes to wake you up in the morning?"

"She is." Rachel rolled her eyes.

Kenzie leaned in and gave her lips a gentle peck. "Good night." Kenzie steadied the door as she latched it, careful to not make a sound. She tip toed back down the stairs to her basement bedroom. Alone. Would she have to sleep downstairs every Christmas until they got married? Was marriage even an option? Kenzie meant it when she said she wanted to provide Rachel everything she wanted, but with Kenzie's dream so close to being in reach, would she be able to have both?

CHAPTER THIRTY-THREE

Kenzie received the call for her song's CCA nomination on January second. She remembered it clearly because she and Rachel were still recovering from the New Year's Eve party they attended. Kenzie had never considered herself old until it took her two days to recover from staying up past midnight. Rachel seemed more excited than Kenzie about the news, and Kenzie didn't know if it was because she wanted to attend the award ceremony or was just happy for her success. More than likely, it was a little bit of both.

The day before the award show, Kenzie sat in a decorated ballroom for the pre-award luncheon. *To Hell and Back* had so many nominations, they took up two full tables. Braxton had received a nomination for her supporting role, and Kenzie was thankful because she knew no one else. She had barely met the big stars at the premiere and knew none of the production members since her contribution to the movie was strictly musical and entirely behind the scenes.

The empty chair next to her pulled back and a well-dressed Cooper occupied it just as the lights dimmed to begin the main program.

"What's going on?" Kenzie whispered in Cooper's ear.

"Global didn't want an empty chair at the table. Braxton couldn't make it. Long story. I'll tell you later." Cooper directed her attention to the main stage where a speaker fed the crowd's egos by recognizing their success in making it this far.

If Kenzie hadn't been obligated to be here, she would have skipped. She was never one for awards shows. Music awards shows were different, in that it was more like a concert and she enjoyed seeing her peers' work. This room was stiff and filled with actors who would do literally anything to win the awards being passed out. If Kenzie had to hear the phrase "It's an honor just to be nominated" one more time, she might stab her eyes out with the fancy fork in front of her.

After the speaker finished, the lights came back on. Cooper's phone buzzed in his pocket. "Okay. Yeah. We'll be right out." He turned to Kenzie. "We need to go chat in the hall."

Confused but curious, Kenzie didn't argue and followed him. Damon was waiting in the hall next to a brunette dressed in a business suit. She had a Bluetooth earpiece in her ear and spoke fast.

"Yeah. Yeah. Okay. Yes. I'm here now." The brunette paid Kenzie and Cooper no attention. She clicked the button on her earpiece and looked up. She stuck out a hand. "Lisa Grant." She gripped Kenzie's hand firmly.

"Kenzie," she said hesitantly.

"Yes, I know."

"Lisa is part of the legal counsel for Global Studios." Cooper tried to fill in the blanks.

"What's going on?" Kenzie asked.

"Braxton has a sinus infection," Cooper answered.

"And that's a legal matter?"

"Unfortunately yes." Lisa answered. "Someone has to perform 'The Other Side of Forever' tomorrow or the nomination gets pulled, and the studio does not want to have that happen."

"Lisa, I got this." Cooper blocked her from Kenzie's view. "Braxton can't sing at the show tomorrow and we are asking you to step in and do it."

"Wait. Really?" Kenzie had never performed for an audience that large, let alone on live television. This was finally the break she needed.

"Really. This is your chance, Kenz. We need you step in and be the next best thing to Braxton."

"Hell yes! I mean, I'm sorry she's sick, but I won't let you down."

"Great. I'll let the studio know that the performance is covered and we will see you tomorrow." Lisa answered a call on her Bluetooth as she left.

Kenzie dialed Rachel right away.

"Hi. What's going on?" Rachel answered in a panic.

It occurred to Kenzie after Rachel answered that she wouldn't normally call in the middle of the workday and Rachel expected her to still be at the awards lunch. "I have great news."

"Oh. Well, what is it?"

"Braxton has a sinus infection!"

"I'm not following."

"Braxton can't perform at the CCAs tomorrow, and they are asking me to step in. I get to do the awards show performance."

"Holy shit! That's huge!"

"Right? I know you get in tonight and we are meeting up, but I think I'm going to be too busy getting ready. I have to nail this."

"About that." Rachel paused.

"Do not tell me you aren't coming." Kenzie knew she was asking Rachel to give up family time for the weekend, but now that she was having the performance of her lifetime, she wanted her by her side.

"I'm coming. I just can't make it tonight. Work is absolutely nuts and there is no way I can break away today. I was going to call you as soon as the luncheon was over."

Kenzie stayed silent.

"I already worked out the details with Damon, and I'll be there. I promise."

"Okay, well it all works out, then." She couldn't be mad. She was going to have to cancel plans with her tonight anyway. But if she hadn't gotten the news, she'd be alone tonight waiting for Rachel to meet her.

"I will be in the seat next to you the second it starts."

"Okay. Travel safe. I'll see you tomorrow."

"I can't wait to see you."

Kenzie clicked the end call button and turned back around.

"This is the break we've been looking for." Cooper put his large hand on her shoulder and gave it a squeeze.

Panicked, she turned to Damon. "I need different shoes."

"What's wrong with your shoes?" Damon asked.

"I can't play piano in heels. Actually, I need two pairs of shoes. One for the piano and then one for the rest of the night."

Damon pulled out his phone and started opening web pages. He ran a hand through his brown hair as he scrolled, a nervous tic he had picked up over the years of trying to comply with diva requests.

Cooper ran his hands over his face. "Why do you need separate shoes?"

"I'm not going to be a foot shorter than Rachel in all the pictures."

"That's the dumbest shit I've ever heard," Cooper said.

"You can't tell me Braxton has never made a ridiculous ask."

"Fair point," Cooper replied.

Damon looked up from his phone. "I can get you the same style with no heel. I'll get it all taken care of."

"Thank you." Kenzie had much bigger problems to deal with then the size of her heels, like how she was going to make sure she took full advantage of this opportunity. It was time to show the studio and the world that she was the next big thing.

Kenzie sat at the grand piano in the empty awards hall. The space echoed more than she anticipated, as it had not been a room designed for music performances.

"Stop, stop, stop." Cooper waved his hands over his head to get Kenzie's attention.

She stopped abruptly and turned to find him in the middle of the hall. She put her hand to her forehead to block the bright lights to make him out.

"You need to stop doing that thing with your face," Cooper yelled to the stage.

"What thing?" Kenzie asked.

"That. Right there." Cooper pointed to the large screen where Kenzie could see herself projected across all twenty feet. Cooper moved closer so he didn't have to shout. He got to the base of the stage and looked up. "You look like you are physically in pain."

"There's a lot more to this than I realized," Kenzie replied.

Cooper hopped up on the stage and joined her on the piano bench. "Everyone is going to be expecting Braxton tonight, and I need you to be the next best thing."

"No pressure."

"No. What I mean is, they are expecting a pretty blond girl to come out and sing a love song. Preferably with a happy look on her face. I need you to be that pretty blond girl tonight."

"You have got to be kidding me." Kenzie did not hide the disgust in her voice at Cooper's characterization.

"Look, I know you are much more than a pretty blond girl. So is Braxton, but this is Hollywood, and we are putting on a show."

"I'm trying, Coop. There's just so much to think about. The lights. The music. My face. I didn't realize how bright it would be and how loud the room is. How does Braxton do this all the time?"

"It takes a special breed. Where is the girl who got put in time-out for grinning so much back at the recording session? I need you to channel her. Give me that face."

"If you call me a girl one more time, I'm going to punch you in the face like a girl." Kenzie balled her hand into a fist to show she wasn't messing around.

Cooper clapped his hands together. "Okay. Let's try this one more time. You don't have to look happy, but you can't look like you're in pain." He hopped down off the stage.

"I wasn't expecting the reverb to be so long," Kenzie called to him.

"It won't be," Cooper yelled back. "Once this place is full, you won't hear a thing."

Kenzie flooded with relief followed by a wave of panic, realizing that someone would occupy every single one of those chairs. She opened and shut her hands a few times and wiggled them over the keys. She made eye contact with the conductor in the pit orchestra and started again. This was all foreign to her. Playing live, playing with an orchestra, playing on a stage of this size. She couldn't fathom how Braxton and the countless other singers she had worked with continually handled this level of attention. She pictured Braxton singing to sold-out arenas and missed the C-sharp minor chord. "Fuck." She slammed her hands on the keys.

"Okay," Cooper called from the audience and approached the stage again. He hopped up and took a seat next to her on the bench.

Kenzie didn't know if she wanted to scream or cry. Tears formed behind her eyelids, more from frustration than anything else. "I wrote the damn song. How can I not hit the notes?"

Cooper put a hand on her back. "Let's think of this another way."

"Okay." Kenzie didn't look up from the white keys.

"Braxton is a performer. You are an artist. There's a big difference."

"Where are you going with this?"

"If you think you are going to miss the chord, don't play it."

"What? You want me to fake it?"

"No. But you have the orchestra behind you, they can cover one chord. This is a performance. It is more important that you look good. You need to sell how the song looks tonight, not the notes behind it."

Kenzie shook her head.

"I know you hate hearing that. I know this isn't what you do, but that's what today is. Braxton has a higher range than you. It's a lot to try and hit the high note and the chord. If you need to, drop it down. The last thing we need is your voice cracking on national television."

"I can hit the note."

"Kenzie."

"I can hit the note." Kenzie knew she was getting defensive, but how could she not? Yes, Braxton did have a higher vocal range than she did, but that didn't mean she couldn't hit one damn high note.

"You haven't hit it yet."

"Because there's so much going on that I can't concentrate!" She slammed her fist onto the keys.

"Exactly. So just humor me, and let's do one run-through where you skip the C-sharp and focus on your face and the high note." Cooper looked at his watch. "Then we have to get out of here because people will start filing in."

Kenzie nodded as Cooper jumped back off the stage. She put

all her focus into this take, and while she didn't love skipping the chord, it worked.

"That'll work, Kenz." Cooper shot her a thumbs-up.

She pushed herself back from the piano bench. Damon waited for her behind a black curtain in the wings. He looked sharp in his black tux. She stopped herself from asking him where Rachel was for the fifth time this hour. She longed for her. She understood that work had kept Rachel home the night before, but that didn't make her miss her any less. She couldn't wait to see those brown eyes and feel her closeness.

"We can head to the green room and you can relax for a few minutes before it's time to take your seat. Don't worry, your shoes are waiting for you."

"Is there a bar in the green room? I need a drink."

"I think I can manage to find you something." Damon ushered her down the white cinder block hallway to a long line of dressing rooms. "You are all the way down on the left. I'll come by in a few."

Kenzie paused when she got to the end of the long hallway. A gold name plate with black lettering read "McKenzie McCall." She ran her fingertips over the lettering and wondered if Braxton ever got tired of seeing her name on dressing rooms. She turned the knob and pushed the door open. "Oh, sorry," she said to someone on the couch. "I thought this was my dressing room."

The woman on the couch put down her magazine and looked up. "It is. I thought green rooms were supposed to be green."

"Common misconception." Kenzie ran and pulled Rachel up into a hug. She hadn't recognized her with her hair pinned up. "Thank God you're here." She leaned her head onto her shoulder. Kenzie pictured her in the salon chair waiting as Charles supervised one of his ladies placing her perfect brown locks in place. "You look amazing." Kenzie pushed her back at her hips so she could take in all of her. "Spin." She held Rachel's hand over her head as she twirled around for her. The blue dress fitted her curves and the modest neckline showed off the perfect amount of cleavage. Kenzie ran her finger along her exposed collarbone, stopping when she got to the diamond necklace on her neck.

"Good enough to be your arm candy for the night?"

"Tonight, and every night." The skin around Rachel's eyes wrinkled at her smile. She loved when Rachel smiled so deeply and genuinely. Charles had done it again. The blue in Rachel's dress perfectly complemented Kenzie's. Her own top was a crisp white flowing into monochromatic shades of blue toward the bottom. They looked like a pair, like they fit together naturally.

"You don't look half bad yourself."

"How did you get back here?"

"Damon is good at his job." She wrinkled her nose. "How was the sound check? Why is your neck all splotchy?"

Kenzie reflexively touched her neck. She had hoped the heat forming was just from being under the lights. "There's a problem with my face."

Rachel ran her thumb across Kenzie's cheek. "What's wrong with your face?"

"It doesn't look good when I sing."

"I completely disagree with that."

"Cooper said it looked like I was physically in pain."

Rachel chuckled.

"He wants me to skip the chords at the bridge."

"What's wrong with that?"

"I can't just skip the notes I don't like."

"Why not? Performers skip notes all the time. At football games, they don't even actually sing, they just lip-sync the whole thing."

Kenzie pushed herself past Rachel and paced toward the couch. "That's where I'm struggling. It's hard to not play all the chords I wrote. But if I want to be a performer, I'm going to have to make some adjustments."

Rachel put a hand on Kenzie's shoulder and turned her around. She put her hands on her hips and pulled her in. "How about for tonight, you just pretend to be a performer? And how about later, I pretend to be your groupie?" Rachel ran her mouth to Kenzie's ear and exhaled. "I won't throw my panties at you onstage," she whispered. "Unless you want me to."

Kenzie's mind raced to pictures of Rachel, later, naked. There was a knock at the door, and Kenzie yelled over Rachel's shoulder, "Come in."

Damon carried a whiskey glass and a wineglass. "Sorry about not telling you." He motioned with his head to Rachel. "She wanted to keep it a surprise."

"It was a wonderful surprise," Kenzie gushed as she relaxed for the first time in twenty-four hours.

Damon checked his phone. "We have about twenty-five minutes until the show starts. I'll come back and get you and take you to your seats. Your shoes are over there." He pointed to a shoebox at the end of the couch.

"Damon, you are a godsend."

He nodded and left the room.

Rachel swirled the wine in her glass. "Now I feel like a groupie."

"Oh my God." Kenzie shook her head.

"I heard you were a real diva about the shoes," Rachel said.

"Not my proudest moment," Kenzie said. "But I stand by it."

"Let's have a toast." Rachel raised her glass. "Tonight is a really big deal, and I hope you can at least take the time to appreciate the moment. To this moment and all the moments we have left to come."

"That's good." Kenzie snapped her fingers. "Let me write that down."

"You never stop."

CHAPTER THIRTY-FOUR

Rachel buzzed with excited energy as they took their seats. Every way she turned her head, an A-list celebrity, musician, or famous athlete was close by. It was surreal. She thought that attending the movie opening would have better prepared her for this night, but she couldn't contain her giddiness. She took in each moment, and every famous person, knowing that her mother and Ashley would want a play-by-play tomorrow. How was it possible this was her world?

Kenzie leaned over and whispered in her ear. "You promised me you'd be cool."

Rachel tried to mask her grin. "I know. I know." She had promised Kenzie she would act less starstruck, but how could she? She had grown up reading celebrity magazines and watching award shows, and now she was here. She still couldn't believe any of it was real.

She smoothed the front of her dress. "I'm cool." Marissa Tomlinson sat in the row in front of them, and Rachel bit her bottom lip to keep her glee from exploding.

"Keep yourself together and I'll make sure you get introduced at the after-party," Kenzie whispered as the lights dimmed.

Rachel bit her lip harder and gave a small nod. After-party? She had been so wrapped up in the travel plans and logistics of the award show itself, she had completely forgotten there would be an after-party. She smoothed her dress again and gave her full attention to the comedian who was the master of ceremonies for the night.

The award show was entertaining enough, with a few tributes

and smaller awards to start the night. Winners from years past graced the stage and made lame jokes. Rachel loved it. The first performance for the best song category started. It was the theme song from the newest children's movie.

"Thank God I didn't have to dress like a fairy princess," Kenzie whispered to Rachel's ear.

"See, at least you have that going for you." She nudged her back.

"Is there a weird echo in here?"

"No." Rachel shook her head and squeezed her hand.

"You don't hear that? That delay?"

Rachel placed her hand on Kenzie's cheek and made the best eye contact she could in the dimly lit room. "No," she said softly.

Resigned, Kenzie nodded and turned her attention back to the stage.

Rachel could feel Kenzie's nerves coming out of her body. She hoped that Kenzie could relax enough to not only find some good memories but knock this performance out of the park. She didn't fully understand what an opportunity like this would do for Kenzie's career. Would this finally be the steppingstone for her own album? Would this lead to Cooper giving songs more radio time?

The end of the night was getting close when Damon came to take Kenzie backstage. "Good luck," Rachel whispered as she left. Kenzie was the last performance of the night, and then her award category would be up shortly.

"Oh my God, Rachel, hi," a familiar, yet somehow deeper voice whispered excitedly next to Rachel.

"Braxton!" Rachel tried her best to be cool. "What are you doing here?"

"The camera is going to pan to us a couple times, and they don't want an empty seat."

"Really?" Rachel hadn't thought about the fact that she could be on camera tonight. That made sense, since she was sitting next to a nominee.

"Yes. I need to look approving or something." Braxton rolled her eyes. "How's she doing? I am so jealous right now."

"She's nervous." Rachel knew she could be honest with Braxton.

"This is such a good performance." Braxton threw her head back like a whining toddler. "She is so lucky."

"How are you feeling?"

"I'm on so many different drugs right now. I feel fine, I just have to be ready for my tour. They did tell me that if I happen to win, I need to really play up my nasal voice in my speech."

Rachel crossed her fingers for her. The lights flickered, indicating the show was back from commercial break and would resume.

"Okay." Braxton leaned in. "Your seat is a better angle than mine, so that's why I moved over here." She spoke fast, and Rachel was finally learning how to keep up with her. "When they cut to us, I am supposed to nod approvingly, and you are supposed to look like you're in love."

"Why are they going to pan to us?"

"In case her face does that thing." Braxton made a pained expression with her face and Rachel burst into laughter at the spot-on impression.

"This really is a production."

"Hollywood, baby."

The room went dark, and a single spotlight shone on Kenzie, seated at the grand piano in the middle of the stage. Rachel held her breath as Kenzie plucked the keys. Her dress sparkled as it caught the light, and Rachel's stomach fluttered.

Rachel's skin tingled as the orchestra came in after the first verse. Kenzie looked confident. Not necessarily smiling, but not in pain by any means. Rachel clenched her fists as the bridge approached. The large screen panned from Kenzie's face to her hands at the keys. Rachel stared intently, knowing what was coming.

Kenzie finally smiled as she hit the C-sharp minor chord and high notes at the same time. She looked relaxed, in control, like she had been performing for crowds like this for years. The orchestra cut out, and it was just Kenzie. Her voice turned husky, low. A voice Rachel hadn't heard from her before. She sang like she was holding gravel in the back of her throat, and Rachel grabbed the armrests to keep herself from melting into a puddle.

Kenzie had never sung like this before. Never with this kind of desire in her voice. Rachel's mind wandered to all the things she wanted to do to her the second they were alone. Those hands, that dress on the hotel room floor. She no longer cared about after-parties or meeting famous actresses. She had to have Kenzie.

The song ended, and Rachel reflexively jumped to a standing ovation. She was grateful that she wasn't the only one. The crowd roared with applause as Kenzie took a modest bow and left the stage.

Kenzie returned to her seat, and Rachel reached for her hand instantly. "That was amazing."

"Yeah?"

"Yeah." She nodded emphatically. "And your face looked great."

"I'm not going to lie, it felt really good." She flexed her fingers. "I am buzzing with adrenaline right now."

"It was really good. So good that I will be finding it on the internet later and watching it on repeat."

Kenzie blushed.

Rachel leaned in. "But not tonight, because I'm going to have my way with the real thing."

Kenzie swallowed hard and shifted in her seat.

Rachel squeezed her hand. "This is your category. Damon says make sure you smile when they call your name, and try not to swear if you win."

"The kids' song always wins. I'm not worried about it."

Last year's winner, a tall man with brown hair and a short, cropped beard, read the nominees from the stage. "And the winner is," he paused as he opened the envelope and pulled the card out, "'The Other Side of Forever' by McKenzie McCall."

Rachel's eyebrows shot into her hairline. "Babe." She nudged her shoulder.

An equally shocked Kenzie met her gaze. "Did he just say my name?" She pointed to herself.

"Yes." Rachel pulled her to her feet.

"Holy shit. I didn't prepare anything."

Rachel kissed her on the cheek and pushed her to the aisle, where Damon motioned frantically.

Kenzie took a few steps toward the stage when Braxton practically tackled her to the ground in a hug. The room laughed at Braxton's reaction.

"Oh my God, you did it!" she screamed.

Kenzie brushed Braxton off her, and Rachel couldn't make out what she said through her smile. An announcer rattled off Kenzie's credentials as she approached the stage to the orchestra's rendition of her song.

Last year's winner met Kenzie at the bottom of the stairs with an outstretched hand. Rachel rolled her eyes. Kenzie didn't need help up the stairs, but she knew it would look good on TV.

Kenzie held the small gold statue out from her body and admired it. The gold film canister on top of the black base caught the light, and Kenzie weighed it in her hands. She stepped forward to the microphone, unable to stop smiling. "Like most musicians, I wrote this song because I was trying to impress a girl."

The room let out a collective laugh. Kenzie composed herself and started again. "And I think it worked, because she's here as my date tonight."

Rachel's cheek's flushed red as the room's attention turned to her.

"I want to thank Global Studios for allowing me to be a part of this production. Braxton, for bringing life into this song in ways I never imagined, and the council for recognizing great storytelling and that music is a key component of that." She looked at the award in her hands. "Rachel, thank you for this moment and all of the moments yet to come."

The orchestra started and Kenzie was ushered off stage.

"Rachel," Damon whisper-yelled at her. "Do you want to go see her?"

"Yes." She nodded and followed him out a side door and down a long hallway.

Kenzie posed in front of a black banner covered with the CCA emblem. She held her award and posed as photographers clicked rapidly. She looked up and smiled wide when Rachel entered the room. She motioned her over as the photographers turned around to see the visitor.

"I am so proud of you." She grabbed Kenzie by both cheeks and kissed her. The sound of camera clicks filled the room.

"Give it a rest, guys," Kenzie said to the room.

"Give us one together," one of the guys yelled out.

Kenzie looked up to Rachel. "You good with a few pictures?"

"Of course."

Kenzie wrapped one arm around Rachel and held the award between them.

"Goddammit," Kenzie let out.

"What?"

"I forgot to change my shoes."

Rachel stood a full head taller than her in her heals. "Want me to take mine off?" she offered.

"No. I love your long legs. I just hate that they're longer than mine."

"You might want to change the way your face looks for these pictures," Rachel joked and posed for the cameras.

"Oh my God!" Braxton's familiar greeting came bursting into the room. "Kenzie, can you believe it?" She showed off her own trophy she had just won for supporting actress.

"How about the two of you?" another photographer yelled.

Rachel stepped behind the cameras as Kenzie and Braxton took pictures together. Rachel took the two of them in. Was this her life now? Award shows and after-parties. It was exciting, something she had never in her wildest dreams imagined, but how did a family fit into this equation? Would Kenzie be running off to accept awards while she was home with their children? Telling her kids from her acceptance speech that it was past their bedtime and they should go to sleep now? Was that the kind of family she wanted? Rachel pushed the thoughts to the back of her mind. Tonight was supposed to be a celebration, but she couldn't help but wonder how this could work in the long term.

❖

The show ended with *To Hell and Back* cleaning up, winning almost all the awards it was nominated for, including best picture. By the time the show ended, it was barely nine p.m. They had a lot of night left.

Damon led them to the car that would take them to the after-party. The studio had put most of the cast and crew up in a nearby hotel, and they had rented the ballroom. Rachel and Kenzie entered the black town car and finally had a moment alone.

Kenzie leaned her head back against the black leather seat and let out a long sigh. "Holy shit."

Rachel ran her hand up Kenzie's bare arm, feeling her smooth skin. "What?"

"It was almost a year ago that I was asked to write a song for an upcoming movie." She looked down and turned her gaze to Rachel. "I think about everything that has happened since then and, just, holy shit."

"You were wonderful tonight." Rachel's mind flashed back to her gravel-filled voice.

"Thank you. And thank you for being here. I normally hate this stuff, but with you, I don't." The car stopped, and they got out to enter the party. "Okay, we can meet whoever you want," Kenzie said to Rachel. "And we'll stay as long as you want."

"Actually, I have other ideas."

"What's that?"

"Let's just say they involve getting you alone." Her voice turned husky.

"Okay." Kenzie nodded. "I need to get my award engraved and make a lap, and then we can go up to the room."

Rachel leaned in and whispered in Kenzie's ear. "If I don't take you in the supply closet before then."

Kenzie stepped back. "We'll make this fast."

Waiters circled the room with platters of champagne, and Kenzie grabbed a glass for each of them. "Here." She handed one to Rachel. "Try and cool yourself off."

Rachel brushed a hand across her hip. "It's not my fault."

They made their way to the back of the ballroom, where a woman took up shop with engraving materials. They took their place in line as Cooper approached them. "Kenz, I knew you could do it." He took Kenzie into a bear hug. He let her go and nudged Rachel "I told you she could do it."

"I never had a doubt," Rachel said.

There was a squeal as Braxton joined their small circle. "I still can't believe it," she said. "This is a dream come true."

"Well deserved." Cooper brought Braxton in for a hug as well. "Girls, we did it." He held his hands out to Kenzie and Braxton.

A woman dressed in evening wear with an apparent Bluetooth earpiece approached the group. "McKenzie, congratulations," she said with a forced smile.

"Thank you," Kenzie said. "Lisa, this is Rachel. My girlfriend." Kenzie motioned to Rachel.

Rachel stuck out her hand. "Rachel Park."

Lisa paid her no attention and turned her attention to Kenzie. "I just wanted to let you know that the studio sends their regards."

"Thanks," Kenzie said.

"The studio wants to talk to you about your album," Lisa said flatly.

"Seriously?"

"Yes. Oh, and we want rights to your next ten songs."

"That's fantastic."

"What she means to say is that she'll arrange for her lawyer to meet with you," Rachel cut in. "Don't forget about the fine print," she whispered to Kenzie.

"Right. My lawyer will be happy to go over any of those details."

"One second." Lisa held up a finger and clicked on her earpiece. "Yes, I have them both right here. Oh. Great idea. Okay, I'll let them know." Lisa appeared to end a call and turned her attention back to the group. "That was the studio. They think it would be great publicity if you and Braxton appeared together tomorrow on a morning show. It'll be great." She motioned to Kenzie and Braxton.

"Sounds fantastic," Kenzie said.

"Damon will get you the details."

They moved to the front of the line. and a woman etched Kenzie's name into her statue. "McKenzie, congratulations." Marissa Tomlinson stood mere inches from them in line. Marissa Tomlinson. The famous actress was actually talking to them. Rachel remembered to breathe.

"Thank you." Kenzie waved an arm toward Rachel. "This is Rachel. Rachel, this is Marissa." Kenzie waved between the two of them.

Any other day, Rachel might have lost her mind, or been too

nervous in her presence, but tonight she had other things occupying her mind. She had her own award winner to attend to. "Pleasure to meet you," Rachel said. She noticed the statue that she had set on the counter. "Congratulations."

"Oh, thank you. It's a pleasure just to be nominated," she gushed, and Kenzie gave a small eye roll.

The woman behind the counter finished and handed the statue to Kenzie. "Thank you," she said as she grabbed it from her. "Okay, is there anyone else you want to see?"

"No, let's get out of here." Rachel grabbed her by the wrist and led her to the elevators.

"Kenzie! Wait!" Cooper yelled just as the elevators were in sight.

"Hey, Coop."

"Get back here, I need you to meet a few people."

"We were actually about to turn in for the night." Kenzie motioned to the elevator.

"The hell you were, get over here."

"It's your night, babe. Let's go back in."

Cooper put a hand around Kenzie and led her back inside. Rachel soon lost them both in the crowd of increasingly drunk celebrities.

"First time?" a woman asked as Rachel waited in line at the bar.

"At an award show yes. It's my second after-party."

"I'm Janice." She stuck out her hand.

"Rachel."

"You're here with that new singer. McKenzie. She was fantastic."

"Yes and yes, she was."

"Oh, you must come with me."

Not having anything better to do or anywhere else to be, Rachel followed Janice to a couch hidden in the corner of the ballroom with a few more people. "We're the WAGS," Janice said.

"The what?"

"WAGS. Wives and girlfriends," another woman explained. "I'm Mary. My husband is a studio exec. He's around here somewhere, and I'm going to drink champagne on this couch until it's time to go."

"Have a seat." Another woman made room for her.

"By this time in the night, only the winners still want to be out partying or people off trying to make deals. I'm guessing your girl is off doing both," Janice said.

"I'm not sure, honestly. One of the studio producers said he needed to introduce her to some people."

"Settle in, girl, that means she's making the rounds."

"Do you all do this a lot?"

"Every major award show, charity gala, and business dinner," Mary said. "Well, everyone except Tom. He's new and we don't know how long he'll last."

"Hey now!" Tom threw a napkin in her direction.

"Tom is dating Marissa, so who knows how long he'll be around."

What world had Rachel stumbled into?

"Now that McKenzie is an award winner, you'll be invited to a lot of these. At least for the next year or so. We should exchange numbers." Janice pulled out her cell phone.

"And you come every time?"

"It always looks better for my husband when I do. Plus, the sex after he closes a deal is amazing. Almost makes it all worth it."

Rachel had been trying to discover that last part out for herself before Cooper had hijacked her evening.

"Rachel, there you are." Kenzie's hand brushed her shoulder. "I've been looking for you. Ready to get out of here?"

"Oh this must be McKenzie," Janice said.

"Hi." Kenzie waved. "I'm going to go ahead and steal Rachel back. I hope you all have a great night."

"You have my number, Rachel. Stay in touch," Janice said.

Kenzie wrapped an arm around Rachel's waist and led her to the elevators. "What was all that about?"

"I think I joined a club."

"A club?"

"Wives and girlfriends. Apparently, they sit in the corner and drink champagne while they wait for their husbands and boyfriends to finish up business deals."

"I'm sorry about that. I really didn't know Cooper was going to do that."

The door to their room had barely shut when Rachel grabbed Kenzie by her hips and turned her around, pinning her to the door. Her hands ran on the smooth fabric of her dress, settling firmly on the top of her hip bones. She leaned in and met her lips. She had waited long enough. There was no foreplay or preamble. She pushed her into the door and kissed her like it was the only thing she'd been thinking about all night.

Kenzie pushed her back. "Hold on."

"Everything okay?"

"I just need a minute."

Rachel raised an eyebrow.

She rested her hands on Rachel's shoulders. "I want this. I do. It's just tonight was a lot and I need a minute."

"Okay." Rachel took a small step back, giving her some space.

"I feel hot and sticky, and I want to shower."

"I like you hot and sticky."

"And we can get that. I just need a minute. Let me shower and then we can pick this back up."

Rachel stepped back and made a motion to the bathroom. "Of course." She didn't think she could wait any longer, but she wasn't going to push it.

She grabbed her tablet from her bag and waited on the king-size bed. She knew someone would have leaked Kenzie's performance already. She undid the straps on her shoes and kicked them off as her tablet powered on. A quick internet search helped her to find exactly what she was looking for. The fluttering in her body returned as she relived the performance, smiling at the few times the camera panned to her and Braxton in the audience. Her arousal grew as she rewatched the bridge, and she willed Kenzie to hurry up.

"What are you doing?" Kenzie said from the bedroom door.

"I told you I was going to watch this on repeat later."

Kenzie shook her head as she stood wrapped in a white bath towel.

"Now, drop the towel and get over here."

The towel made a thump as it landed on the floor. Kenzie reached for Rachel's hand and pulled her up. "You're overdressed."

"I need your help." She motioned to the long zipper on the back of the dress that was just out of her reach.

Kenzie spun her around, grabbed her by her hips, and pulled her into her. She kissed the nape of her neck, making a line of kisses up to her ear. "I can help," she whispered. She continued kissing Rachel as she undid the zipper. "Thank God there's a zipper this time."

A cold breeze wafted on Rachel's back as her dress opened, exposing her. She gasped as Kenzie slid her hands on her hips, then up her body to her shoulders. Her warm hands took their time. They made it to her shoulders and slid the straps off her, allowing the dress to fall to the floor. Rachel stepped out of the dress and spun them around until the back of Kenzie's knees were level with the bed. With her hands on Kenzie's shoulders, she pushed her down and straddled her lap, her own knees feeling the down hotel comforter. Her heat radiated from her, and she sensed that Kenzie could feel it too.

Kenzie wasted no time and ran a finger between Rachel's legs. "You weren't kidding." Kenzie easily ran her hand up and down her clit with no friction at all.

"I've been waiting all night." Rachel's chest heaved as Kenzie easily inserted her thumb inside her, curling it at just the right angle. Rachel ran her hands from Kenzie's shoulders to the back of her neck, holding on as she writhed at Kenzie's touch. It didn't take long, as she had been worked up all evening picturing Kenzie and thinking about getting her alone. She tensed around Kenzie's hand and relaxed her whole body at last.

Rachel slid off the bed, kneeling on the floor in front of Kenzie's split legs. She pushed her thighs open and blew on her warm sex. Kenzie placed her hands behind her and leaned back. Kenzie's breasts rose, then fell, and her nipples grew hard with arousal. Rachel slid her arms under Kenzie's thighs and pulled her to the edge of the bed.

She took Kenzie in her mouth, licking, sucking, and working her tongue through all of her folds. She went fast, then slow, trying to draw it out. She fit her whole mouth over the bundle of nerves and sucked hard.

"Oh God," Kenzie said. "Right there." She threw her head back and shut her eyes tight.

She sucked harder, licked faster, wanting to give her the release she was on the edge of achieving. Kenzie moaned and fell back onto her arms, and Rachel continued to lavish her as her wet center grew even wetter.

❖

Hours later, sated, Rachel fell into Kenzie's arms and let her hold her close. While she was exhausted, her mind wouldn't stop racing, and she knew sleep wouldn't come. "Babe?"

"Mmm?" Kenzie made a noise with closed eyes.

Rachel tensed. It was a conversation that needed to be had. She hadn't planned it to be tonight of all nights, but her mind was not going to quiet until it was out in the open. "I want to talk about our future together."

"Okay. What about it?" Kenzie sounded half asleep.

"You know I think you're great at your job."

"But?"

"Your work hours are all over the place. Sometimes you don't get up until ten a.m. and you drop whatever you're doing to go sing a lunch hour set. Cooper calls you and you take off at a moment's notice and I don't always know when you'll be home."

"Um. Okay. I wasn't expecting that." Kenzie rubbed her eyes. "I guess I need to be fully awake for this conversation."

Rachel opened her mouth to speak and then closed it.

"Where is this coming from?"

"Sometimes it seems like you're irresponsible."

"What?"

Rachel's phone buzzed uncontrollably on the nightstand. Text after text rang in rapid succession. "Sorry, let me silence that." She reached for her phone. Multiple texts from her mom and sister had come through. "My mom says congratulations," Rachel put her phone on silent and set it face down.

"That was nice of her."

"Why isn't your phone blowing up?"

"It probably is." Kenzie shrugged. "I turned it off."

"What do you mean you turned it off?"

"There's this button on there and it makes it so the phone does nothing. No one can call or text or email."

"What if something important happens or someone needs to get a hold of you?"

"I'm with you. My mom never calls, and Damon knows where I am if something changes. Who else would need to get a hold of me?"

"This is what I mean."

"Why I'm irresponsible? Because nothing you said makes me irresponsible. You are right that my work hours are different, and I don't have an office I go in to, but that makes me unconventional. Not irresponsible"

"No, I just..." Rachel ran her hands over her face and cupped them over her nose. "I don't want to be a WAG."

"What's a WAG?"

"Wives and girlfriends."

"You don't want to be my wife or girlfriend?"

"No. That's not what I'm saying. The women you found me with tonight, that's what they call themselves. They sit in the background and wait while their husbands or whoever go off and make deals at these events."

"You know that that's not what's going to happen, right?"

"Kenzie, you just signed an album. You kicked ass tonight. You're literally about to take off."

"Thank you." Kenzie stroked Rachel's shoulder. "But it's not going to be that fast. The album still has to be recorded, then released, and I probably won't even do a tour."

"You'll perform shows, though."

"I will, but nothing like Braxton or what happened here tonight. Yes, there might be more awards shows in the future, but I can assure you, you will not get stuck sitting with the WAGs."

Rachel propped her head up. "You know how you have a road map for your life? And you plan out how things are going to go?"

Kenzie shook her head. "No. Not even a little bit."

"Okay, well, us type-A personalities plan things out. For me it was basketball, then law school, then starting a family. That's always been the goal."

"Let me guess." Kenzie rubbed her arm. "You are the high-powered attorney coming home to your white picket fence in the suburbs with 2.5 kids, a dog, and a wife?"

"Not quite, but close."

"And I don't fit it into this fantasy of yours."

"Kenzie, things with you are exciting and fun, and it feels so right. I have never had a relationship like this."

"But?"

"This life is just so different from what I imagined for myself. What I've been working toward for myself."

"Rach, that picture sounds awful."

"What?" Rachel pulled back. "Which part?"

"Okay." Kenzie backtracked. "Not the part about having a family with you, but the whole suburbs, 1950s family picture. It sounds awful. What are we going to do if we want to go out to dinner? Drive into the city?"

"How often do you think we'll go out to dinner?"

"Well, we both know I don't cook, so…"

Rachel stayed silent.

"And who's going to cut the grass? I'm not going to cut the grass," Kenzie said definitively.

"I'll cut the grass."

"You'll come home after being in court all day and then mow the lawn? And make dinner because we can't go out to eat?"

Rachel thought about it. "Well, that won't work all the time. We'll just hire someone to mow the lawn."

"Oh no. We are not hiring a gardener. I will not have our little girl go to school and not realize that not all the kids in class have a gardener."

"Little girl?" Rachel pictured a younger version of Kenzie heading off to elementary school.

"Of course."

"Just one?"

"I think we need to see how we handle one before we get too far ahead of ourselves. Not that I don't love planning our life out, but why is this coming up now, in the middle of the night?"

"I want to meet with a fertility doctor."

Kenzie sat up. "That seems a little cart before the horse, doesn't it?"

"The wait list is six months and I want to get on it. I need a plan."

"Plan?"

"We keep putting off talking about it. We both say we want a family, but we aren't doing anything to make it happen. I need a plan. I need to know what the process is, the cost, what I'm in for."

"Your dad will kill me if we have a baby without getting married."

"Why would you say that?"

"Your dad is definitely more traditional when it comes to how families should look. Do you want to get married first?"

"In a perfect world we'd be married first."

Kenzie ran her hands over her face. "Rach, this is moving kind of fast. Kids, marriage."

"We keep talking about forever."

"We do. So doesn't that mean we have time? Like forever?"

Rachel touched her stomach. "Unfortunately biology doesn't have forever. If we're serious about having a baby, we need to start looking into this sooner rather than later."

"Right."

"Unless that's not what you want?"

"No. It is. I guess I always just imagined that my career would be much further along before I had kids. It just always seemed like something in the far away future, but you're right. Mother Nature is working against us in this case. Can I go with you to the appointment when the time comes?"

"Yes. I want us to do this together. All of it."

"Come here." Kenzie reached out her arms and pulled Rachel in.

Rachel melted into Kenzie's body, their bare skin making contact. God, they fit together so perfectly.

"The plan is, I love you," Kenzie said.

Rachel started to turn but Kenzie tightened her grip and held her in place.

"I love you. And before you tell me that isn't a plan, it is. I love you, and I'm going to do anything to give you the life and the dreams you want."

"I love you too." Her heart melted saying the words out loud. She still hadn't gotten tired of it. Kenzie was holding her and caring for her in ways that no one ever had. That no one ever could.

Kenzie planted a kiss on the top of her head. "Even if that means having major life conversations at all hours of the day."

Rachel looked up. "Not the best timing, I'll admit."

"Rachel, I'm all in. So if you're worried that I don't want this"—she motioned her hand between the two of them—don't be. I may never work in an office, but I promise you, we can make us work."

"Okay." Rachel planted her lips on Kenzie's. It wasn't the plan she envisioned. None of it was thought out, and she didn't know if love was enough of a plan, but Kenzie sounded so sure. Maybe that was all they really needed.

CHAPTER THIRTY-FIVE

K enzie shifted uncomfortably on the plush red studio couch. The bright, hot lights made the room feel like the interview was on the surface of the sun and not a Hollywood soundstage. She already sweat through the white button-up blouse the show had picked out, and she hoped it wouldn't come across on TV. An always cheerful, Braxton sat on the couch next to her. "Can you believe it, Kenz?"

Braxton was no stranger to talk shows, and Kenzie knew she was loving every second of the attention. Kenzie's tongue went dry. She couldn't speak. She reached for the black morning show mug on the end table next to her and wished for a sip of anything inside it. Water quenched her thirst, but she longed for something stronger. A shot of Jack right now would be perfect. She thought about getting Damon's attention, but the producer started counting them back from commercial break and Kenzie knew she had no chance.

"With us in the studio today, we are thrilled to have the two hottest ladies in music right now, and yes, you heard me right," Joan Kelsey, the big-haired TV personality, said as the show came back from commercial. "I'm pleased to say we have McKenzie McCall and Braxton with us today." She paused, and the audience erupted. The flashing red "Applause" sign blinked furiously, and Kenzie wondered if anyone would have clapped had it not been for that.

"Ladies." Joan clapped her hands together. "You certainly had a great night last night." She motioned to their CCA awards staged on the coffee table in front of them.

Braxton scooted forward. "We did! It is such an honor to be here today."

Kenzie tried to relax her face. She was sure she wasn't smiling. Her plan was to say as little as possible. Speak only when spoken to and let Braxton do all the heavy lifting. She was going to have to get much better at these events before her own album came out.

"Now, Braxton." Joan shifted her focus to her. "You were unable to perform last night."

Braxton reached her hand to her throat. "I contracted a sinus infection, and in an effort to ensure my tour could go on as scheduled, my doctor advised me to rest my voice."

"And how are you feeling now?"

"So much better." Braxton perked up. "I am so ready for the tour next week and getting to see all of my amazing fans."

"Well, we are certainly glad to hear you're doing better," Joan said through her plastered-on smile. "And while we missed seeing your live performance, it was such a treat to see you, McKenzie."

Video of the CCA performance flashed on the large screen behind them. Kenzie tried hard not to grimace at seeing herself on screen, suddenly very aware of her face.

Joan cleared her throat and shot a look to Kenzie.

"Oh, thank you." Kenzie searched for words. "I'm no Braxton, but I tried to be the next best thing." She looked to Braxton, who took in all of her compliment.

"So, what's next for you two ladies? Braxton, more movies on the horizon?"

"Oh, I hope so. But right now, I am hyperfocused on the tour and then my upcoming album." She squealed.

"Speaking of," Joan cut in. "McKenzie, rumor has it you are recording an album. When can we expect that?"

Braxton's eyes pierced her.

"Very soon. It's in the works and we hope to have something to announce in the near future." She had yet to tell Braxton, but they both knew this had been Kenzie's goal all along. She couldn't have been that surprised.

"Speaking of behind the scenes…" Joan flashed the picture of Rachel and Kenzie posing in front of the CCA banner right after Kenzie had won. "Is it true that this tall drink of water actually inspired the song?"

Kenzie studied the screen behind her. Rachel looked amazing with her hair pinned back, and the dress hugging her in the glimmering light. She kicked herself again for not remembering to change her shoes. "Yes, you could say that," Kenzie finally answered.

"And you wrote it to impress her?"

Kenzie shifted uncomfortably. She didn't think this would get so personal.

"At least that's what you said in your speech," Joan said.

"Yes, you could say that too." Kenzie fumbled over her words and knew she sounded unintelligent.

"So, will there be songs about wedding bells in the near future?"

The splotchy part of her neck turned red hot. "Uh..." She shifted in her seat. "It's not something we've really talked about."

"Oh really? Even with a love song like that?"

"I hope we have a long future together." Long future together? What did that even mean?

"Well, you two look great together, so I hope we get lots more songs. Speaking of, how about a performance? Will you sing for us after the break?"

"Really? I'd love to!" Kenzie didn't know she'd get this chance. Two television performances in as many days. She'd wished she'd had time to warm up, but if she was going to perform, she'd need to be ready at a moment's notice.

This performance was much smaller. The live audience still applauded and gave Kenzie a standing ovation when finished, but didn't have nearly the same gravitas as performing at the CCAs. There was nothing like sharing the songs she wrote with the world. Yes, she loved Braxton's renditions, but being able to put her own flare and spin into it was a new kind of high. "The Other Side of Forever" would never be *her* song, but she would perform it every chance she got.

The producer signaled the commercial break once the applause died off.

"What the hell, Kenz?" Braxton threw her mic pack off her back and stormed off the stage.

Kenzie followed close behind with one of the production assistants trying to grab the mic off her.

Braxton burst into the hallway, then spun around. "That's *my* song. You're just going to start performing it now?"

"I'm not. They asked me to play. What the hell was I supposed to play? You know that's what they were expecting." Kenzie freed herself from the assistant's grasp. Braxton crossed her arms and stared at her.

"Seriously? You're going to act like a child?" Kenzie said.

"Ladies! Great news! We're headed to New York," Cooper announced as he joined them in the hallway.

"I'm not going anywhere with that song stealer." Braxton turned around and faced the wall.

"New York? When?" Kenzie's mind spun. How was she going to tell Rachel she was headed to New York instead of home? She had just promised Rachel she'd find time to make their relationship work, and now she'd be heading off to the other side of the country.

"We are wheels up in an hour. I don't know what the hell this is." Cooper motioned between Braxton and Kenzie. "But you better fix it."

"Why do I have to fix it?"

"Because the older sister always has to fix it." He clapped her on the shoulder and left.

Kenzie saw Damon out of the corner of her eye. "Will you get Rachel on the phone? Please?" She needed to tell her right away that she wasn't coming home but was heading back to her current least favorite city.

"Braxton, I am not a song stealer, and you know it. They asked me to play it, so I did. You would have done the same thing."

"Fine. You're right." She turned around to face her. "But what? I'm just supposed to find another songwriter while you go off and record your own?"

"Braxton, listen to me." She grabbed her by the shoulders. "You know that I love working with you. I am going to continue to do everything I can to help you. That doesn't mean that I don't have dreams of my own. I can want something great for me and for you." She stared into Braxton's eyes, willing her to believe her.

Braxton caved. "Okay. Fine But I will not be competing with you for backup dancers."

Kenzie rolled her eyes. "I will get my own."

Braxton brought her in for a hug and squeezed her tight.

"Kenzie, I have Rachel on the phone." Damon pointed to the phone in his hand and handed it to her.

"Rachel, hi."

"You were amazing."

"Thank you."

"Why didn't you tell me you were going to play? I would have told more people to watch."

"I didn't know. They asked me literally two minutes before."

"Not bad for no warmup."

"That's what I thought. Hey, so I just found out I need to go to New York."

"New York? For how long?"

"Damon?" Kenzie covered the microphone as she yelled. "How long are we going for? He thinks a week."

Rachel sighed.

"I'm sorry. I literally just found out."

"Speaking of Damon, I don't like it when he calls me from your phone."

"Okay?" Kenzie's mind spun from the sudden conversation change.

"You're my girlfriend. When the phone rings and it displays your picture, I expect it to be you on the other end."

Kenzie relaxed a little at Rachel's use of the word "girlfriend."

"You're right. I won't have Damon call you for me anymore. I'm sorry, I was just in the middle of fighting with Braxton and needed to talk to you too. This is such a cluster."

"Fighting with Braxton? What's going on?"

"She's pissed that I sang her song and am recording an album."

Rachel let out an audible scoff on the other end of the phone. "Can I pick you up from the airport?"

"You don't have to do that. They'll send a car."

"No, I want to do it. Let me do normal girlfriend things."

"Normal girlfriend things?"

"You know? Rides to the airport, taking you to dinner. That kind of thing."

"Okay. Deal. You can pick me up and then we'll go to dinner and do normal girlfriend things."

"I can't wait."

Kenzie finally could relax. "Okay, Damon is telling me we need to go. I'll call you tonight. Hopefully from a mold-free hotel."

CHAPTER THIRTY-SIX

Rachel answered her phone quicker than she thought humanly possible when Kenzie's name flashed on the display.

"Hi, babe." It had only been four days, but it was the longest Rachel had been apart from Kenzie in months, and she yearned for her. They had a night apart here or there, as Kenzie had to go to California or other cities on occasion. Or the nights when it didn't make sense for them to stay at the same apartment, but by and large, four days was the longest stint apart, and it surprised Rachel how much she was looking forward to seeing her.

"Hi there, beautiful. How's your day?"

"I actually have some good news." Rachel was waiting to tell Kenzie in person but couldn't keep it in any longer.

"Oh yeah? Let's hear it."

"The fertility clinic had an opening and can get us in Monday!"

"That's fantastic! Way sooner than we thought."

"I know! I was going to tell you when I picked you up tonight, but I can't keep it any longer. Speaking of, are you headed to the airport?" Rachel looked at her watch and did the quick math. It would be almost three p.m. in New York. She would be on her flight soon and home to her in five hours.

"About that…"

Rachel braced herself for the news coming.

"Do you know that show with all the comedians that airs live on Saturdays?"

"Yes, doesn't everyone?" Rachel didn't know where this was going.

"I didn't, at least not until an hour ago. Anyways, I guess they have a musical guest, and this week's backed out. Then Global decided that since Braxton was already in New York, she should do it. Plus, it will help kick off her tour."

Rachel needed her to get to the point. She had already resigned herself to the fact that Kenzie wouldn't be home tonight, but now she needed her to get to the details of it.

"And the studio thought it would be fun if Braxton sang and I played piano."

"Oh." That was all Rachel could muster.

"This is a huge opportunity. People know who I am right now, but seeing me next to Braxton would do wonders for my brand."

"Right," Rachel said. This was what Kenzie had been working toward all along. "This is a great opportunity."

"I know Braxton is really excited about it."

"Braxton is excited about anything that involves a crowd."

"That is so true. Hey, why don't you come out? We can make a weekend of it. I'll take you to a fancy dinner or something."

"No, I can't do that." Rachel shook her head.

"Why not? It's the weekend. You won't have to work."

"River and Ash have soccer games this weekend. I promised them I'd go. Plus, we had to miss last weekend's for the awards show."

"Dammit. That's right. Tell your dad I'm sorry I missed it," Kenzie's voice was barely above a whisper.

"You can tell him yourself next time. This won't be the last soccer game."

"I'll make it up to you."

"You always do."

"And I'll make it up to the kids. Things are just so busy right now. It won't be like this forever. I promise."

Rachel thought about that. If Kenzie kept writing award-winning songs, it would be like this forever. What was the likelihood of that? Knowing Kenzie's talent, pretty likely. She thought back to the night of the awards show and pictured Braxton and Kenzie posing with their trophies. How many more nights like that would there be? The celebrity life was fun for a night or two, but could that be their life together? "So, you'll be home Sunday?"

"Yes. Braxton starts the tour Monday, so there is no way it will get delayed any further."

"I'm still going to pick you up at the airport."

"Duh. You're my girlfriend and I expect you to do girlfriend things. Plus we have the big appointment on Monday. I wouldn't miss it for the world."

Rachel's heart tingled.

"Okay, one second." Kenzie yelled to someone. "Rachel? I have to go. Damon is giving me the signal. I'll call you later?"

"Of course. I'll talk to you later."

Rachel hit the red end button and stared at the phone in her hand. She had changed her lock screen picture to the one of her and Kenzie at the CCAs. It was fun to get all dressed up for the night, but now she would have given anything for just a normal night in.

CHAPTER THIRTY-SEVEN

H i, Dad." Ashley waved.

"Is Mom at her new spot?" Rachel asked.

"She sure is." Her dad had not only managed to angle the SUV into the parking spot so her mom could see the soccer field but had gotten the same spot every weekend. The game started, and the conversation shifted to cheers for the kids and the team. Ash ran, full force, in control of the ball all the way toward the goal. He kicked it and it sailed out of bounds, missing altogether and rolling onto the next field over.

"That's alright, Ash!" Rachel's dad cheered. "That was a great shot!"

Rachel turned to her dad. "I seem to remember that if I had missed a wide-open shot like that, you would have yelled something much different. Something more like 'a good player would have made that,' if I recall."

"Yeah, well." Rachel's dad shrugged. "I'm a granddad now. Being overly cheerful is the grand part."

Rachel shot him a look.

"It's hard to know what you're doing in the moment." He turned and faced Rachel. "Raising you girls, I thought I was doing the right thing. But now, I stop and think that maybe I pushed you too hard in certain ways."

"Pushed too hard? What are you talking about?"

"Just with sports. I think maybe I should have let up a little bit and let you have more of a normal childhood."

"Dad, basketball was my dream. You didn't push me to do anything I didn't want to do."

"Good." He settled into his chair. "I'm glad to hear you say that."

"I don't think you could have stopped me, even if you wanted to."

"Once you get your mind set on something, you follow through. You have always been like that. Basketball, law school, you are a determined person."

"I like to have a plan."

"That you do. Is Kenzie almost here? The first half is almost over."

"She's working," Rachel settled on saying. It was too much to try and explain.

"On a Saturday?"

"Yes. Her schedule has gotten busy in the last week."

"I won't pretend to understand how her job works. I just thought that after our chat, things would be different."

"What chat?"

"At Christmas."

"What all did you talk about?" Rachel hadn't asked Kenzie any more about it since that night. She hadn't thought to.

Rachel's dad had the eyes of someone who had been caught. "Nothing." He brushed her off.

"No. Not nothing, Dad. Clearly, you think there was something."

"She'll tell you. I shouldn't have said anything."

"Dad, I'm not going to let this go."

"It's pointless to argue with you. It always has been."

Rachel smiled.

"I told her it would be a good idea if you married before you started a family," he said nonchalantly.

"You what?"

He waved his hand out. "I know that you have a plan for your life, and that involves kids and marriage, and I needed to make sure she could provide that for you."

"Dad, why would you do that?" Kenzie had met her dad one

time, and he was pushing marriage on her. That would be a lot for anyone to handle.

"Because I know that you want a family, and I didn't know when I would get her alone again. But more importantly, I told her she needed to start coming around more. Guess we can see what she thinks of my opinions."

"It's not that she doesn't want to be here."

"And yet she's never here."

Rachel wanted to defend Kenzie. She wanted to stick up for her, but her dad had a point. Kenzie wasn't there. She hadn't shown up to these events even though she knew it was important to Rachel.

"Kenzie does what Kenzie wants, and I just think you deserve something better."

"Dad! What?"

"I'm sure it's fun to get all dressed up and attend fancy parties, but is that really the future you want? You need stability. Someone who is going to put your needs first and in the way that you want them. Not just someone who does whatever she wants."

"That's not how our relationship is." Yes, Kenzie was off working, but that didn't mean she didn't care for Rachel and provide for her in other ways. Ways her father couldn't see.

"I'm not trying to strike a nerve or anything, sweetheart, I just know what you want in life, and I want to make sure you are with someone who can make all of your dreams come true."

"Thank you, Dad. I am."

"If you say so." The moment was gone, as Ash had just gotten the ball again and started his way down field. "That's it!" Rachel's dad yelled. "Come on!"

She cheered and gave high fives with her sister and Patrick as Ash floated the ball just past the goalie and into the net. What would a marriage with Kenzie even look like? She couldn't even show up to a soccer game for a niece and nephew. What would happen when it was their own child playing in the game? She needed to push those thoughts away. Of course she would show up, that was just her dad's voice in her head.

Rachel's phone buzzed between soccer games. Her chest fluttered like it always did when Kenzie's picture filled the screen. "Hey, babe."

"Hi." Kenzie's voice was chipper.

"How's New York?"

"I have amazing news!"

"That's great. Let's hear it."

"They want me to be the opener on Braxton's tour!"

"What?" Rachel's stomach dropped. She left her chair and went to find a place away from screaming kids.

"Cooper talked with the studio, and they are going to have me open. We hit the road tomorrow. Can you believe it?"

"No." Rachel was supposed to pick Kenzie up tomorrow. She could not believe it. They were supposed to go to the fertility doctor on Monday and start planning their future together.

"This is it, Rach! The tour. The album. It's happening!"

"That's great." She gave the best support she could. This wasn't part of the plan. Rachel accepted that Kenzie was going to sell albums and live an unconventional life, but nothing had prepared her for this. "When do you think you'll be home?"

"I have no idea. The East Coast portion goes through summer. I'm sure I can fly home for a bit when we have breaks. Then we will be on the West Coast this fall and possibly international. I still can't believe it."

"Summer?"

"That's probably the earliest, yeah."

"So how does this work?"

"Well, I get on the bus and tour city to city. I didn't have a lot of time to practice, but I know I can throw a set together."

"No. I mean us. How do we work? You were supposed to come to the appointment with me Monday."

"Shit. That's right. You want me to video conference?"

"Video conference? Seriously?" Her dad's voice echoed in her head. *Kenzie does what Kenzie wants.*

"I'm giving you the best option I can here, babe. Things are happening really fast."

"If I'm not going to see you until summer at the earliest, and you're going to be living on a bus, how does that leave time for us?"

"We'll just have to make time for us."

"When, Kenzie? When you're trapsing around from city to city?" The whole goal in moving the appointment up was to try and get pregnant sooner. She certainly didn't want to embark on this journey all alone.

"Whoa. Where is this coming from? This is a huge deal for me."

"It is. And you need to take it. I just don't see how this works for *us*."

"What are you saying?"

Rachel swallowed the lump forming in her throat. What was she saying? Was she really doing this? Over the phone at the soccer field? "I'm saying I don't think I can do this. I don't see how I fit in this. I don't see how a family fits into this with you not here."

"Rachel, this is my dream. I have come too far to turn back now."

"And I'm not asking you to."

"But you won't be a part of it."

"I don't see how I can be."

"So you're just going to give up? You're not even going to give us a chance? This is just a hurdle. Something we can work through, together."

How could they work through it together when Kenzie had made the decision for them? "I think this was always too good to be true, Kenzie. I think deep down we both know this could never work in the real world."

"Work in the real world? What are you talking about? Have we not been living in the real world for the past year? Rachel, I love you. No amount of distance is going to change that. Yes, I don't know when I'm going to see you in person next, but that shouldn't stop us from being together. That shouldn't stop us from trying."

"I have to go. Good luck with the tour." She ended the call. It was cold. It was callous. But it needed to be done that way. She couldn't build a life with a partner who wasn't around. Or a partner who made major life decisions without even talking to her. Kenzie wasn't signing up for a weekend away. The tour with Braxton was months long and she didn't know when she would be back. Rachel needed stability, and as much as she did love Kenzie, in this instance, that wasn't enough of a plan.

CHAPTER THIRTY-EIGHT

Sweat beaded on Kenzie's hairline under the stadium lights. After weeks of opening for Braxton, she still hadn't gotten used to the heat they produced. "You all have been a great crowd. I'm going to do one more before we bring out my very good friend, Braxton!" The audience always went wild whenever she said Braxton's name. It was who they were here to see, after all. Braxton knew how to bring the energy and make a memorable performance reach every fan every night.

Kenzie couldn't match that energy. Not now, maybe not ever. Since Rachel wouldn't return her calls or texts, it was like her world was without color. Her world was tilted on the wrong axis. As much as she had worked for and wanted her big break, it meant nothing knowing that Rachel wouldn't be there to share it with her. She would trade it all to have Rachel back. But how could she even take that kind of gamble when Rachel wouldn't talk to her?

Kenzie finished her last song and the house lights came on, giving fans a quick break before the main event. She got several compliments and words of affirmation as she exited the stage for her dressing room. Cooper waited for her inside. That was unusual. "We need to have a chat." Fuck.

"Are we taking a walk?"

"No. Too many people around. So we'll just have a chat here. You want to sit or stand?"

"I'll sit." She flopped onto the red sofa. She wasn't going to like whatever came next.

"We're going to go a different direction for the rest of the East Coast leg of the tour."

"What does that mean?" Kenzie knew different direction meant—not her, but she wanted to hear him say it.

"It means we need someone who's going to pump the crowd up, not someone who's going to go out and sing sad songs for thirty minutes each night."

Ouch. He wasn't wrong, but that didn't mean it didn't hurt. "I can change the set list if that's the problem. It's not like I had a whole lot of notice."

"It's not just the set list, Kenzie. You know I think the world of you, but you don't have it right now."

"What does that mean?" Kenzie had heard of the it factor before, but she'd never been rejected for not having it.

"It means get over her or get her back."

"What?"

"Rachel. Either get over her or get her back."

"It's not that simple."

"It's exactly that simple."

Kenzie grabbed her chest. "It feels like I can't breathe without her. I don't know what the hell happened. She just gave up. She didn't even give us a chance. How can I get someone back who doesn't want me?"

"Then get over her."

"Get over her? Did you hear me? I can't breathe without her, Cooper. My body doesn't have oxygen."

"Then get her back."

"You are like a broken record."

"And you are a heartbroken woman who needs to get it together."

Heartbroken. She was. Truly. For the first time, this was what heartbreak felt like. Like someone had reached into her chest and torn her heart in two. Nothing could ever put it back together. She had written breakup songs and thought she knew how to describe it, but nothing in her life had ever hurt like this. How could she just get it together?

"So go home and take some time. Get your mind right, and we'll chat once we get to the West Coast leg. This doesn't change anything with your album. That's still a go. We just need someone more peppy to bring the energy up, and that isn't you."

He wasn't wrong. Peppy was not a word to describe any aspect Kenzie's life right now. The last thing she wanted to do was go home. Home was a place where Rachel wasn't. Home was a place where Rachel never would be again.

"You'd be surprised what people are willing to try," Cooper said. "You might have a chance you don't know about."

Kenzie doubted that very much. Rachel hadn't answered a single one of her calls or texts. She didn't have a chance at all.

CHAPTER THIRTY-NINE

R achel swirled the wine in her glass, waiting for Ashley.
      "Did hell freeze over? I don't think you've ever beat me
before." Ashley took the spot across from her.

Rachel didn't love going back to Pressed, but again it was close
to work and an easy place to have a conversation. At least she knew
there would be no chance of running into Kenzie, since she was still
on tour. "I know my sister's time is valuable and I didn't want to
keep you waiting. I took the liberty of ordering." She pushed a glass
in Ashley's direction.

"Thank you." Ashley took a sip. "The wine selection here is so
good."

"It is." She had to hand it to Jenni. She did a phenomenal job
with the wine menu.

"So how are things with Kenzie?" Ashely waggled her eyebrows.

Rachel was dreading this part. It had been weeks and she hadn't
told her family yet. Part of her was still hoping it wasn't true. Kenzie
had made attempts to call and text, but what could she say? "We
broke up."

"You what?" Ashley rattled the table.

"We broke up."

"What happened?"

"They asked her to open the tour for Braxton."

"That's great! She's been working on getting a break like that
for a long time."

"Yes, well, she didn't know when she would be coming home

and I didn't see how any of this would work. I can't just be someone who sits at home and waits."

"So your girlfriend gets the job of her dreams and you break up with her?"

"That's not at all what happened."

Ashley pinched the bridge of her nose. "Let me ask you this. If Kenzie was a lawyer and got offered a job working at the Supreme Court, what would you say?"

"I would tell her that's a fantastic opportunity."

"Would you tell her to take it?"

"Of course."

"Would you break up with her?"

"Probably not. Why would I?"

"Because she would be living on the other side of the country and you don't know when you would see her next."

"Right, but she'd have an apartment or something and we would work it out."

"Okay, but how is any of that different? She just had one of her dreams come true. Yes, it looks a little different, but it's not *that* different."

"But she doesn't even know when she'll be back," Rachel whined. She knew it sounded silly. Distance wasn't impossible to overcome. Lots of people had long distance relationships.

"The tour has an end, doesn't it?"

"Yes."

"So, she won't be gone for the rest of her life."

Rachel sipped her wine. She needed something to do. The flavors cascaded over her tongue and took her mind to a happier place. A place where Kenzie was singing and she was sipping wine and listening to her.

"Is this really about the distance?"

"She just up and made a major life decision without so much as consulting me."

"Okay. I think we might have found the crux."

"Isn't that a red flag?"

"Yes and no. It was a major life decision, but not one that was a complete surprise to you. I think you probably could have talked about it rather than just end things altogether. It certainly seems like there's a way to make it work."

Rachel put her head in her hands. "Why does it have to be so hard?"

"Because if it were easy, everyone would do it."

"You think I made a mistake?"

"I think you got scared and overreacted."

"What other kinds of decisions is she going to make without consulting me? If this is her dream, if this is what she wants her career to be, there could be opportunities that come up for the rest of our lives. I can't just sit around and wait. I'm not going to raise a family on my own."

"Or maybe you figure out something that can work for the both of you. Plus, you will never raise a family alone. That's what amazing Aunt Ashley is for. You think I won't be there to help?"

"I wish I didn't miss her so much."

"Heartbreak is a real bitch."

"I just don't see a way to make this work."

"Well, maybe you need to get a little more creative. Sometimes the picture you have planned out isn't the best one."

Was there a way to make this work? Could Rachel and Kenzie work long distance? How did a family play into that? How did Rachel fit into that? Rachel thought she knew what she wanted her future to look like, but maybe she had gotten the picture all wrong.

CHAPTER FORTY

Even though Rachel had been the one to end things, it didn't make her heart hurt any less. Kenzie had tried to get her back. She called, texted, emailed, everything short of showing up at Rachel's doorstep. Rachel needed a clean break. She knew that if she saw Kenzie in person, Kenzie would say all of the right things and make her believe they could somehow have a life together. Her mind flashed to one of Kenzie's many voicemails, begging her to let her show her the plan she had. She couldn't do it. She'd worked too hard and come too far for the life she wanted to get derailed now. Plus, how could Kenzie show her a plan when she wasn't around? She still didn't have an end date to her leg of the tour.

In the weeks since breaking up with Kenzie, she had stopped listening to the radio altogether. Braxton was still topping charts with "The Other Side of Forever," and Rachel couldn't handle hearing it. Not only that, but she knew Kenzie had her fingerprints all over the industry. It was a matter of time until a new breakup song would come out, and it would be about her. She would probably be a song on Kenzie's new album.

She exclusively listened to podcasts or talk radio on her commute, as she couldn't handle anything else. At her office, her new background music of choice was classical. She needed music in the background to feel productive, and this was the safest option. She put her headphones in, ready to tackle her growing inbox.

She'd grown to love a classical station. She skipped all the piano pieces, for obvious reasons. Just hearing a piano gave her flashes of Kenzie's hands. The way her touch was so soft against the keys. She couldn't do it. The current Beethoven she had on was between movements when a vaguely familiar tune came on. She checked her phone. It was still on the classical station. She took her earbuds out and headed down the hall. As she suspected, Kenzie was playing the piano. She waited in the doorframe, not wanting to make her presence known.

Kenzie moved her hands across the keys and hit the wrong ones. "Fuck," she said to no one.

Rachel couldn't help but laugh, and that caught Kenzie's attention. She snapped her head toward the door. "Oh, sorry. Was I too loud?"

"No." Rachel leaned against the long table. "Is that something new you're working on?"

"No." Kenzie shook her head. "It's pretty old, actually. I don't have anything I'm working on right now."

"Oh?" Rachel studied her. Her face looked different. Her eyes held a sadness to them she had never seen before. She looked like she'd lost weight and hadn't been sleeping. "I didn't know you were home."

"Yeah. I got benched. I'm off the tour for the foreseeable future. I might get to do some more shows later. I'm not sure."

"I thought Cooper said things were going really well for you." Rachel didn't recognize the woman in front of her. She was a ghost of Kenzie. A shell of the person she had been in love with.

"Yeah. Well. Things change." Kenzie's voice was flat. She pulled the wooden cover over the keys and shut it. "I'm closing my studio."

"I thought it was doing well."

"It is."

"So, you can focus on your new album, then?"

"Oh no." Kenzie shook her head. "That's already done. But I think I'm going to try and get out of that the rest of the global contract. That's part of why I'm here today."

"Get out? What will Braxton do? Aren't you contracted to write her more songs?" The news hit Rachel harder than she expected.

"She'll be fine. She's on tour now, so she won't need another album for a year or so. Cooper will find her someone to finish what we've already been working on."

"What will you do?"

"I don't know." Kenzie stared off into space, past the piano. She squinted her eyes and turned her head. "I think I'm going to move."

"To where?"

"I don't know." She shrugged. "My mom wants me to go see her in New Mexico. I'm not going to move there. Well, maybe I will." She paused, seeming to think about it. "Probably LA or Nashville."

"Those are both great places for songwriters."

Kenzie leaned back. "Yeah. I think I'm done with that."

"What?"

Kenzie looked her in the eyes. "There are only so many ways to describe heartbreak, and I don't want to do it anymore. It's someone else's turn."

The words knocked the wind out of Rachel. In all of her thinking about her own future and what she wanted, she forgot that she had hurt someone else in the process. "When do you leave?"

"I don't know." Kenzie stared off at the wall again.

Typical. Of course, Kenzie would have no idea where she was going next, even on such a major life decision.

"End of the week, I think." She turned and faced Rachel. "Speaking of, I have a few boxes of your stuff. Nothing major, but I'm sure you want it. I can have it sent here or to your place. Just let me know."

Ah, yes. The worst part of a breakup. Separating your stuff back out. They didn't have a lot together, so it wouldn't be much, but still an awful process. "I can come get it." Rachel didn't need to put any more burden on Kenzie.

"I'll be home tonight, unless you have plans."

"No. No plans. Can I come by after work?"

"Yeah. Okay. I'll see you then."

"If it isn't my favorite client," an overly cheerful Nina called from the doorway.

Kenzie forced a smile. "And my favorite lawyer."

❖

Rachel knocked on the door to Kenzie's apartment. It was such a strange act. An apartment she had basically lived in for the last several months, and still held a key to, and here she was, knocking. It didn't take long for Kenzie to answer the door. She had changed after her business meeting earlier and wore yoga pants with an oversized sweatshirt. Her hair was pulled back with loose bits framing her face.

"Come in." She motioned Rachel inside.

Rachel stepped into the apartment. Everything was so different. Empty. Boxes of Kenzie's stuff were in neat piles, and a sheet was draped over the piano. She didn't think it was possible for Kenzie's place to feel any emptier than it had before, but it did.

Kenzie motioned to a small pile by the door. The brown cardboard boxes had a "R" written on each box in black permanent marker. "Those five are yours. I can help you get them down to your car."

"What's with all the blue tape?" Various lengths of blue painter's tape covered the floor.

"Oh. Nothing." Kenzie waved her off. "It was a silly idea I had a couple of weeks ago."

A couple of weeks ago? That was how long they had been broken up for. Was this part of her frantic voicemails? "What was it?" Rachel couldn't keep her curiosity at bay.

Kenzie looked like she was going to put up a fight, then gave in. "Walls."

Rachel furrowed her brow. "Walls?"

"Yeah. Apparently, some people need them. Or did need them. I had a whole plan."

"Show me."

"Rachel, we don't have to do this."

Rachel had to know. She couldn't help it. What was the plan Kenzie had? "Please?"

A reluctant Kenzie grabbed her tablet off the coffee table. "It's pointless to argue with you." She powered it up. "Can you see this okay?" Kenzie brushed her shoulder as the tablet opened a picture app.

"Yes." Rachel nodded.

"So where the tape is, that's where a wall would go. If you look on the screen here, you can see what it looks like in the room." She handed the tablet to her and Rachel took it with both hands.

"So here, behind the couch, that's a wall?"

"Yes." Kenzie followed behind her. Looking at the screen over her shoulder. "If you look to your left, you can actually go through the door and see the room."

Rachel side stepped through the imaginary door. "It's pink."

"This would have been our little girl's room. It wouldn't have to be pink. It was just to get some thoughts out there."

The mention of the little girl tugged at her heartstrings. She moved the tablet around the room. A crib with an animal mobile hanging over it was placed in the middle. It was the perfect nursery. "What's that door there?" She pointed in front of her.

"That's the bathroom. We'd need more than one. You can walk through it, and then there's an adjoining room on the other side."

Rachel winced as she ducked through the fake door, then realized how silly it must have looked.

"If you keep going, that's the third bedroom. I figured it could be your office for now. Then if we have another, either the kids would share, or we can build you an office downstairs."

It was just a quick mockup, but Kenzie had put so much detail into these rooms. There was a beautiful desk in the corner and a dark brown leather armchair with a reading light. It would have been a great space for Rachel to get work done. "What else?" Rachel turned around and looked at Kenzie.

"Okay, well, the piano would stay here." She motioned to the piano. "But just past it, that's where the new kitchen would go."

Through the tablet the tiny burner and fridge had been converted to a designer kitchen. Blue cabinets flanked the wall, with appliances on the far wall. "Blue?"

"I was just playing around." Kenzie shrugged. "I don't need a kitchen anyway. But this part is cool." She reached her hand to the tablet and slid her finger across it. "See, the gate is built in. It slides out and then we don't have to worry about kids or dogs in the kitchen."

"I kind of like the blue," Rachel said without thinking.

"Anyways, that was the plan." Kenzie reached for the tablet.

Rachel went to hand it to her when a different door caught her eye. "What's that?" She looked at the brick wall, then looked again through the tablet revealing a new door.

"Oh. Nothing." Kenzie reached for the tablet, and Rachel held it just out of reach. "Come on, don't do that."

"Show me what's behind the door," Rachel said playfully.

"Fine." Kenzie gave in. Rachel handed the tablet over, and Kenzie set it down. "That's where the door will go, but we have to go this way now." Kenzie led her out the front door and down a hallway Rachel had never noticed before. They climbed a flight of exposed stairs and stopped at a metal door that read "Roof access only."

"What's this?" Rachel asked.

"You'll see." Kenzie pulled out a key and undid the lock on the door. She pushed it open for Rachel.

Rachel squinted as her eyes adjusted to the bright sun shining on top of the roof. She spun around and took in the spectacular view from the top of the building. "I had no idea this was up here." Blue painter's tape covered the roof flooring as well. "What goes here?"

"Well, we have options," Kenzie explained. "The play structure goes over there. Swings, slide, the whole thing. Then, in that corner, we can either grow real grass or put turf in. I would prefer turf, but I don't really care."

Rachel could picture it clearly. Little kids running around, swinging on the rooftop playground. Her eyes widened at the exposed ledge not ten feet from them.

"That's where the plexiglass goes," Kenzie explained. "We don't want to obstruct the view, but we need a guardrail. It'll be six feet high, so there's no chance anyone would fall." She motioned with her hands to show where the wall would go.

"Is that?"

"Mt. Hood? Yes."

Mt. Hood's perfect white peak glimmered against the blue sky background. It was picturesque, and Rachel envisioned herself, a glass of wine in hand after a long day in court, coming up here and letting the world below them go.

"And since not every day is as beautiful as this one, we can put a cover over the swing set. That way, no matter the weather, we can still come up here and enjoy it."

"You would have done all of this for me?"

"I would have done all of this for us." Kenzie emphasized her words.

"What's that?" A small black box rested on the ledge.

"Oh shit. That's where that is. Thank you. I've been looking for that." Kenzie grabbed the box and put it in the pocket of her sweatshirt.

Rachel raised a questioning eyebrow.

"It doesn't matter now." Kenzie put both hands in her pocket.

Rachel's throat closed and her mouth went dry. The realization of the mistake she had made hit her hard. She had been so caught up in the life she thought she wanted, thought she needed, that she had never stopped to consider alternatives. Alternatives that actually looked better than anything she could have imagined.

"I got scared." She looked into Kenzie's eyes.

"I know." Kenzie rocked back and forth on her heals.

"This is a great plan." Rachel held her hands out, motioning to the rooftop area.

"I thought so." Kenzie's tone was flat.

"When I get so focused on something, I can't stop and see other options."

"I know that about you."

Rachel wanted to feel her touch. She wanted to reach out, but she restrained herself. "I got scared because things were moving differently than I thought and then I didn't give you a chance to explain because I knew if I did, you'd use your words to convince me. You always say the right thing."

"Some would call my words award-winning." Kenzie shuffled her toe against the ground.

"I'm being serious."

"I can't give you the picture of the life you want."

"I know. But I'm beginning to think I was too focused on what that looked like instead of who it would be with."

"I can't give you the white picket fence in the suburbs. I just can't do it. But I thought this might be a nice compromise." She shrugged.

As much as she had tried to tell herself Kenzie was wrong for her, that she couldn't give her the life she wanted, standing in front of her on this rooftop, everything suddenly clicked into place. "Is this still something you'd be willing to compromise on?"

Kenzie squinted her eyes. "Are you saying what I think you are?"

"Yes." Rachel held her breath, waiting for the answer. She knew she had screwed up and hoped that Kenzie could find it in her heart to take her back.

"You can't run when you get scared." Kenzie took a step closer.

"I won't."

"Things aren't always going to turn out the way you planned or pictured them, and you can't just leave when that happens."

"I know."

"I'm unconventional and sometimes irresponsible."

"I don't know that I'd go that far, but I would like to be included in major decisions. You can't just go running off on tour without telling me."

"Rachel, those weeks on tour were some of the most miserable of my life. I thought I had what I wanted, but I didn't. None of the success meant anything without you next to me. I am not used to having someone in my life that means this much, and I promise that I'll never do anything to lose you like that again."

Rachel didn't know how much more of this she could take.

Kenzie paused a long moment. "You really like the blue kitchen?"

Rachel couldn't help from smiling. "I do. It's not what I ever pictured, yet somehow it's perfect."

Kenzie took a step forward, and Rachel reached for her and pulled her into herself. Their bodies fit perfectly together like they had so many times before. Kenzie lifted her head. "What did you think of the pink bedroom?"

"That was my favorite part." Rachel put both her hands on Kenzie's cheeks and kissed her. She needed Kenzie to feel her in more than a physical way. She needed her to know that she was here to stay and never going anywhere.

Kenzie pulled back suddenly, panting. "There's one more thing."

Rachel answered between her own breaths, "Okay."

"If we're going to do this, then I need you to be all in."

"I'm all in." Rachel raised her right hand.

"That's not enough." Kenzie shook her head. "If we're going to do this, I'm not going to do it as your girlfriend. I love you and I have meant every word I have said to you. I want to get to the other side of forever with you." Kenzie looked into Rachel's eyes and held her gaze.

"Okay." Rachel nodded.

Kenzie reached into her sweatshirt pocket and retrieved the black box. "This is for you." She pushed it into Rachel's hands.

"What is it?"

"Open it." Kenzie eyed the box.

Rachel opened the lid, then shut it immediately. "Holy shit."

Kenzie took the box from her hands and opened it, revealing a white gold band with diamonds leading up both sides to a large princess cut center stone. "Marry me."

"You left that up here on the roof?" Rachel's head was spinning.

"Well, in my defense, I thought you would be taking it home a few weeks ago. Then I never came back up to the roof. And did I not just say I'm irresponsible?"

"You did."

Kenzie took the ring out of the box and held it out. "You didn't answer me."

Rachel held out her left hand. "Yes." She nodded. "Yes, I'll marry you."

Kenzie slipped the ring on her finger. She grabbed Rachel by her hips and pulled her in for a hug. "I love you," she whispered in her ear.

"I love you too." Rachel pushed her back then held her left hand up, admiring the ring.

Kenzie leaned up and met her lips. Rachel kissed her cheek, then made her way to her ear. She gently bit her earlobe and pulled at it. "Take me to bed."

"Our room still doesn't have walls. I hope that's okay."

"It hasn't stopped us before."

EPILOGUE

"Okay, folks, I'm going to sing one more before we welcome my great friend Braxton to the stage!" The crowd erupted at Braxton's name as they always did. Kenzie hadn't planned to open for Braxton again, but when she came to town and begged her to play, she couldn't resist. She never got tired of seeing "McKenzie McCall" in bright lights. Her own album was out and doing well, and she welcomed any extra listens that a Braxton crowd might bring in.

When Rachel asked her to take Park as her last name, Kenzie didn't even have to think. She said yes immediately. She was happy to have a family with one name. She would keep McCall as her stage name, so to speak. She had an alter ego now. By day, she was Kenzie Park, seemingly stay-at-home housewife and expectant parent. By night, she was McKenzie McCall, award-winning songwriter and performer. The performances would be winding down in the near future, but only temporarily. She was looking forward to the change in her life. Songwriting had been her love for a long time, and she was ready for something new.

The small diamond band on her left hand caught the stage lights and glimmered. She hadn't wanted a wedding ring. She had gone so far as to tell Rachel she couldn't wear one—what with all the playing she did, it would be too cumbersome. If she continually took it off, they both knew she would inevitably lose it. She could wear a chain around her neck, or something similar, but a ring? That was too much.

Rachel insisted. She told Kenzie it was important to her. A

symbol. She wanted the world to know that Kenzie was taken. Rachel said the ring could be small. It didn't need to be flashy. A simple gold band would do, but it was important to her. As usual, it was pointless to argue, and Kenzie decided she could at least give it a try. She let Rachel pick it out and surprise her. Since she didn't care, she could give up control of that part. She didn't know how much she loved wearing her diamond band until their wedding night.

It was a small ceremony at the end of June. Kenzie had wanted to marry Rachel the night she proposed. She told Rachel to call one of her judge friends and they could get married right then on the rooftop with Mt. Hood as their witness. Rachel, per her usual self, needed a plan. Rachel agreed to a quick engagement, and they were married weeks later on a rare sunny day. Kenzie looked at her hand during the reception dinner, and the diamonds sparkled.

Rachel leaned in and whispered in her ear, "If it's too flashy, we can get a different one."

"No," Kenzie said. "It's perfect."

"Good." Rachel squeezed her other hand. "I'm never going to get tired of seeing it on you."

Kenzie caught herself staring at her ring now when something else flashing grabbed her attention. A strobe light from behind the wings. A voice spoke in her earpiece. No one should have been talking. She pushed it into her ear, trying to make out the words.

Kenzie had originally told Cooper she couldn't perform tonight. Braxton was performing a special Valentine's Day show just outside of Portland. Kenzie and Rachel were expecting their little girl literally any day now. The due date was February eighteenth, and Kenzie had pointed out to Rachel this would be their last Valentine's Day with just the two of them, and they should do something. Rachel reminded Kenzie that she hated Valentine's Day. She had always hated Valentine's Day, and while she loved her very much, this was not a day they were going to celebrate, now or ever. She should go and open for Braxton, as this would be her last chance for a long while. It was too convenient that Braxton happened to be playing in town and there was no way Kenzie should miss it. Kenzie protested, saying that something could happen. Rachel could go into labor or need something. But Rachel assured her that she would do everything in her power to not have their baby on February fourteenth.

The voice said something about Rachel and labor. Kenzie's heart stopped. Her hands stopped playing. She reached for the microphone. "I am so sorry. My time is cut short. My wife is in labor, so I have to go, but you will all have a great time with Braxton!" Even with the confusion, the crowd cheered. How could Rachel be in labor now? She had been fine all day. She had insisted that today would not be the day. She hadn't even had a slight contraction.

Kenzie ran to her car. How had Rachel gotten to the hospital? Her mother probably. Why hadn't Rachel called? Kenzie fished for her keys and phone in her bag and got into the driver's seat. She looked at her phone. It was off. Shit. Old habits died hard.

She powered on her phone as she drove to the hospital; she knew it wasn't far and hoped she hadn't missed much. Her phone buzzed alerting her to ten missed texts and three voicemails from Rachel. She decided not to listen to them.

She raced into the hospital, to the mother and baby floor. Mike was in the waiting room, playing on his phone.

"Mike," she panted.

"They're in room 2C." Mike looked up from his phone. Kenzie thought she was making inroads, showing up to family events. She hadn't missed another soccer game, but missing this, being late to the birth of her own child, that was going to take some making up for.

"Mike, I'm—"

He held a hand up. "I'm not the one you need to explain to."

"You're right." Kenzie spun around, looking for the right room.

Mike pointed to the right. "That way. Go. Before you miss any more."

The words stung. Kenzie had been trying, but it didn't change the fact that she was late yet again. She walked briskly reading room numbers until she found 2C. She opened the door to see Rachel, in the hospital bed, her mother leaning over her. Both turned at the door opening. "Hi." Kenzie gave a small wave. "I got here as soon as I could."

"I saw." Her eyes were strained and sweat beaded the top of her hairline.

"What do you mean you saw?"

"Thank goodness for streamers. I was watching the whole thing online. Your panic was kind of cute."

"I'm sorry it took so long, but I'm here now." She reached for Rachel's hand.

Rachel's mom looked up at Kenzie. "Well, I'll leave you two. Looks like you have it from here?"

"Yes." Kenzie nodded emphatically.

"I'll be right outside." She stroked Rachel's head and then excused herself.

Rachel gritted her teeth, and Kenzie squeezed her hand. "I can't believe I'm having our baby on Valentine's Day," she said between labored breaths.

Kenzie tried not to wince when Rachel clamped down hard on her hand. "You can be as mad at the universe as you want, but right now we have bigger things to focus on."

Rachel bit her lip and nodded. Kenzie comforted her the best she could. The doctor came in several minutes later. "Well, ladies, look like this one is ready to meet you. And a little early."

Kenzie stroked Rachel's head. She kept the stray hairs out of her eyes. She reminded her to breathe. She told her she was doing great and how beautiful she was.

At 11:59 p.m. on February 14, they welcomed Erica Abigail Park into their family. They counted fingers and toes again and again. "She is absolutely perfect," Rachel said, holding her between the two of them.

"She is." Kenzie had climbed into the bed to cuddle her exhausted wife.

Rachel's eyelids went heavy and Kenzie pulled her in close, looking at both of her sleeping girls.

"You know what's funny?" Rachel said, eyes closed.

"What's that?" Kenzie kept her voice soft.

"I think I finally like Valentine's Day."

About the Author

Kel McCord lives in a small town in Oregon with her wife, two dogs, and more gardens than she can possibly keep up with. Her family continues to grow, and their nest may never be empty, which is fine because there is no greater joy than seeing your kids happily partnered and welcoming grandbabies into the mix. When not writing, she enjoys reading, running, skiing, and endlessly taking her wife on vacation.

Books Available From Bold Strokes Books

The Art of Love by Ali Vali. When Mimi and Bianca both set their sights on Jolly, sparks fly, loyalties are tested, and hearts collide as they navigate the unpredictable nature of their hearts. (978-1-63679-719-9)

Chasing Her Scent by MJ Williamz. When Sheridan Rousseau walks into Lisette Mouton's charming little bookstore in Quebec City, she unknowingly holds the key to a mysterious box hidden in a secret room. (978-1-63679-900-1)

Heart's Run by D. Jackson Leigh. Hoping to recover an escaped racing mare, stock transporter Tobie Mason locks horns with local wild horse advocate Maggie Wilkes. (978-1-63679-825-7)

Scandalous by Kris Bryant. When a Hollywood actress trades places with her twin sister, everyone's in an uproar about getting duped, but Lindsay's more concerned about finding out which twin she made out with. (978-1-63679-874-5)

The Secrets of Rhydian Hill by Ronica Black. A doctor in need of a new start. A woman running from a killer. A love story that could end in tragedy. (978-1-63679-880-6)

Feeling Lucky by Krystina Rivers. What happens when, despite suddenly having enough money to buy almost anything, Lucy and Tanner start to discover that maybe all they need is each other? (978-1-63679-876-9)

Iceberg by Gun Brooke. When Lady Arabella hires Zandra, she never expects to find love, especially not as a disaster looms on the horizon. (978-1-63679-908-7)

It Happened One Semester by Aurora Rey. After a Pride night hookup, can eager new Assistant Professor Hudson Greene and Dean of Advising Callie Shaw overcome the odds and ace falling in love? (978-1-63679-814-1)

It's Kind of a Bad Idea by Sarah G. Levine. What happens when an emotionally unavailable serial dater meets the one woman she can't help but fall for—who happens to be the one woman who told her not to? (978-1-63679-920-9)

Thankful for You by Tagan Shepard. Everyone deserves to find their person. Maybe Karen has finally found hers? (978-1-63679-884-4)

What Happens On Location by Nan Campbell. How can Helen produce a successful movie when its director is the woman responsible for the demise of her marriage? (978-1-63679-904-9)

When Love Comes Around by Radclyffe and Ronica Black. Can Maya Sanchez and Nolan Wright trust each other enough to build something real, or will the past tear them apart? (978-1-63679-930-8)

Anywhere with You by Margo Glynn. On a road trip through the Great American Southwest, two friends discover nature, hope, and each other. (978-1-63679-907-0)

Burning Bridges by Lesley Davis. Can Clancy and Jude crack the case of eight missing women—and the secrets of their own hearts? (978-1-63679-872-1)

Dreams Entangled by Sophia Kell Hagin. Amid self-doubt, secrets, a pandemic, fear of attack and attempted murder, Pirin and Gracie's attraction turns to love, and their lives will never be the same. (978-1-63679-892-9)

Echoes of Love by Catherine Lane. As Hazel's and Jo's paths intertwine, they're swept up in a whirlwind of long-buried secrets, sizzling chemistry, and memories that won't be denied. (978-1-63679-835-6)

The Fame Game by Ronica Black. Wild child Hollywood actress Luna Kirkman begins dating Hollywood's leading man, only to fall for his straitlaced sister instead. (978-1-63679-858-5)

Moonlight Obsession by Sheri Lewis Wohl. All it takes to stop a clever killer is moonlight, love, and a silver bullet. (978-1-63679-831-8)

My Boyfriend's Wife by Joy Argento. Amid betrayal and heartbreak, can two women discover a love that could heal their pasts and rewrite their futures? (978-1-63679-866-0)

Tapout by Nicole Disney. A struggling MMA fighter finds her edge in an underground ring, but as she falls for the magnetic and ambitious promoter behind the matches, their dangerous world threatens to destroy everything they've fought to rebuild. (978-1-63679-924-7)

An Extraordinary Passion by Kit Meredith. An autistic podcaster must decide whether to take a chance on her polyamorous guest and indulge their shared passion, despite her history. (978-1-63679-679-6)

Heart's Appraisal by Jo Hemmingwood. Andy and Hazel can't deny their attraction, but they'll never agree on the place they call home. (978-1-63679-856-1)

That's Amore by Georgia Beers. The romantic city of Rome should inspire Lily's passion for writing, if she can look away from Marina Troiani, her witty, smart, and unassumingly beautiful Italian tour guide. (978-1-63679-841-7)

Through Sky and Stars by Tessa Croft. Can Val and Nicole's love cross space and time to change the fate of humanity? (978-1-63679-862-2)